A DARK AND STORMY KNIGHT

KERRIGAN BYRNE

OLIVER
HEBER
BOOKS

To my Anam Cara.
I recognized you instantly and never looked back.

The devil's breath was a persistent cold prickle on Cutter Morley's neck. He'd awoken with a start in the wee hours of the morning, propped up against the doorway to St. Dismas where he'd taken refuge. Vicar Applewhite had fallen ill, and so the rectory was locked against vagrants today. More's the pity. He'd not been able to scrape together enough money to afford a flea-bitten room for the night, but the fact that his twin, Caroline, hadn't met him in the abbey courtyard meant she'd found a roof to sleep beneath.

Or a protector willing to allow her into the warmth of his bed for a pound of flesh.

She wasn't a prostitute. Never that. She was just... desperate. They both were.

But not for long. He'd a plan—one he'd implement just as soon as he was old enough, or rather, as soon as he looked old enough.

He was so close. Just one or two more winters. One or two more inches. No one was right sure of their ages... maybe thirteen or fifteen. Probably not older, but his recollection of the first handful of years was cagey so he couldn't be sure.

They'd no papers.

The slick of oily disquiet Caroline's new sometimes profession wrought within him was a mild hum compared to the symphony of peril and impending doom sawing at his nerves.

It haunted him as he set off from Spitalfields to Shoreditch, increasing with every step until he lifted his grimy hand to swat at the itch and smooth the hair at his hackles back against his neck. He had a hard-enough time staying warm with only the moth-eaten jacket he'd filched from a rubbish heap, but something about this day frosted the marrow in his bones.

He thought to lose the disquieting demon in the Chinese tent city, hoping it could be distracted by inhabitants of the cloyingly fragrant opium dens just as easily as he was drawn by the sizzles and aromas of food cooked in the out-of-doors. His gut twisted with longing, but he found no opportunity to filch a breakfast. People were extra wary today. Perhaps they, too, felt whatever portent hung in the air.

He wandered through throngs of peculiar and elegant Jews, his ear cocked to the lyrical Crimean accents of those escaping the violence in Russia, Prussia or the Ukraine. He thought their industrious bustle would perhaps chase away this unfathomable sense of bereavement. But alas, he made it all the way down Leman Street with the healthy sense that calamity watched him from the shadows of the palsied, rotten buildings, waiting to strike.

It wasn't a matter of if, but when. Or... no... perhaps it had already happened. The thing. The terrible thing. And the world held its breath waiting to suffer some awful consequence.

Turning down Common Doss Street, he loped up to number three, a ramshackle place mortared with more mold than grout.

Mrs. Jane Blackwell land-lorded over the only seven

rooms free from vermin. At least, vermin other than that of the human variety. In Whitechapel, vermin were as inescapable as the toxic yellow fogs belched up by the Thames and thickened with soot from the refineries.

Cutter didn't need an invitation to shoulder into the doorway of the Blackwell common house, he'd been doing it since he was a lad.

The sharp smell of lye cut through the noise and stench wafting from men and women of dubious nocturnal vocations who had already begun drinking beer for the day at half noon. It drew him to the back of the house where a square of garden was connected by several alleys cobbled with grime. Clad in a dark frock and a soiled apron, Mrs. Blackwell stirred laundry over a boiling pot.

"More discarded bastards in these sheets than in all of Notting Hill," she muttered with a grimace. "I'm charging Forest extra if he's going to wank all over me linens, bloody pervert."

She glanced up when Cutter ambled over, her marble-black eyes crinkling with a good-humor quite lacking round these parts. In a place where most humans were anything but humane, where corruption was the only legitimate business and vice the only escape, Jane Blackwell was a warm, if rough-handed oasis of compassion.

Cutter would have given his right eye for a mum like her, or any mother really. She was a crass and vulgar woman, but he knew nothing else. She'd inherited these rooms from her father back before the pernicious poverty had taken over Whitechapel so completely, and an addiction to gin rounded out her inheritance. Or rather, drained it.

On top of her rents, she could charge tuppence a week more for her laundry services, and when she was of a mind to be dry, the money kept her and her son, Dorian, in luxuries like meat, cheese, and sometimes milk.

No wonder the lucky bugger was so tall and broad when they'd only dipped their toes into their teen years.

So long as Mrs. Blackwell kept her broken teeth— courtesy of Dorian's missing father— behind her lips, she was still a handsome woman. Her night-hued hair remained free of grey, and curled from beneath her cap in the steam of her laundry. She'd clutched Cutter to her breasts from time to time in a fit of sodden sadness or effervescent good spirits, and he'd be lying if he said he didn't enjoy it. He enjoyed it twice when he got to rib Dorian about it until his best mate blushed and boxed him one.

"I'm going to marry your mum," he'd taunt before dancing away. "Then I'll raise ya proper."

"Sod off," Dorian would reply irritably.

"Don't worry, I won't make you call me Da."

"I'll call you worse than that, you poxy cock."

At the thought of future scuffs, Cutter directed a half-grin at her, the one he knew made his cheek dimple, and he hefted what little sparkle he had left into his eyes. It was the first time he'd felt close to warm all day.

"Hullo," he greeted. "Did Caroline breakfast here?"

"I ain't seen her, Cutter," Jane greeted with a noticeable slur and a lack of any T's whatsoever.

He reached for the back of his neck and rubbed once again, even though little needles of gooseflesh stabbed at every inch of his skin by now.

"Dorian about?" he asked.

"In the kitchen fleecing doxies out of their hard-won earnings wif his dice last I checked." She swiped at her forehead with the back of her wrist and wrinkled her nose at him. "I've a mind to boil your wee arse in

4

my pot next, ya noxious goblin. I can smell you from here."

Cutter's testing sniff of his own person was interrupted by a strong arm around his neck as he was pulled in for a grapple choke that might have resembled a boisterous hug if one was feeling generous.

"Oi! I think you smell awright." Dorian's voice seemed to deepen by the day, though Cutter's had changed over a year ago, much to Blackwell's competitive consternation. "I've heard there's a dead body or some such washed up at Hangman's Dock." His mate's dark eyes gleamed with a greedy sort of mischief. "Wot say we go and work the crowd?"

Working the crowd was their language for relieving the distracted onlookers of their watches, coin, and pocketbooks.

"Maybe later." Cutter rubbed at his chest as the dread that had dogged at him now bared its teeth and struck, wrenching at his heart with an icy pain.

Pain meant weakness. And one never showed weakness here, not even in the presence of those he knew the best. He always covered his pain with humor if not indifference.

"Your mum just offered to bathe me." Cutter waggled suggestive brows and summoned a cheeky smile from lord-knew-where. "Now toddle off, son."

A hot rag hit him square in the face, eliciting a very unmanly squeak of surprise.

"Wash your face, you little deviant, and then both of you make yourselves scarce, I've work to do!" Jane's bellow was softened with a wink, and Cutter gave himself a half-hearted scrub before he tossed the soiled rag back to the laundry pile and threw Jane another smile.

This she returned with a curse and a shake of her head.

He'd felt this strange sort of veneration for her since

the first time Dorian had brought him and Caroline around. She'd allowed them to curl up in the kitchens and sleep like dogs by the stove in the winter and eat whatever crusts they'd helped clean from the tables. The next morning she'd sent them to Wapping High Street with strong warm tea in their bellies and a few pointers on how to beg.

"You're two golden-haired angels, inn't ya?" She'd tugged their noses fondly. "You'll empty more pockets than a naughty peep show, eyes that big and blue. 'Specially you, darlin'." She'd pinched at shy Caroline's pale cheeks and tugged at her golden ringlets.

And so they had. For years, Cutter and Caroline worked the streets of London, his sister drawing upon the kindness of those who would stop to offer a coin, while he learned to divest them of the rest with a pick of the pocket and a nimble getaway.

Sometimes they'd be caught, and Cutter would take the beating meant for them both. Those were often their most profitable weeks, as he could use the pitiable bruises and abrasions to solicit more charity.

This kept them fed until they'd passed their first decade and were no longer young and wretched enough to pity. People began to solicit them rather than offer them kindness, and eventually Cutter learned to answer the beatings he received with violence of his own.

Because he lacked the brawn of other boys, he relied on reflexes more advanced than most, and he'd mastered a slingshot as well as his sleight of hand, earning him the moniker, "Deadeye."

It was that name the streetwalkers of Whitechapel squawked as he tumbled into the common room with Dorian, loping toward the front entrance.

"Bugger me at both ends, you ladies ever seen an angel and a devil so 'andsome?" A girl they ironically called "Dark Sally," jabbed at one of her friends, who gathered at the long-planked table nursing sharp beer and waiting for darkness so they might ply their trade.

Cutter knew instantly he was the angel, as Dorian's wealth of shiny, black hair and sharp, satirical features made the comparison bloody obvious.

"I don't see no ladies here." The older plump prostitute named Bess gave an overloud bark of laughter before peering over at the boys. "I've swived plenty of devils in my day, but I'd bonk an angel with pretty eyes like that for free." She reached out an almost masculine hand to Cutter. "Come over here, darling, and let's see what you're packing."

Cutter didn't raise his eyes from the floorboards as his cheeks burned. "Any you seen Caro?"

"Look! Someone who still blushes in this shitehole," crowed yet another woman. "I'll bet you a pence he's a virgin."

"Caroline, you seen her or not?" he asked again.

Bosoms bounced as shrugs passed around the table, though it was Dark Sally who spoke. "She took up with an old watchmaker last I heard." She turned to Bess. "Remember the one, had an orange to share and it weren't even Christmas."

"I'd do right sick things for an orange," muttered a girl he didn't recognize. "Little bitch swiped him up before anyone got the chance at him."

"Careful, you," Bess threw a soiled handkerchief across the table. "That little bitch is his sister."

"I like virgins," sighed a thin, waspish woman around her sip of beer. "They 'aven't learnt to be cruel yet, and it's over quick enough. Right grateful they are." She sized Cutter up with a look that made him squirm.

"At that age, they'll pay you for another go in five minutes!" said Bess.

"And, what they lack in skill they make up for in eagerness," added another.

Dark Sally's eyes turned from kind to malevolent as she speared the boys with a hatred they weren't yet old enough to understand or to have earned. "Don't no man 'round here bother with skill," she sneered. "They'll grow to be no different."

A roar of laughter followed the lads out into the yard as they escaped the loud and bawdy women only to be swallowed by the crowded din of the streets.

A bitter autumn wind reached icy fingers through their threadbare clothes, and Cutter snapped the collar of his jacket higher, though it did little good. He rubbed at the back of his neck, and again at the empty ache in his chest.

Something was fucking wrong. Off. Missing.

"Fleas at you again?" Dorian ribbed.

"No, I just…" Cutter could think of nothing to describe what he was experiencing. "I'm cold is all."

"Where's the coat you got from the Ladies' Aid Society this spring?" Dorian asked, shoving his hands into his pockets. "That jacket you've on wouldn't warm a fleeced sheep."

"The sleeves barely came past me elbows anymore," he answered, giving his newly elongated limbs a wry stretch. "Besides, Caroline's was swiped from a doss house while back, so I gave it her."

Dorian nodded.

A tepid humiliation lodged next to the demon dogging Cutter, and he glanced over at Dorian to suss his friend's thoughts. "Caro's not like them whores in there," he rushed to explain. "She's just…well she won't let me spend me rifleman money on a room while it's still above freezing, so she does what she's got to."

"I know." Dorian gave a sober nod, his shoulders

hunching forward a little more. "She wants out as bad as we do."

"Maybe worse."

"We've almost enough, Cutter." A thread of steel hardened his friend's voice and worked at his jaw as he looked so far ahead, he might squint into the future. "I bet our haul today will cover at least one of us."

"But we go together," Cutter reiterated.

"Together," Dorian nodded, and they knocked their forearms.

A few months past, Cutter had hatched a scheme on the day the royals had paraded through High Street to celebrate the betrothal of a princess.

Dazzled by the accompanying regimentals in their crimson coats and rifles, he'd decided that in the space of a year, he and Dorian would be tall enough to lie about their ages and join Her Majesty's Army whereupon they'd be paid a penny a day. Enough to keep Caroline in rooms, and even send her to the regimental school. Enough to get medicine for Jane Blackwell's deteriorating health.

Enough to buy a future that didn't end in an early grave or worse, prison.

But that took papers...documents of birth they didn't have, and forging papers took money. So, they all kept whatever savings they could scrimp together in a tin hidden in Dorian's wall, waiting for the day they'd have enough.

"All's we have to do is evade the coppers until then." Dorian shoved his chin toward a pair on their beat, cudgels already out though there was no disturbance. "They'll give you nickel in Newgate for just about anything these days."

"You'll still marry her, won't you?" Cutter's soft question was almost lost to the din. "Even after the watchmaker. Even after—"

A rough punch landed on his shoulder. "'Course I will, you toad. Caro's me first kiss and everything, and...we all gotta do what needs doing to survive."

Dorian less than some, Cutter didn't say.

Because it wasn't his fault he had a mum, a roof over his head, or at least one or two guaranteed meals a day. Besides, Dorian and Mrs. Blackwell were generous whenever they could be.

"Maybe, if I'm going to marry Caroline, Mum would let her sleep in my corner with me."

Cutter's head snapped up as he speared Dorian with a glare.

"Not like that." Dorian lifted his hands in a defensive gesture. "I won't touch her or nothing. Just... so she wouldn't have to sleep somewhere else. With... anyone else."

Cutter had to swallow around a thickening throat before he could reply.

"You would do that?"

"'Course. We're family." Dorian shrugged him off. "I'd ask for you both if Mum didn't rent out every inch of space we own at a premium."

"It's all right. I can fend for meself."

They skipped, dodged, and slithered through the masses toward the docks, answering the calls of the other street lads, most of whom either feared or venerated them. Dorian, because he was strong as a cart horse with a punishing temper to match, and Cutter because of his aforementioned dead eyed aim and his sharp fists.

Cutter threw them convivial retorts out of habit alone. For some reason, the worse he felt the more stalwart he was at maintaining a pretense of normality.

If anyone knew you were down, they'd kick you for it.

So he did his best to conceal the devil of dread riding him today.

They arrived at Hangman's Dock the same time the coroner's cart did, so they had to act quickly before the police scattered the crowd.

"Look," Cutter pointed above. "There's a landlord charging a fee to get a glimpse from his fire escape. I'll wager there's at least a handful of shillings in that box."

"He's our mark." Dorian made a quick assessment of the buildings and boathouses above the river. "Think you can climb that drainpipe there, and get to the roof above him? I'll create a diversion and lead them away while you swipe what you can from the box."

"I'll swipe the whole bloody box, see if I don't." Cutter nodded and spit in his hands before raking them through the dry bank silt and rubbing them together. They'd just have to get to the other side of the crowd and then, he'd grasp the drainpipe, shimmy hand over hand until he'd scaled the two stories, and scoot onto the roof poised to drop into the spot the blighter would abandon once he tore off after Dorian.

This was one of his favorite ruses.

Cutter didn't care about the corpse. Hell, he'd seen his fill of death after the last typhus epidemic raged through the East End, what was one bloated river find?

Boring, was what.

He followed his friend as they shouldered and shoved and jostled as many people as they could, their enterprising hands dipping into every place and coming up with coin more often than not.

When they broke through to the front and took a breath, they each fished out their finds and shared a grin when they counted almost two shillings' worth between them, more than a day's wages around these parts. Today might make them rich, if they played it right.

They were about to scamper around the half-circled arc to dive back into the other side toward the building when the entire crowd made a collective gasp and took a step back, leaving them strangely exposed.

He barely heard the disbelieving whispers, so intent was he on his mission.

"She's in shreds..."

"What sort of animal...?"

"...no more than a child..."

Cutter turned his back on the river and made to dive back into the safety of the throng when Dorian's hand clutched his wrist with an iron grip.

He said nothing, but he didn't have to.

The demon that had haunted him all day now roared.

It scratched and clawed and cut deep enough to sever a limb. That was truly what it felt like. Something had been cut out of him. Off of him. Something vital and dear. Gone.

Amputated.

He already knew before he turned to look.

Before he saw the strands of identical golden hair sullied with river filth waving like soft reeds in the little dam created by a concrete dock. Before he registered the red abrasions at her wrists and bare ankles, or the ridiculous pattern of last spring's coat, the one he'd given her, only one arm haphazardly shoved into the sleeve.

Before it dawned on him that even such polluted water was never so red.

The coin in Cutter's hands fell to the earth. He stepped on them as he lunged forward, her name released to the sky by the devil who'd stalked him. Surely it had to be. Because no human creature could have made such an inhuman scream.

Caroline.

CHAPTER 1

LONDON, 1880, TWENTY-FIVE YEARS LATER

*P*rudence no longer desired to be good.

Or, rather, to be *a* Goode.

It was why she stood at the gate to Miss Henrietta's School for Cultured Young Ladies at midnight, her chest heaving and her resolve crumbling. She'd come all this way. And she wanted this. Didn't she?

Just one last night of freedom. One night of her own making. Her own choosing.

One night of pleasure before her father foisted her off on the highest-ranking noble desperate enough to have her at nine and twenty.

Three months. *Three months* until her life was irreparably ruined, and she'd have to love, honor, and obey the most notorious spirit-swilling, mistress-having, loud-mouthed, and fractious idiot in all Blighty.

George Hamby-Forsyth, the sixth Earl of Sutherland.

He'd marry her because she'd an obscene enough dowry to cover his debts and still maintain a generation or two.

Not because he loved her.

God, what a fool she'd been!

13

For the umpteenth time, the tragedy of her gullible nature slapped her until her cheeks burned. Had it only been yesterday she'd found out her happy engagement was a farce? That everyone around her knew she would be wretched and humiliated, and still expected her to go through with it?

That the two people closest to her in the world hadn't loved her enough to tell her.

The scene forever tormented her, illuminated just as clearly as it had been in the brightness of the late afternoon sun the day before. Every decision she'd made a perfect mix of timing and luck until she'd stumbled upon her own tragedy.

Pru had been pleasantly exhausted after spending a day with the seamstresses for her extensively fine wedding trousseau. Her sister Honoria had accompanied her, along with their oldest friend and neighbor, Mrs. Amanda Brighton of the Farley-Downs Brightons.

"Do let's go to Hyde Park," Pru had gestured expansively toward the park in question, shaking Amanda's arm in her eagerness. "I'm dying to sweep by Rotten Row and take a few turns on Oberon."

"I'm game for it." Honoria, her eldest—already married—sister, had lifted her nose and squinted into the distance where the horse track colloquially known as *Rotten Row* bustled with the empire's aristocracy, both human and equine.

Amanda was more Honoria's age than Pru's—which was three years older—but she and Amanda shared a blithe and energetic nature that made them natural mischief-makers and thereby the swiftest of friends.

Honoria, though a beauty, was born to be a dreary proper matron, and fulfilled her vocation with dreadful aplomb.

"I wouldn't at all mind examining the new stags on the market," Amanda said with a sprightly grin lifting her myriad of freckles. She tucked one arm into Pru's and the other into Honoria's, and nearly dragged them both toward the square.

Prudence's ride along the row had been every bit as exhilarating and satisfying as she'd imagined. Friends and acquaintances had called out their hearty congratulations, which had produced the sort of smile that she felt with her entire self.

It'd dimmed when she'd a brief encounter with Lady Jessica Morton, who was the reason everyone had called her "Pru*dunce*" in finishing school. But even her spinster nemesis had gritted out her felicitations. Had Jessica's smile been on a dog, it would have been called a snarl, and Prudence had to fight a spurt of victorious wickedness.

Jealousy was such an unflattering color.

Oh, it wasn't her best quality, this, but it *had* felt indescribably good to "win," for lack of a better word. Her entire life, she'd come in second. Second eldest and second prettiest of the four so-called, "Goode girls."

Second married, as well.

But to an Earl! And not just *any* Earl, but one of the most marriageable bachelors in the realm. Her happy engagement was delicious any day but became pure truffled pleasure when trotted out in front of Jessica.

Bidding a cheerful farewell to the retreating back of her childhood antagonist, Pru had handed Oberon to one of the grooms, and set off to meet the ladies for tea.

Bouncing her riding crop off her thigh in high spirits, Pru had searched for them, eager to share her bit of gossip about her conversation with Jessica.

She found Honoria and Amanda on a bench with their heads together. They admired a group of smartly dressed young men prancing about on thoroughbreds and sipped thin glasses of lemonade that sweated in the summer heat.

She was about to call out to them when she fumbled her riding crop and dropped it, kicking it behind a tree.

Cursing her constant clumsiness, she scampered after it, and was still stooping to retrieve it when Amanda had said, "How bold of Lady Jessica to approach Pru in public."

Honoria retrieved a compact mirror from her reticule and checked the hue of her perfect lips, the pallor of her dewy skin, and tucked a stray dark hair back beneath her hat before snapping it shut. "I detest Jessica Morton. She tormented Pru endlessly in school."

Amanda made a sour face, as if her lemonade had suddenly become too tart. "I'd thought her affair with Pru's fiancé concluded, but now I'm not so certain."

Honoria's excessively pretty features pinched into a frown of disapproval. "George and Jessica? Are you quite certain?"

Heedless of her new wine velvet riding jacket, Prudence had pressed her back to the tree, less a furtive move than a collapse. She needed something to hold her up.

George...*Her George*...and Jessica Morton?

When? Why? And how? And how many times? And... *When?*

Certainly, she'd never assumed he'd been a saint, not with his roguish good looks, but now that they were to marry, she'd thought he'd have no need for other women.

That she'd be enough.

That their love would contain all the passion he'd require.

Amanda swatted at an insect with the fan previously hanging from her white-gloved wrist. "I heard about it at the Prescott Ball, Maureen Broadwell and Jessica Morton complained that Sutherland is a base and venal lover. She said, and I quote, 'That man can read a woman's body like a blind man can read music.'"

Honoria's breath hitched on her sip of lemonade and she hid a series of delicate coughs behind her handkerchief.

Pru swallowed back her own sob. The Prescott Ball had been only a fortnight ago. George had been her escort...and these women had been discussing him in such a manner as he waltzed her on the tops of clouds.

"Poor Pru," Amanda tutted, waiting for Honoria to finish her coughing fit before adding, "Don't you find it a bit disgusting how many bastards Pru's dowry will keep up once George has his hands on all her money?" She sighed, then shrugged it off as if it were no more disappointing than a broken fingernail.

Bastards?

Pru had tugged at the high neck of her gown, fighting for breath.

All she'd ever wanted was children.

To tuck chubby little limbs into bed. Kiss scraped knees and tears. She wanted to hear the peals of laughter when their strong daddy would toss them in the air and allow them to climb on his back.

George had been that man in her dreams. So dashing and virile.

He already *had* children?

Honoria had leaned forward, looking intently toward the track as if searching for Prudence's form. "Poor Pru, indeed. George has convinced everyone that he loves her. Even William...even me. I suppose we should tell her."

William Mosby, Viscount Woodhaven, was George's closest compatriot, and Honoria's husband.

Now that Pru thought about it, Honoria hadn't seemed particularly pleased with the betrothal, and she'd always assumed it was because Pru was marrying an Earl when William was merely a Viscount, and thereby his social inferior.

She'd been so absurdly blind.

Amanda let out a disenchanted sigh. "Pru needs to learn how the world works, eventually. That it's not all ponies and balls and butterfly nets."

Honoria sucked her lip between her teeth, a gesture she made whenever she was conflicted. "Though, I'd hate to ruin her wedding for her, and it's not as if she can break the engagement now. I should have warned her off George ages ago, but William expressly forbade it."

Amanda nodded, smoothing the creases from her cream gown. "It's kind of us, I think, to maintain her frivolous naiveté for a bit longer."

"Yes. Kind." Honoria's famous composure crumpled for the slightest moment, uncovering the features of a woman beset by abject misery. "She's a lifetime to be disappointed by a husband."

Pru clapped two hands over her mouth to keep from saying anything. From screaming in the middle of the bustling park loud and long enough for all of London's elite to hear. She couldn't face them yet. She couldn't sort through her hurt and anger and humiliation enough to land on a single thing to say.

Frivolous naiveté? Was this *really* what they thought of her? Her best friend and her elder sister? Honoria... the woman she'd idolized for the whole of her life. The bastion of feminine perfection against which she'd been measured. The loveliest debutante to grace Her Majesty's halls in decades.

And Amanda? The naughty sprite who'd collected all her secrets and her sorrows. Who'd bounced and giggled through life with nary a care.

"Speaking of disappointing husbands...mine will be back in town tomorrow night," Amanda distracted Pru by saying. "And so, I think *that* one with the muscular legs will be my next acquisition." Amanda pointed in the direction of the riders, and Pru blinked through gathering tears in confusion.

Her friend had never expressed a great interest in horseflesh, and her husband was more interested in estate acquisitions than equine. He owned half of Cheshire.

"I've always admired your taste," Honoria said approvingly.

Amanda leaned in closer. "Lady Westlawn told me he brought her to completion twice in one night. *In fact*, he was so skilled, she gave him one of her coveted diamonds." The sound Amanda made was laced with enough licentiousness to bring about a biblical plague.

Pru gaped. They weren't speculating about horseflesh at all. But the men astride!

"To the Stags of St. James." Amanda lifted her lemonade for a "cheers" in the fashion of a bawdy sailor at a public house. "Are you certain you won't try one?"

Honoria clinked her glass with Amanda's but set it down at her elbow. "As tempted as I am, William has me on a tight leash."

"That doesn't mean you can't come and look," Amanda offered. "That's nothing more than window-shopping, really."

"No. I suppose it doesn't." Honoria stood and drifted toward the Row, a trailing Amanda in her wake.

Pru couldn't stand any more. She'd fled home and immediately begged her father to break their engagement.

He'd blustered through his stately beard. "You and your sisters are beautiful enough to tempt men away from their mistresses, Pru. I dare say Honoria did, and you're almost her equal." He patted her head with the sort of fond deference he showed his hounds. "Sutherland is an Earl, a vital man of true English blue blood and the...passions and tempers to match."

"But, Papa," she'd sobbed. "He'll humiliate me. He'll make me a laughingstock."

"Nonsense. Sutherland has always been a discreet man. This marriage is your duty to your family, so don't let your doddle-headed fancies of romance get in the way of that, do you hear me? You will say nothing of this to Sutherland and when he next comes to court you, you'll keep a civil tongue in your head, or I'll not be responsible for what I do!"

A distraught and sodden Pru had then taken her shattered soul to her mother, asking her to mend it. Begging her to intervene.

"It is the practice of men to have mistresses, dear. And you'll find it's a blessing in the end..." With that crisp reply, she'd nailed the coffin shut on any hope Pru had of reclaiming a sense of herself.

Something had hardened in her then. A fist of rebellious anger clenched around the last glowing shard of her heart.

The very next day, she had called upon Lady Westlawn and not-so-discreetly inquired about the Stags of St. James.

Which was how she'd ended up here. At the garden gate to Miss Henrietta's School for Cultured Young Ladies.

St. James, she was told, was not a reference to the park or buildings, but to the patron saint of riding.

Of all the vulgar things.

As she stared at the gate, Pru gathered her resolve. She wouldn't be like George. Nor would she be like Amanda. Once she'd taken a wedding vow, she'd keep it, regardless of what George decided to do. And if any children resulted from their marriage, she'd teach them to do the same.

One deceit did not merit another.

But tonight, she'd take a lover. A man who was nothing like the Earl of Sutherland in all his dark, brutish glory.

She'd claim a night of pleasure for her very own. One night she controlled with her desires and whims, and where *her* satisfaction was the object of the deed.

Because from what she'd heard, she'd live without it for the rest of her life.

Pru pulled the hood of her cloak down to shadow her face from the gaslights perched atop the wrought iron gate and tapped on the third bar three times.

A footman melted from the shadows, a pretty lad, barely old enough to shave.

He gave her a curt nod. "Do you have an appointment, madam?"

What had Lady Westlawn told her to say if she hadn't made prior arrangements at Hyde Park? Oh yes.

"I'm here to peruse the night-blooming jasmine."

The gate swung open on silent hinges and she took in a shaking breath. Thresholds, she'd heard were dangerous. Places of in-between, where fairy folk and demons could meddle with the living.

Or so superstitious ancestors once believed.

Tonight, she could believe it. Out on this street, she'd done nothing to speak of. She was no one of great importance. Prudence Goode. A second daughter of second-rate nobility.

A virgin.

To cross this threshold, was to be forever altered. Did a night like this always seem so monumental? Did the specter of fate seem to hover above every woman's head upon making such a decision?

Something intangible drifted above the lamplight but below the stars. Something sentient and dark. Perhaps a bit dangerous and wrathful, though she somehow wasn't afraid.

Destiny was on the other side of that gate, it told her. More than her virginity would be taken tonight.

No. Prudence shook her head. No, not destiny. What whimsical tripe.

She wasn't here to court fate...only fantasy.

It took two tries to swallow her nerves before she picked up her skirts, stepped over the threshold, and lost her breath to a marvel.

For a moment, she wondered if she had, indeed, been snatched by the Fae.

The gardens at Miss Henrietta's School for Cultured Young Ladies might have been a fairy patch. Strings of beads and ribbon flowed from curious shaped hedges and foreign willows with lush, wilting limbs. They glimmered and sparkled in the dim lamplight along lustrous cobbles, illuminating paths to dark places.

More importantly, they created concealing shadows, some of which were already full of revelry. The grounds were vast for the city, and the manor house glowed gaily on the other side of the garden.

She was not to approach the house, she was told. The ironically named school for cultured young ladies was anything but. Miss Henrietta's was one of London's most exclusive and expensive brothels where *men* took their pleasure among a menagerie of women.

The Stags of St. James, however, made discreet house calls.

And in the summer on certain clear nights...they rutted out-of-doors.

Except, Prudence realized as she ventured onto the grounds, the out-of-doors was not so rustic as one might assume. The gardens at Versailles might weep for the luxury here, and if one wanted to find a place to feel ensconced in privacy, one needn't look too far.

"Approach any stag you like, madam, so long as he is not engaged by another," the young footman startled her by appearing at her elbow. She'd quite forgotten he was there. He leaned down to whisper, "They'll lock horns for the likes of *you*."

"Who—who would you recommend?" she murmured, instantly regretting the ridiculous question.

The footman didn't even break his perfect form. He might have been engaged by a Duke, not a derelict debutant looking to debauch herself.

"Adam is in the orchard, seeking his Eve," he proffered, gesturing toward a copse of trees, as if he directed her to pluck an apple, rather than the original sin. "Let's see…Daniel is bound in his den in anticipation of devouring, if you are feeling the role of lioness tonight." He pointed at a dark shadow in a glass enclosure covered by ivy.

"There's Goliath, the barbarian who might be tamed by the right gentle hand. Or David, if you prefer someone…younger. More eager."

Prudence stopped, suddenly seized by indecision and a not little fear of lightning, even on such a clear and cloudless night. "I'm sorry but are all of the—er—stags given religious names?" she queried. "Seems rather blasphemous, doesn't it?"

He gave her a mockingly chiding look. "Go to a church if you want to judge, Madam, we're all here to commit a cardinal sin, maybe several."

A decent point, that. She nodded and mumbled an apology, suddenly feeling very itchy and out of her element.

With a jovial wink that told her all was forgiven, he bowed. "If you're feeling indecisive, I encourage you to take a turn around the garden, let it dazzle your senses, and see what entices your...vigor."

That seemed like an excellent idea. She'd come here for a thing. An experience. Why the devil hadn't it occurred to her that what she was coming here for...was a person?

A man.

A man of her own choosing.

How very novel. She'd only ever thought to be chosen. Women were always waiting, hoping to be picked or plucked by the right man. Selected like a trinket in a shop, to be taken home and trotted out at expensive gatherings.

Tonight, she was the shopper. She would pick the man she wanted and pay him to do what she desired.

But who? Did she want David or Goliath, Adam or Daniel?

A hero or a heretic.

A saint or a sinner...

Venturing deeper into the fairy garden, she allowed her senses to take it all in. The gentle breeze ruffling at the ribbons and drapes of chiffon and silk along the path. The slight sound of running water in the distance. A giggle from that dark corner. A groan from that Bedouin tent over there.

She refused to look too far into the dark, and so she kept her eyes often skyward, up to the stars.

Which was why she never saw the dark shadow crouched behind a hedgerow by the fountain.

CHAPTER 2

*C*hief Inspector Carlton Morley stalked his latest villain from the putrid slag pots of industrial East London all the way to Mayfair. Three young men had been slaughtered, and no one had connected their murders until today.

Until him.

The victims had been from several different boroughs of London and none of them had known each other, but their deaths were identical. No one had noticed the connection until the files had made their way to his desk, because detective inspectors from differing stations rarely had cause to collaborate with each other.

But they all answered to him.

The cases had been closed. Deemed unsolvable or without enough evidence to proceed through lawful means.

But Morley had other means at his disposal... and there were many forms of law and justice. The Queen's Justice. The law of the land. Divine justice. The laws of nature.

And the justice of the streets. The laws of which were unwritten but universally heeded.

The laws of the land were necessary to uphold, and he'd devoted his entire career to doing so.

But the laws of the streets afforded him the means to mete out justice where the system had failed.

And they'd failed these murdered men. Strapping, handsome lads, well-liked by their families and communities, all employed among the working class. And yet none of them seemed to be struggling to get by. Each of them lived above their station, kept family members fed and comfortable in clean and respectable dwellings on pittance a day.

The question was how?

The answer had led him here.

Miss Henrietta's School for Cultured Young Ladies, of all the unimaginable places.

And since he'd obtained the information that'd led him here by means not strictly legal, he couldn't very well walk through the front door, let alone obtain a warrant.

So, he'd taken to the dark, as he'd done with alarming frequency these days, disguising himself every now and again with a simple black mask he'd had lying around from one of the Duchess of Trenwyth's multitude of endless charity functions.

His view to the garden was impeded by impenetrable hedges or stockades of ivy around wrought iron, if not a full stone wall on the west side. He ultimately decided to circumvent the locked gate by scaling a nearby wych elm. He balanced out on a limb until he feared it would no longer hold his weight, and vaulted over the gate, expertly avoiding impalement on the iron spikes.

Morley landed in silence among the shadows and kept to them as he stalked along the circumference of the property. He waited and watched, his entire body attuned to danger, to a possible threat. A villain or a murderer.

A couple strode nearby, and he melded with the dark as a tall and elegantly handsome man bent to whisper something scandalous into the ear of a woman ten years his senior and two stone his heft.

She tutted, flirted, and then her companion swept her into his embrace, pressing her against the column of a gazebo. He kissed her passionately before he grappled with the latch of a small outbuilding and shoved her inside.

What the devil?

A tree branch snapped around the corner of a hedge. Morley drew his knife, took two readying breaths, and burst from around the corner, dropping into a fighting stance.

Only from this angle could he have seen the gagged and blindfolded woman beneath the tree, holding its lower branches for purchase as a man brutally thrust into her from behind.

Something in the muffled sounds she made froze him in place. They were yips and mewls of encouragement. Unmistakable in their ardor.

Bemused, Morley sheathed his knife and blinked rather doggedly at the fornicating couple until the man noticed him and made an impatient gesture for him to go.

His hips never lost their rhythm.

The woman was enjoying herself, but the gentleman checked his watch as though... he kept track of the time?

Morley backed away, turning to the garden and seeing it for what it truly was.

If someone had told him he'd already died and gone to Elysium, he might have believed them. For this resembled something of a pagan paradise. Friction and fornication hinted at everywhere, if not flagrantly happening.

No one *exactly* fucked in the open, but neither was a gazebo, a sheer tent, a hedge maze or a copse of carefully placed trees considered a proper place for a romp.

Even the air was sweeter here, whispering of lilacs and gardenias rather than the singular smells of the city. The garden sparkled like the very stars might visit to watch the debauchery. It was a dream crafted by honey-hued lighting and fluttering fabrics.

Of all the bastardly bacchanalian bullshit.

Morley retreated to a borderline pornographic fountain and crouched behind a hedgerow, grateful that the sound of the water covered the thinly veiled noises of carnal revelry.

A small mercy that, because his body was beginning to forget how exhausted he was and respond to the wickedness of the atmosphere.

It was how they got you, these places. Inundated one with sex and fantasy until instinct took over and a man forgot who he was. Became a needful, terrible creature, one led around by his cock rather than his reason, until he found his pocketbook emptied by his own weaknesses.

A brothel. He grimaced. He'd broken into a brothel of all places whilst searching for a killer. He must have taken a very wrong direction, or he'd stumbled upon another humungous clue.

Either way, he couldn't exactly begin an interrogation at—he looked at his watch—half one in the morning. Tucking the watch away, he scrubbed at his face with both hands before adjusting the mask over his eyes.

God's blood but he was tired.

He'd been waylaid on his way here by a contingent of the High Street Gang, who'd taken one look at his darkly elegant attire and decided he was an easy mark.

He'd kicked nine shades of shit out of four men and had left them tied to the corner for the next copper on his beat to find.

With a note, of course, as was courteous.

He'd broken up a domestic brawl that'd spilled out onto the streets, and gave a boy on the cusp of manhood a pence to sleep beneath a different roof than his ham-fisted father.

A man on Wapping High Street had mistaken a charwoman for a nightwalker and had been about to force his attentions upon her when Morley had picked up a palm-sized stone, and made a spinning slingshot of his cravat. The rock to the temple had felled the attacker, and Morley didn't stay to check if he was even alive. He'd shrugged off the woman's cries of gratitude and had been on his way.

He was no hero. These were just things he did, sweeping up small crimes while he chased nightmares through the night.

Back when he'd attempted to sleep, he'd been tortured by them. Eventually, those nightmares had seeped into the daylight, following him from the dark until they filled every corner of every room. Shades and specters. The ghosts of those he'd killed, of those who'd endeavored to kill him. Of the souls he'd failed to save and the monsters who'd escaped justice.

For decades they'd haunted him, tormented him endlessly each time he dared close his eyes. Until he'd done something about it.

He *became* the thing from which nightmares ran.

He rid the night of monsters, so he could continue to be the man he was during the day without sinking into a miasma of slow and indelible madness. He was both the system of justice and the shadow of it.

Because the shadow could do what the system could not.

Because he still had a dead-eye, sharp fists, and even sharper blades.

Because he'd sold his soul to a demon for justice years ago, and every subsequent sin merely deepened the fathomless pit into which he'd been thrown.

Every time he'd thought he'd hit the bottom, he realized he was still falling.

That the depths could always be deeper. That the night could always be darker. That the world could always be colder.

That honor didn't seem to mean much anymore, and he continued to fight a war that might have always been lost and for a cause that was nothing more than an illusion.

He'd been fighting for so long. For so many endless years, and for what? These days, every victory felt as though it made as much difference as a teardrop to the Thames.

And still he hunted, because what else could he do? Collect a wage until the inevitable forages of time and regret came for him as they did for everyone else?

A snap of a whip and a snarl came from the glasshouse covered in ivy. Morley squinted over at it, watching the shadows take shape, illuminated by one dim lantern inside.

If he wasn't mistaken, a woman rode a man, but not his hips...Morley squinted...his face. Her pleasure sounds filtered through the fountain to him, hot and demanding.

They reverberated down his spine and landed in his loins.

God, it had been too long since he—

Another astonished sound broke his intent concentration, this one behind him. From his crouching position, he turned his neck to watch a woman's windmilling arms fail to balance her before she crashed down upon him like a felled tree, toppling them both to the grass.

Morley swam in a sea of skirts and petticoats, taking a slap to the jaw for his troubles, though he was fairly certain she hadn't meant to strike him.

The woman draped across his lap writhed and wriggled, apparently as surprised as he. He attempted to gather her up as one might a child, one arm behind her shoulders and the other beneath her knees, but she didn't seem capable of holding still enough for him to manage.

"Upon my word," she exclaimed from behind mountains of silk. "I'm frightfully sorry! Are you hurt?"

Morley opened his mouth to assure her he was unharmed, but she didn't wait for a reply.

Her next sentence was spoken in one breath. "I'm forever ungainly, clumsy, my sisters call me, and in a place such as this it's rather impossible not to look everywhere at once and I was honestly attempting to look nowhere at all and you're rather dark—" She finally crested her skirts and wrestled them beneath her arms to look at him. She took a breath to amend... "No, not dark. Dazzling."

Morley blinked down at her, suddenly wishing he'd ever thought to steal a moment from crime reports and newspapers to crack the spine on a book of verse.

Because the woman in his arms was a poem, and he hadn't the words to describe her.

His hold of her became suddenly very careful. Delicate, like one would hold a teacup in a lady's parlor rather than the tin mugs at the Yard.

"Oh," she said breathlessly, as if discovering clarity. "It's you. You're who I've come looking for."

Even through his building confusion, some strange

part of him was *as glad* she'd—quite literally—stumbled upon him as she seemed to be.

He shook his head, trying to dislodge the sensation.

As Morley always did when out about his nocturnal business, he adopted a bit of his childhood cockney accent. "Do I know you?"

The lanterns painted the shadows of her ridiculously long eyelashes across cheeks that could have been chiseled from the whitest of Roman marble. Those lashes fringed wide, dark eyes two sizes too large for her delicate features. The effect intensified her dramatic expression as she seemed to take him in with identical wonder.

"Yes, you'll do rather nicely, I think," she breathed, apropos of nothing. Her voice, alternately husky and sweet, seemed incongruous with this place. There was temptation in it, but no sin. Innocence, but also desire.

She leaned forward on his lap, and he became very aware that he held her like a man held his bride when crossing the threshold.

The thought terrified him, and yet he couldn't seem to let her go.

"Which one are you?" she asked as though to herself as she conducted a thorough examination of his features. "I can't think of any biblical hero you'd resemble...and none with a mask, besides. I like a bit of mystery."

He cocked his head at that. Biblical? This was all lunacy. He neither knew this woman nor did he want to. If she was a prostitute, she was a bloody good one, but he was no customer. He should lift her to her feet and send her on her way. He'd work to do and—

The soft scrape of her fingers against his shadow beard froze him in place. She watched her own hand with a dazed, almost unfocused gaze as she discovered the line of his jaw with a featherlight touch before cupping it in her small palm.

The tender curiosity demonstrated in the motion unstitched something hard within him.

"No…" she whispered. "No, you're no hero."

He could do little else than hold his breath, his every sense hanging upon her next words. What would be her verdict, he wondered? Would she compliment or condemn him?

"You're an angel, aren't you? An archangel, perhaps. Or a fallen one? A warrior…" she decided. "But… for which side?"

"I'm no angel," he warned. "I'm nothing but a shadow." Morley hated to disappoint the fanciful woman, hated to dispel whatever magic she was weaving through him with her touch. But it was better he told the truth. Better for them both.

"How ridiculous of me, I beg your pardon. I'd like to say that I've been caught up in all this fantasy, but it'd be a lie. I'm like this all the time." At this she gave the ghost of a giggle, and the sound was more pleasant than the rush of the fountain beneath which they'd fallen. "You're a very solid shadow, sir, if I may say so." Her gaze finally focused to resolute. "How much?"

He frowned. "How much?"

"How much?" she encouraged meaningfully with a thrust of her sharp chin. "For you? The—er, footman told me to select any one of the Stags of St. James who were not previously engaged. And I've decided upon you. I want to make love to you—or rather, I want you to make love to me. But only i-if you don't have other women—er—plans. I mean, that is, prior engagements."

"Prior engagements?" he echoed.

Her hopeful features fell into a petulant pout. "Did someone already make an appointment at Hyde Park for tonight?"

"No," he said carefully, wondering what to do next.

She brightened immediately. "Excellent. Then...tell me how this works. I've never...hired a man to make love to me before. And I confess I'm ignorant of how else to proceed rather than plainly. So, would you do me the kindness—er—the honor?"

Morley blinked down at her as three things had just become inexorably clear to him.

The first was this woman talked incessantly when nervous, and her babble was oddly endearing.

Second, she was from a wealthy family, likely blue-blooded and likely married.

And tertiary...he'd lived probably nearly forty years and had never met a woman he'd so keenly desired to fuck.

A hunger awakened within him with all the ferocity of a hibernating beast. It had teeth and claws and tore his decency to shreds before going to work on his restraint. His heart kicked at his ribs, which restricted in turn, relieving him of breath.

He was a moral man, goddammit. Lawful and without prejudice or vice. He'd lived as a veritable monk for more years than he cared to admit, and there was good reason for it. He should bloody well stand up and take his leave of her. Right now.

Except, what if she didn't go home? What if she lingered in search of a different stag?

That wasn't going to bloody happen. He wouldn't let it.

He could throw her over his shoulder and return her to her father. Her husband. Or whatever woebegone individual had the responsibility for her safekeeping.

He made to do just that when another variable struck him.

What if she returned tomorrow night? What if she took her pleasure with another man?

What if... he missed his chance?

The hungry demon within him snarled at this, raked his claws and expelled scalding fire through his veins like a hell-spawned dragon until Morley had to force himself to inhale and expel a protracted breath.

He was no kind of man to consider such a proposition. He was neither starving for coin nor lacking in romantic prospects.

No, this was ludicrous. Nothing more than a flattering fantasy.

He opened his mouth, preparing a gentle rejection. "What do you want me to do to you?"

His lips slammed shut. The question had ricocheted through his mind since the moment she'd asked him to name his price. But it'd been the *last* thing he'd expected to escape his lips.

Blotches of color stained her pale cheeks, but she didn't look away. "I-I'd like you to do...whatever it is women pay you for the most often." She reached into her hooded pelisse and retrieved a satchel of coins. "The skill you're most proud of. The thing that makes them come to you on a night like this."

Morley didn't know what women *paid* for sexually, but he knew enough about people to reply. "A bird like you knows her mind. She don't come looking for a man like me 'less she has some idea of what she intends to get from the encounter."

What the bloody hell was he saying? He wasn't even considering this... so why—

She made a wry sound. Half laugh, half gasp, as she reached up to smooth at the collar of his shirt, which had bent when he'd torn off his cravat. Something in the nervous gesture touched him. Something that had

KERRIGAN BYRNE

begun to unstitch him the moment she'd fallen, and now was quickly unraveling.

"My fiancé. He's a selfish lover. I don't think he'd ever..." She trailed away for a moment, before imparting information about a man Morley hoped to never meet, lest he murder the bastard. "I found out that he—well, he's not faithful. And understand he doesn't have to be—that most men of my class aren't. But *I* will be. If I take a vow of marriage, I shan't break it, but I've said no vows yet." She tilted her head to look back up at him, a defiant little furrow appearing beneath her dramatically arched brows. "He does not own me *yet.*"

Tears colored her voice, though none had fallen, and something inside Morley twisted. Pain did not sit comfortably on features such as hers. She'd a visage that glowed with an inner light, even in the sinful dimness of this lusty place.

She didn't belong here in the dark, committing sins on the ground. Hers was a face for the sun. She was a spoiled woman experiencing her first heartbreak. Learning her first terrible truth about the world of men in which she lived.

She didn't know the first thing about pain.

And yet...the courageous way she fought her threatening emotion, tied him up in knots.

Christ, this shouldn't be happening. That he was even entertaining such an idea was lunacy. This woman was obviously an emotional disaster he didn't need and there was a killer to find.

And yet...she was warm and fragrant, and they were surrounded by sensual indiscretions, the sounds of which glided through this infernal glade with increasing intensity. She smelled like a delicacy waiting to be devoured and his mouth would not cease watering.

So he held her, his cock hard as a diamond, and Lord save him if her eyes were not dilated black with passion. He knew he could give her what her fiancé would not, and that knowledge ate him up inside.

Inflamed as his body was, as hungry as the demon within him seemed to be, he gave one last feeble resistance.

"Making love to me won't make nights with him any easier," he warned.

"I know," she whispered, dropping the coin purse on the ground next to him so she could trace the hollows beneath his cheekbones with those soft, questing fingers, angling down toward his lips.

Morley's terse mouth softened involuntarily as her featherlight touch sensitized the rim of his upper lip as she charted whatever curve she found there.

"I—overheard tell that there are those of you who can bring a woman to completion with—with your mouth. I find I'd—very much like to know how that feels. And then... I'd like you to..." Her lashes swept down again as she battled with her own breath for a moment. "Lady Westlawn told me that some of you could make a woman come for you more than once..."

Morley swallowed twice before he could bring himself to cede defeat.

Of all the injustices and indignities he'd encountered in his long, lonely life, the one chewing at his soul was the idea that either of them would live one more night without knowing what it felt like for her to orgasm against his tongue.

And then again against his cock.

Though he cradled her as one would an invalid or a child, his fingers curled around her limbs as the hunger tore through him, spilling hot and victorious through his veins.

Sweet Christ but he was going to devour her.

And she knew it as well as he did.

He saw it in the slight widening of her eyes, in the parting of her lips. In the way her body stiffened a little, and then slackened, settling into his arms with a sigh of submission.

That sigh was his ultimate undoing.

He lowered his head, lifting her to meet him. He didn't so much kiss her as consumed her, his searching, burning mouth parting the pliant pillows of her lips, delving into the honeyed depths he found there.

If this was Elysium, then she was ambrosia. And with her in his arms, he felt like a god.

He broke the kiss before long to cast about for a place for them to go.

"The fountain," she panted, sliding her hands to lock behind his neck so she could pull him back down to her mouth, her eyes homed in on his lips.

"You'll be exposed," he pointed out, realizing how ridiculous he sounded even as he said it. But now that he'd decided to have her, he was jealous that even the stars would have the chance to see her beauty, let alone anyone who should happen by.

"Only to you," she whispered, sliding out of his grasp and lifting herself to perch on the wide stone ledge.

The path with the row of dim lamps ended at the far side of the Italian style stone, leaving their side of the fountain cast in shadow. He could barely make out her features, but she must have been able to see him plainly enough.

She might have been a sea goddess commanding the stone deities behind her to spout her element into the night, anointing her wealth of carefully arranged dark hair with little gems of mist.

"I'm… I don't know if I can bring myself to disrobe," she said in a small voice.

"I'll do it." He lifted onto his knees and reached for her, but she intercepted his hands with hers, lacing thin fingers with his own.

"I mean to say, I'm too reticent to do this in the altogether."

She wanted to keep her fine silk dress on... and he'd be goddamned if he didn't find that oddly arousing.

And helpful. His lust had teeth, and something told him that if he were to unwrap this woman, he wouldn't last long enough to fuck her well.

She was too beautiful, her scent too alluring, and that look on her face. That coy mix of vulnerable vixen was going to drive him beyond all control.

God help him, he was doing this. With her. *To* her. A part of him knew he'd live to regret it, and he couldn't bring himself to care.

A hard life had turned him into a hard man. Harder and colder with every lonely year that passed. And all he did was work and fight. Work to keep the hard man from becoming an evil one, and fight the evil he recognized in others. Fight to keep it from devouring his city, as it had his family.

And here was someone soft. Soft and...beleaguered by a familiar loneliness. Asking for him to share a few moments of pleasure.

He was too soul-weary to resist such an enticing bargain.

Releasing his hands, she curled her fingers in her lap, bunching her skirts and lifting the powder blue hem to uncover lace boots and stark white stockings.

It was an invitation not to be denied.

Morley plunged his hands beneath the folds and frills, drawing them up shapely, silk-covered calves until he reached her knees. He parted them, filling the space he made with his body.

With her sitting up on the ledge, and him on his

knees, their faces aligned. He claimed her lips once again, marveling that there was a mouth on this earth that tasted like hers.

He delved into the warmth, a velvet intrusion. A parody of what he would do to her elsewhere. Her little, warm tongue made gentle slides against his, tentatively testing his restraint.

Finding the edge of it.

A fire of anticipation immolated in his loins, and he suddenly ached to taste every part of her. To rip her dress open and see if she was as pale as the night suggested. If iridescent veins adorned her breasts and the thin, tender skin on the inside of her thighs. He wanted to mark her with little bites of his teeth, to show the man who had never pleased her that someone was able and oh so willing.

He hitched her skirts higher, hands venturing from her knees up her thighs, finding curious frills, silk garters bedecked with lace and little bows attached with delicate stitches.

His hands played there, plucking at things and testing textures while he savored her mouth for as long as his inflamed body would allow.

Her hands didn't remain idle.

They rested on the buttons of his coat, releasing them with jerky, uncertain motions until she could wrench it open and slide her hands inside. She explored the width and breadth of him until her arms locked around him.

The uncertain tenderness in the embrace was too much for him to bear.

Morley broke the kiss, pulling back to assess her. To watch her widening eyes as his fingers threaded higher, following the silken expanse of flesh until he met the barrier of her thin cotton drawers.

She tucked her lips between her teeth and trembled, but didn't look away.

"Tell me again what you want." He hardly recognized his voice, the dark, growling street accent, the insolence and lust.

She gave a delicate swallow before answering. "I-I can't say it."

"You want me to kiss you?" he prodded, covering her mound. "Here?"

She gave a little jump, and her knees clamped his hips, as if they might have closed had his body not impeded it.

"Yes," she replied with a bashful whisper.

Feminine heat radiated from beneath the thin barrier of her undergarment, and Morley leaned in to lift her hips and draw it down to her ankles.

He wanted to kiss her again. He never wanted to stop kissing her, and because of that, he didn't allow himself to do so.

Kissing her was dangerous. As was the sweet detention of her arms.

A man could find himself a willing prisoner of such shackles, and he hadn't the inclination. He hadn't expected such sweetness. Hadn't been prepared for the answering emotion evoked in his body.

Best he keep this carnal.

Lowering himself down, he ducked his head beneath her skirts. His shoulders widened her legs and she leaned back, giving him the sense she'd rested her hands on the stone.

In the pure black beneath her skirts, he used his other senses to guide him.

He breathed in the scent of her. Fresh floral soap, feminine musk, and something that reminded him of ripe, summer berries.

He stilled for a moment, just feeling the sensation of what he'd cupped in his hand. The slight tickle of soft hair. Warm, pliant flesh, which parted in a seam of liquid heat.

He separated her folds with a slow slide of his finger, and she clenched around him with surprisingly strong legs.

"Already so wet," he murmured, delighted.

"Er—should I—?"

"Should has nothing to do with this." He pressed his shoulders forward, fighting the reflexive tightening of her trembling thighs. "Relax."

She gave a tremulous sigh, but then she obeyed, her thighs going slack and her heels returning to the ground.

He moved his finger then, wondering if any woman had been quite so soft, so small, so incredibly hot. He allowed himself a gentle, caressing exploration as he pressed a worshipful kiss to her thigh.

She was highly responsive, this woman. She twitched and tightened to his every motion, her breath hitching over little catches in her throat. His finger drew from the well that sprang from the center of her and painted gentle wet swirls on the little nub of engorged flesh.

Christ, she was so ready.

He wouldn't even have to work for it.

Unable to wait any longer, he lowered his lips to hover above the very core of her.

"Whatever I do, do not scream," he warned.

In an instant she was tense again. "S-scream?"

But he did not answer her question.

Because he'd parted her sex with one long, powerful lick.

CHAPTER 3

*P*ru screamed.

Or, at least, she threw her head back and opened her mouth, but somehow her throat closed over the sound, releasing a choked whimper instead.

Dear God. This was *happening*. The most beautiful man she'd ever seen up close was now beneath her skirts.

Licking her.

There.

One of her hands clamped over her mouth, trying to contain the scandal of it all, the pure, wet, unadulterated wickedness.

A sound from beneath the silk of her skirts and petticoats filtered through the night. A growl, or a groan, she couldn't tell.

She couldn't listen. She could only feel.

After that first sinuous lick, he paused. His breath a warm devastation against her sensitized flesh. His shoulders wide against thighs that had never parted before tonight. Beneath skirts that had never lifted.

She bit into her finger, forcing herself not to ruin the moment with incessant, anxious questions.

Was he uncomfortable under there? Did he have

one taste and decide against more? Was she different than other women, or boring and the same? Better or worse? Did he want to stop? She'd understand, of course. Perhaps she hadn't prepared properly. She'd bathed and used the finest perfumes and lotions, but what if such an act took a preparation she'd not thought of?

He was doing his job, she reminded herself. This was his vocation... and people often found parts of their jobs distasteful.

And did them regardless.

But the very idea painted her entire self with mortification. Because, dash it all, despite her intentions in coming here, she couldn't help but want to please him. Because that was who she was. She wanted him to like what he was doing to her.

She wanted him to like... her. This masked man whose name she did not know. Whose eyes were as wintry as the Arctic and hot as blue flame.

And he didn't. He hated her. She knew it. She'd read him all wrong and now that he'd tasted her, he was trying to figure out a way to extricate himself from the situation without causing either of them humiliation.

Too late for that. She should just—

"Get rid of him."

"What?" Prudence realized her hand had muffled the question, but her skirts muffled his words so they might be not even having a conversation at all.

He shoved the ruffles and gathers of her skirt up to lift his head and spear her with a look of such brutality, such carnal dominance, she flinched. God he was... almost frightening. Even with his smartly contained golden hair, a stubbled jaw a few shades darker, and his regal demeanor, had she met him on the street she'd have been terrified of him.

He still held her thighs open, and the absurdity of their positions drenched her in unease.

And other things.

"Your fiancé. Get rid of him," he ordered.

"B-but—"

"If there is a man on this planet who would prefer another woman to you...to this..." he thrummed a rough-skinned thumb over her slick and aching sex, eliciting a soft whimper from her. "He doesn't deserve it. He shouldn't be allowed to reproduce. Moreover, he should be shot. Drawn and quartered, and wiped from memory."

Even as he growled the savage words, Pru felt herself take a breath of relief. He was being kind, of course he was. But the sentiment was appreciated.

Necessary, even.

All her boldness seemed to have deserted her and she suddenly felt like what she was. A hapless maiden who knew nothing of men. Of the world.

Who was at the mercy of this stark stranger, spread before him, waiting for him to dine upon her.

Lapping up his compliments like a starving animal.

It occurred to her to thank him for his kindness, but her words were lost as he bent back to her, this time pressing a reverent kiss to her sex.

Unable to stand the wicked view, Prudence tossed her skirt back over his head.

His chuckle was a sinful vibration against her, and it tightened something low in her belly. A warning of what was to come.

She gasped as he pressed his lips into her, delving through her folds with slow, languid licks.

He unlocked her with his lips. Undid her with his tongue as he stroked and slipped over the swollen, aching core of her, eliciting pleasure she'd never known existed. She'd the sense that he savored this as she did, which was ridiculous. He did this every night. To every sort of woman.

No wonder they gave him diamonds. He'd been at it all of two seconds and she'd have handed him her entire dowry had he requested it.

And maybe her heart.

She closed her eyes, escaping from the whispers of guilt and shame her upbringing instilled in her. Focusing instead upon the tactile sensations of the moment. The soft, almost intangible coolness of the fountain's mist kissing her upturned face like snowflakes in the summer.

A miracle. Just like his tongue.

The tendrils of pleasure elicited by his ministrations diffused through her blood, and then seemed to be called back to her core by a tightening low in her belly. A harbinger of happening. A pulsing, pounding, throbbing thing that rushed at her from a great distance.

Something she was afraid to miss and equally frightened of being run over by. Like a train or a stampede of wild horses.

"Oh," she fretted breathlessly. "Oh, dear. I—I think I—"

He lifted his lips from her… stealing the sensation away to her utter consternation and relief.

"Don't think," he ordered in the voice of a man quite used to giving orders.

"Don't stop," she begged, her hand blindly reaching for the head hidden beneath her skirts.

He made a low sound of amusement, breathing a cool stream of air against her overheated flesh. He whispered something she didn't quite catch and was too overwrought to clarify.

But she thought she heard the word "forever" before his tongue returned to flicker against the little button of pure sensation.

His touch was eternally light. Barely there, even, but it infused her with such an electric pulse her entire body tightened and jerked with it, as if he'd plugged her into one of Edison's own machines.

She arched and bent with such strength she feared she might snap her spine in two, and he rewarded her by sucking that little bead of flesh into his warm mouth, rolling it gently with his tongue.

A raw sound escaped her, and she returned her hand over her mouth, leaving the other to support her against the stone ledge, all she had keeping her from diving backward into the water.

The wave crashed over her before she even realized it had formed upon the horizon. A crest of such unimaginable, inconceivable euphoria dismantled everything she knew about herself.

She came apart in his hands, against his mouth, and hoped to never again be found.

This was bliss. Rapture. Heaven. And a bit of the other place, too. Because once she'd begun to tumble into the grips of ecstasy, she already understood it was fleeting. That it would inevitably end, lest she die from the intensity of it.

For surely nothing like this could last.

Inevitably his mouth softened, gentled, and returned her back to herself. A self she wasn't certain what to do with. She was a weak, trembling, over-wrought mess, and she couldn't seem to remember her own name let alone consider what to do next.

So she sat and breathed, because such was the extent of her functional capacity.

She'd expected pleasure... but not that.

Not her unaccountable unraveling.

He left her, sliding from beneath her skirts, and used one of the many ruffles of her petticoats to wipe his mouth before he rested back on his haunches so that they might take the measure of one another.

She couldn't see much of his body, as he was dressed in all black and the night was a moonless one. The lamps filtered through the fountain and cast the shadows of water against his skin. Like a mirage of tears. An entire ocean of them.

They bled down his stark cheekbones creating hollows beneath, and the effect somehow caused her heart to swell in her chest.

"You look... as if you are in pain," she ventured, doing her best to lift her boneless arms to reach for him.

"I'm hard as fucking marble." A crass, almost cruel admission, one that brought her body back to astonishing life.

"Bloody hell," he panted, running the back of his hand over his mouth again as if to rid it of her flavor. Stopping in the middle of the motion, he curled his fingers into a fist and bit down on his knuckle. Composing himself just long enough to command, "Stop looking at me like that, woman, or I won't be responsible for what I do next."

Little trills of danger thrummed through her veins. Something primitive and ancient in this garden of delights. Something as old as the first stories, when a man found a woman who tempted him to sin.

The stories had always offended Prudence as she'd obediently sat in church, listening to holy men blame Eve for everything. For the knowledge of good and evil and the ability to bear fruit. For life, itself.

And for temptation.

Why would God, in all his infinite wisdom imbue them with these forces of nature so powerful, there was barely the sentience to deny them? Didn't it make sense that a more pagan deity was responsible? Perhaps one with golden hair and electric eyes. With savagely beautiful features and an expression of half hunger, half wrath.

Eve was not tempted by the devil, but by the power of the very impulses already inside of her. She'd been in Eden, much as Pru was now, and had stared across at a man who'd looked at her just like that, infusing her with power and fire and subtle submission.

How could she have possibly denied him? How could she have denied herself?

Prudence slid from the fountain to her knees before him, little more than a puddle of pleasure and need. Her hands explored him a little, tested the mounds of muscle beneath his coat before slipping it up over his shoulders and down his corded arms.

He was hard and she was soft. He was stone and she was water.

Wet, ready.

Willing.

He watched her as she came to him, his eyes strangely wary and uncertain. His skin pulled taut over the shape of his bones.

The moment she freed his arms from his coat, he took over. He draped it on the moss before guiding her to it and following her down.

He kissed her gently, and she tasted a lingering essence of herself.

It tasted like sin. Reminded her of where he'd taken her. Someplace like paradise.

She opened her legs to welcome the lean intrusion of his hips and he took every inch of ground she ceded.

He distracted her with soft, probing kisses as he reached down between them. Lifting her skirts to her waist, fumbling with his trousers.

No romantic words punctuated his kisses and none were needed. Though his desire was rough and apparent, his mouth was gentle and endlessly restless. He dragged his lips up her jaw, breathing in great gasps, as if he could lock her scent in his chest. He pressed them to her temples, her eyebrows, her lids and the tip of her nose.

Prudence kept her eyes closed, under the guise of appreciating his attentions. All the while preparing to give him what George no longer deserved.

Her virginity.

She didn't tell him. She couldn't say why, exactly. Maybe because he treated her in this moment like no one else had. Like someone whose need and knowledge matched his. Someone who could take what he was about to give her with all its primal desire and no little bit of masculine anger, and provide him a little of the pleasure she'd only just experienced.

Lord knew, he'd earned it.

He returned his mouth to hers just as his fingers stole into her cleft once again, sliding against even more abundant moisture than before.

She squirmed a little, anxious and anticipatory. Wanting him to stop. Wanting him to get on with it. Not knowing what to say or do other than to cling to him.

Yes. That was it. She reared up, wrapping her arms around his trunk, and buried her face against his neck. She breathed him in, a scent like cedar and stringent soap and perhaps a bit of creosote, as if he'd been in a trainyard recently.

Her breath warmed and moistened the scant space between their skin, and she inhaled greedily as his arms locked around her.

"Please," she whispered.

He stole her next words with a strong thrust.

Prudence bit her lip so hard she tasted blood. She'd

expected pain. Or maybe pleasure. But not this unbearably magnificent medley of the two.

Her intimate muscles were not exactly as welcoming as she wished them to be at first, but after the initial thrust, they seemed to clench at him. Pulling him inside.

He'd claimed to be hard, but she realized she'd never truly had an idea of what that word meant. He was like heated steel inside of her, over her, around her. He was everywhere she wasn't and also where she was.

He was her entire world, and yet still a stranger. He blocked out the sky and the breeze and the darkness, her lonely pain and her fears for the future. Reducing her entire frame of existence down to this.

To the place where they joined.

She suddenly wished for daylight. For a filter of illumination through which she could appreciate his nude form. She wished she'd seen exactly what it was he'd pressed inside of her. But for now, all she had was this. Darkness and experience.

And what an experience it was.

With a dark growl, he withdrew slow and deliberate. He held her to him like a coveted treasure as he curled his back to sting into her again. And then again.

Each gliding, slick thrust was easier to bear than the last, easing the way for the pleasure he began to pump from his body into hers, chasing away the lingering shadows of pain.

He made dark, needful, animal sounds. She reveled in the catches of his breath and the sheer wonder in the wordless questions he kissed into her mouth.

He took pleasure as he gave it, and she thought, that was what lovers ought to do.

For he felt like a lover, even though love had nothing to do with what they did here in the dark on the earth.

It was more like a rite. A swiftly intensifying, carnal ritual. One blessed by witches who would have burned once upon a time. As she was burning now, immolating as he thrust pure liquid heat into her with increasing brutality.

She pulled away from his arms, not because she wanted space but because she wanted to see what gathered between them. Because that celestial tide of pleasure was threatening to separate her from herself once again, and she had to make sure this time she was not alone.

That he came with her.

Come. This is why it was referred to as coming. Because no one quite stayed where they were, inside of themselves, inside of each other.

They came, and went, somewhere else entirely.

She looked up at him and instantly noticed that he was closer to that place, that he was afraid he'd leave without her.

His features were a mask of exquisite torment, more beautiful than any piece of art she'd ever seen. She gasped up at him with every motion, as he thrust her into the ground. Her legs widened, strained. Her body seized, and he barked out a harsh sound.

He reached between them and with three magical strokes of his finger, he brought the pleasure crashing into her and sent them both careening into the night.

They came together.

Locked in some paroxysm of bliss that might have looked like a contortion of pain. Neither of them seemed capable of sound, only straining, taut and impossible motion.

Her entire body pulsed around long, liquid warmth he buried deep into her womb, and *God* if that didn't heighten the entire experience.

She returned to herself before he did, it seemed, her

body slackening to the earth as his still thrummed with spasms of pleasure. It seemed to drop him suddenly, and he collapsed over her. Not with his full weight, but with a delicious heaviness that compressed her into a puddle of pleasant affection.

He rooted around in the pool of ruined ringlets at the nape of her neck, breathing deeply, pressing reverent kisses to the sensitive skin. She fought the shrugging giggle as long as she could, but alas her ticklish neck broke the moment.

He rolled to the side, sliding away and arranging himself back into his trousers before she had the presence of mind to peek.

A consummate professional, he was.

They lay next to each other beneath the stars for an eternity, or maybe only a moment. Their breaths synchronized as they deepened and slowed.

A drowsy sense of satisfaction stole over her limbs, and Prudence was the first to roll to her side, acutely aware of the slick aftermath left against her thighs.

He was still far away, she realized. Somewhere in the night above them, unable to return back to the troubles of life below.

She understood a little, she thought. Morning would bring no pleasure to her, especially not after trust had been broken by those she'd once considered closest to her. But her sadness felt like a phantom next to what sort of bleak emotion settled on his features, and she thought to dispel it with a compliment.

"Whatever you charge, sir, it's not enough." She sighed contentedly. "You are a master of your craft."

"Never enough…" he murmured, his eyes still somewhat unfocused, his chest still struggling a bit for breath.

It made sense, she thought, he'd done all the work. She'd just lain there and enjoyed herself.

Feeling at a loss herself, she pushed herself up on her hip like a depiction of a mermaid, legs stretched out to the side. How did one conclude such an interaction? And why didn't she want to?

It wasn't an interaction, was it? But a transaction.

And yet she felt an odd sense of attachment to him now. Was this normal? She could ask, but something told her the question would drive him away.

"Are you cold?" She gathered his coat from beneath her and did her best to brush off errant blades of grass.

He finally glanced over at her, then at his jacket, as if seeing it for the first time. "No. But thank you." He sat up and took it from her, donning it deliberately. "Are *you* all right?" He asked the question as if he dreaded the answer, but his features didn't at all convey what his voice had.

She wished she could identify his expression, but it was a certain kind of inaccessible. Pleasant, but arch. Remote, but attentive. Intense, but polite.

Very carefully so. As if he was suddenly wary or mistrustful of her.

Had she done something wrong?

"Never better." She summoned her most dazzling smile, wishing she had the strength to open her lids past half-mast. That she didn't suddenly want to cry, not because she was sad, but because something powerful had just happened and her emotions hadn't been prepared for it.

"Do you ever—that is—do you care about the women with whom you've spent the night?" she ventured. "Romantically, I mean?"

His gaze flicked away from her, and he stared at the gate, as if hoping the exit would draw closer.

"I don't allow myself the luxury of romance," he answered, and Pru believed she'd never heard anything more honest. Or more depressing.

"Do you ever want to, in spite of yourself?" She was a sentimental fool, but something within her burned to know.

He shook his head adamantly. "Terrible things happen to those I care about."

His answer piqued both her curiosity and her compassion, but he stood before she could reply, and reached down to help her up.

He lifted her with such surprising strength. He was neither overly tall nor was he more than elegantly wide. But rather superbly fit, his every inch hardened with well-used muscle.

She'd first-rate knowledge of that.

"Is it gauche of me to express gratitude?" she asked. "Other than remuneration, that is."

His face softened and the glaciers of his eyes melted behind his mask, his gaze touched every part of her face. "Is your coach nearby? How are you getting home?"

"I'll manage, thank you." A part of her deflated. Of course, he was gently telling her it was time to go. Bless him, for keeping up at least the appearance of concern. "What are you called?"

A sad smile touched his lips as he lifted a lock of her hair that'd escaped its coiffure. He tucked it back in place, smoothing it down with such a tender motion, her throat ached. "It doesn't matter. I'm just a shadow."

Bending down, he retrieved her drawers from where they lay discarded by the fountain and turned to give her privacy. She turned as well, bending to step into them.

"But what if I—" She almost toppled when trying to step into the second leg of the garment and had to steady herself before going on. "What if I'd like to find you again?"

"You won't, I'm afraid."

She drew her underthings up over her stockings and garters. Glad that they'd absorb the dampness that lingered there, until she was able to return home. Wriggling into them, she dropped her skirts and petticoats and smoothed them down her thighs.

Thighs that had just been spread for him. For the man who didn't want to tell her his name.

She whirled back around. "I'm Pru—"

He was already gone.

CHAPTER 4

hree Months Later
    "Congratulations, Morley, you're famous!" Millie LeCour lowered the periodical she read from across the carriage and wriggled dark brows at him. "They're calling you the *Knight of Shadows.*" She leaned deeper into Detective Inspector Christopher Argent's side so she could show him what she read. "Sufficiently ominous, don't you think, darling?"

    "Terrifying," he replied with his distinct brand of prosaic nonchalance. He didn't spare the paper a glance, but he tilted his head to inhale the very nearness of Millie before pressing a careful kiss into her coiffed dark hair.

    Morley's grim mood darkened to thunderous. "Bloody journalists," he muttered, hoping his companions would believe the papers solely responsible for his ire.

    And not their nuzzling nonsense.

    It'd never much bothered him before that night with— No. *No*, he didn't allow himself to dwell on that. To transpose sylphlike features over Millie's bold ones, if only because she shared the slight build and black hair of the woman who haunted his dreams.

Because he'd almost convinced himself the most memorable night of his life had been exactly that. A dream. A strange fabrication of fancy. A hallucination induced by exhaustion, an overtaxed psyche, and vacuous lack of sex.

"Oh, I realize you two men are of the opinion it's sensational and absurd," Millie continued. "But if you think about it, a villain setting out to commit a crime might think twice if he's worried about running afoul of the *Knight of Shadows*." Reaching up, the celebrated actress smoothed an errant auburn forelock away from Argent's soulless eyes. She touched him with the absent fondness of a longtime lover and Morley had to look away from them both. He sought refuge out the window in the bustle and unaccountable brightness of a late-summer London morning.

"And don't be too sore at the writers," she prodded Morley. "Anyone in my profession would commit *murder* for that sort of free press."

He'd committed murder for it too...

The Knight of Shadows. Another farce. Another mantle he'd thrown over his own shoulders almost purely on accident. One night, ages ago, Chief Inspector Carlton Morley had been denied legal entrance to a brothel where he knew evil men sold young, desperate foundlings to disgusting clientele.

He'd a suspicion the Justice involved in his denial was a customer.

The voices of every victimized child he'd ever known had torn through him. Dorian, Ash, Argent, Lorelai, Farah...

Caroline.

He could not abide it. *Would not* allow it. Not anymore. Not in his city and especially not within his own departments of Justice.

His questionable decision fortified by more brandy

than he'd like to admit, he'd tied a mask over his eyes, and broke out the tools of a trade he'd long since deserted.

And a boy he'd long since buried.

He thought he'd left Cutter Morley in the grave he'd dug, but neither was it Sir Carlton Morley who'd shot every pimp in the brothel dead before sending the youths to refuge at St. Dismas Church in Whitechapel.

That night something had eased within him. A sense of helplessness he knew every police officer carried around with him.

The shackles the law locked upon its enforcers were both right and necessary. And yet, they created certain loopholes that became leashes whereby a lawman might be forced to watch an atrocity happen without being able to take recourse.

After years of fighting, of watching the system of which he was a part of, fail so many, mainly those unfortunates believed by most to reside beneath notice, he could stand by no longer.

He was the knighted war hero Chief Inspector because he had to be, and he'd become the Knight of Shadows because London had needed him to be.

How many bodies were there now? The pedophile watchmaker on Drury Lane. The murdering rapist in Knightsbridge. A maniacal doctor who performed gruesome experiments on his immigrant patients, often resulting in disfigurement or death. Two brothers who'd taken everything from their infirmed aunt and moved into her house, effectively keeping her prisoner whilst they spent her meager income.

He'd meant to merely evict them, but one of the men had pulled a pistol on him. And well...Morley's dead-eye had done the job for him.

Then there'd been—

"The public so loves a memorable sobriquet." Millie interrupted his thoughts.

"The public are idiots," Argent reminded her.

"A public you *both* protect, I might remind you." Millie smacked him square in the chest, and Argent smirked down at her.

"If you ever hit me and I find out about it..." He tonelessly poked fun at her petite stature and feeble strength.

Though, Morley supposed, most anyone seemed diminutive next to the ginger giant.

"Think of everyone we know with anointed designations they never thought to give themselves," Millie ticked their connections off on her fingers. "The Rook, The Demon Highlander. The Blackheart of Ben More, The King of the London Underworld, though I suppose those two only count as one..." She trailed off and turned to her husband. "How did you escape without a moniker?"

Argent gave a rather Gallic shift of his shoulder. "If an assassin becomes famous enough to be recognized, it's time for him to retire."

"I'm glad you did," Millie said with feeling. Though the man hadn't retired because of any sort of infamy, but because he'd met his match. Her. The woman he'd been hired to kill, and instead fell in love with.

Morley supposed he should be concerned about how many people were privy to his nocturnal identity by now. Argent had guessed that Morley had begun to spend his nights as a vigilante before he admitted it, only because he and the former assassin were once after the same villain on the same night.

And what Argent knew, Millie knew also.

Morley had confided it to his childhood best mate, now known as the Rook, which meant his wife, Lorelai, knew. And probably also the Blackwells, Dorian and Farah.

The press had begun to follow his exploits but, as Morley had predicted, the descriptions of him scraped from the recollections of villains and survivors were notoriously unreliable, lost in the miasma of misinformation that was the London press.

They all remembered a mask covering the upper quadrant of his face and the fact that he often wore a hat.

He wore many hats. Both figuratively and literally.

Morley sighed before admonishing Millie. "You of all people know better than to believe what you read in the papers. I don't do half the good they credit me. Or, rather, this bollocks Knight of Shadows doesn't."

"The fact they've guessed you're a knight means it is possibly getting dangerous out there for you," Argent warned.

"I think the title is a coincidence." Millie waved a dismissive hand. "With that mask on, he could be anyone. The public has merely distinguished him by merit of his service on their behalf. Though everyone's *dying* to know. I saw an advert for him in the lonely-hearts column just yesterday." She turned to Morley, pursing her lips playfully. "If you're interested, a Miss Matilda Westernra is just nineteen and wants you to know you've touched her virtuous heart. I dare say stolen it."

"That's disgusting, I'm twice her age." Morley shifted in his seat. "Besides, I've no interest in touching or stealing hearts, lonely or otherwise."

"If you don't wish to touch her heart, I'd wager she'd let you touch her—"

Millie scowled at her husband. "Christopher, if you finish that sentence, so help me."

"What? I was going to say virtue."

"Like hell you were."

Morley realized it spoke to the esteem in which Argent held him that he was allowed such an unfettered view into the man's personal life. Even though Argent worked for Morley, only a fool would consider himself Argent's boss.

And Morley was no fool.

Except, it seemed, when it came to women.

"Knight of Shadows." Argent grunted in a manner a kind man might have called a laugh.

A fit of hysterics for the terse giant.

"Sod off," Morley muttered, as their carriage pulled alongside Holy Trinity Cathedral, and the footman opened the door.

Five years hence, if anyone had told Morley he'd be sharing a carriage with Christopher Argent, the Blackheart of Ben More's former right-hand assassin, he'd have laughed at them.

Or punched them.

But here they were, climbing the stairs on a perfectly good workday to attend a rather mandatory society wedding.

"How'd you get roped into this?" Morley queried out of the side of his mouth. "I wasn't aware you knew the couple."

"I don't," Argent said, looking around rather mystified. "Millie had me try on a new frock coat she'd had made for me, and suddenly I had some place to wear it."

Morley chuckled at that, but then Argent shrugged. "Actually, I think...she knows the bride, Prudence Goode, through her sisters who volunteer at the Duchess of Trenwyth's Ladies' Aid Society." Argent lifted his chin to the door where the father of the bride stood to shake hands. "When Millie realized their father was your immediate superior, and therefore mine, she said we both had a reason to attend."

Morley and Argent shared a look of chagrin. The

second daughter of Commissioner Clarence Goode, Baron of Cresthaven, was marrying some Earl from somewhere, and if Morley was absent from the festivities, as he longed to be, he'd hear no end of it. Attendance was expected of him. And Carlton Morley always did what was *expected*.

So that his sins were never *suspected*.

As he mounted the stairs to the chapel, a raven cackled from where it clung to the stone banister, taunting him and twitching its wings.

A raven on a wedding day. Wasn't there some wives' tale about ravens being harbingers of death or doom or some such? He paused, staring at it intently, transfixed by the brilliance of its feathers. Brilliant, he thought, because while the bird was black, it reflected the entire spectrum in the sun with a glossy iridescence.

Just like *her* hair had done when the lamplight had shone through the water...

He shook his head, trying to dislodge the thought.

Most of the time he was glad he didn't know her name. Because then she'd become too real. He couldn't shrug that night off as some fantastical dream that'd happened to someone else.

Other times, he longed for her to be something other than a pronoun.

Her.

Blinking, he turned from the blasted creature, taking the stairs two at a time to catch up to his compatriots.

He had to stop this lunacy. To cease searching for her in every slim, raven-haired woman of passable good looks he saw on the streets. Or the park. Or Scotland Yard. Or in a bloody church.

The city was full of dark-haired beauties, it seemed, and that fact had threatened to drive him mad.

One night, when he'd been unable to stand his longing, when his body had screamed for release and his every sense was overwhelmed by the memory of her, he'd gone to Miss Henrietta's School for Cultured Young Ladies, and had lurked near the fountain.

If only to prove to himself it had actually happened.

He'd touched the smooth stone of the fountain ledge where she'd perched and lifted her skirts and the mere sight of her shapely calves had driven him past all reason.

He swore he could still taste her, summer berries and female desire. He'd waited for her, his raven-haired miracle, and she'd not come.

Not that he was surprised. He'd told her she wouldn't find him again.

And he'd meant it.

Morley rubbed a hand over his face, scrubbing at a smooth jaw where she'd once found it stubbled, wanting to wipe her from memory.

The Commissioner had disappeared into the church as he'd dawdled in reverie, and he'd missed the entire reason he'd attended this blasted wedding to begin with. To be seen by Goode, and thereby make his excuses to leave.

This had to fucking stop, this...obsession with her.

The entire affair had been a mistake. He'd never in his adult life done anything so ridiculous. So dangerous.

So...marvelous.

He hadn't been himself that night. He'd been stretched at the end of a long-frayed rope. His will weakened by exhaustion and a seemingly futile struggle between him and the entire world. Between the two parts of himself. He'd been weak, there was no gentler word for it. Weakness wasn't something he allowed, in himself or those who worked for him.

This had to stop. He whispered a solemn vow then

and there to never look another dark-haired maiden in the eye. Never search for her sharp jaw and arched brows, or her delicate ears with elfin tips.

What would he do if he found her, anyway? She thought him a prostitute or, if she were a clever woman, she'd have worked out that he was the so-called Knight of Shadows because of his mask. Because he hadn't taken her money. Because if she'd asked at Miss Henrietta's or approached any of the Stags of St. James, they'd tell her he wasn't among their ranks.

Either way, she'd a secret that could crush him in the telling of it—not that she'd come out smelling of roses.

Even so.

It was better to stuff the entire misadventure into the past and forget it. Forget *her.*

The church bells tolled the hour, or maybe the event, as Morley stepped into the already uncomfortably warm church. The organ music ground at his nerves, and he hoped to sit next to a large woman with a very busy fan, so he might not expire from the heat. How long was this bloody thing supposed to last? Did he have to go to the soirée after? If he made certain Commissioner Goode saw him at the ceremony, he could pretend he was lost in the crowd later.

"Sir. *Sir.*" Someone clutched at his jacket, and he whirled to find a white-faced reverend at his elbow. "Sir Morley? Chief Inspector Carlton Morley?" the short, rotund old man whispered his name and title as if it were an illicit secret.

"Yes?"

"You *must* come with me. Oh God in heaven. Never in my life..." The Vicar's words trailed away as he furtively skipped his gaze over the guests now trying to step around them since they'd stopped in the middle of the aisle.

Instantly on alert, Morley glanced over at Argent, who made a baffled gesture.

"*Please.*" The Vicar's pallor was alarming. "Don't make a scene."

Argent stepped forward. "Should I accompany—?"

"No! Only Sir Morley." The reverend was tugging on his jacket now, dragging him toward the back of the chapel like a recalcitrant child might his dawdling nanny.

"We'll find our seat and save you one," Millie offered, tugging her husband in the opposite direction.

Morley followed the frantic priest down an empty stone hall with vibrant purple carpets. "Lord Goode and the Viscount Woodhaven sent me to find you right away. There's been a— Well, the groom. The *bride*. Oh my God, of all the nightmares. So much blood."

When Morley entered the sitting room, he froze.

Not because of the blood, though it *was* everywhere. Soaking into the floral carpet, spreading past it onto the grey stone floor. Coloring the bodice of the bride's cream dress in a dappled spray. Saturating her hem and train where she stood, paralyzed, in the puddle draining from a man's neck. The dripping knife still clutched in her trembling, blood-drenched hands.

The fucking priest had been right.

Of all the nightmares...

It was *her.*

CHAPTER 5

*P*rudence was locked in a chamber of red.

She drowned in it. It filled her lungs so she couldn't breathe. Her ears so she couldn't hear. She could even taste it, or could she? Metal stained her tongue, but her mouth was as dry as sandpaper. Her throat wouldn't allow her to swallow. She choked on her gall and grief.

William was yelling. He'd found her like this. Poor William. She'd never liked Honoria's husband because of this tendency of his...always making such a ruckus.

"You bloody viper. You lunatic!" the Viscount accused. "How could you kill him? In a church of all places?"

"I-I couldn't!"

Well, that wasn't strictly true, now was it? She *could* have cheerfully murdered him many times over the past three months.

"I didn't," she amended. *She hadn't.*

Pru looked down at her hands. Back at George. Over at William's purple, puffy complexion, then down at her fiancé.

The blood wasn't pumping anymore but draining

67

slowly. Staining her dress. Everything and everywhere. The pool spread; the blood followed her as she stumbled back a few steps. A train of condemnation.

Oh God. She was going to be sick.

Except had nothing left to throw up, not since she'd emptied her stomach this morning.

"Prudence, don't you *dare* move! What have you done?"

When had her father come in? She should be relieved, shouldn't she? He'd know what to do.

She lifted the knife to show him. Someone had stuck it into the place George's shoulder had met his neck. This long, long, *long* knife. All the way in. Why would they do that? Where had they gone?

It was so cold. *So cold.* And it had been so warm before in the crowded church. Warm enough to complain about it. They were both screaming at her. Making so much noise they could almost be heard over the bells. Wedding bells. *Her* wedding bells.

It all clamored so loudly it was deafening, and yet also very far away. Bells and bellows. Her father shouting questions. William calling her every sort of name.

Prudence tried to speak, but her throat wouldn't allow it. Her tongue was stuck. Too dry.

Why was she still holding the knife? Why couldn't her fingers uncurl?

George. What happened to you? She stared down at him, unable to blink. His long body remained face down where he'd landed. His skin no longer ruddy from drink, but white. Whiter than hers, even.

Poor George. He'd been merry this morning. Insufferable and already drunk. And now...

The door opened. A man entered.

And the pandemonium stopped.

Everyone obeyed his command for silence and, for the first time, Pru's throat relaxed enough to allow a full breath. The sick sense of impending doom released the band around her ribs and her stomach stopped threatening to jump into her esophagus.

Everything would be all right. *He* was here now. Even though the world was upside down, he would know how to put it right.

Except... who was he?

She couldn't look away from the blood.

"*Prudence*," her father barked, as if he'd been saying her name for a long time. "This is Chief Inspector Sir Carlton Morley. You tell him *everything*, do I make myself clear?"

"I don't...want to hold this anymore," she whimpered, unable to peel her fingers from around the knife. God it was so big. It had been stuck in George's muscles.

She moaned.

"Let me have the knife, Miss Goode." A deep, cultured voice came closer, and a hand covered with a white handkerchief relieved her of the weapon. She'd never been more grateful for anything in her life.

"That's one of our daggers!" Reverend Bentham exclaimed. "It's a holy relic."

"It's evidence, I'm afraid," the Chief Inspector said. "You can request it back once this affair is settled."

That word. *Affair.* It made her want to cry.

Gaining some strength, Prudence lifted her head and lost what was left of her breath.

Those eyes.

They had once been liquid for her behind a mask. They had watched her come apart.

He'd made her come.

Chief Inspector? There must be some mistake. He

was…a stag. No, not that. A shadow. Or he had been on a night nearly three months ago.

Pru gaped at him, dumbfounded, searching a face she'd committed to every corner of her memory.

He was at once the same and yet vastly altered. His hair a shade lighter than gold in the gleam of the noon sun through the windowpane. His suit a somber grey. His jaw sharp, clean-shaven and locked at a dangerous angle.

Her lover had been rumpled and dark, his hair the color of honey, or so she'd thought on a moonless night. He'd emanated sex and menace. Hard hunger and brutal masculinity.

The Chief Inspector was all starch and serenity. A dapper, terse, and proper gentleman clad in a fine cut jacket with an infinite supply of decorum.

But that strong jaw. The sinfully handsome features cut sharp as crystal and then blunted with the whisper of ruthlessness. All of this slashed clean through with a sardonic mouth.

It *was* him.

She was sure of it… wasn't she? No one else had eyes so light, so incredibly elemental. Like the color of lightning over the Baltic Sea.

Those eyes bored into her now. Flat, merciless, and unsympathetic. He regarded her as if she were the last person *alive* he wanted to see.

As if she were lower than the earth upon which they'd sinned.

If she'd any hope that this man would be her ally, it was dashed upon the rocky shards of his glare.

"What happened here?" he asked her evenly.

Pru felt her face crumple with confusion. He didn't sound like himself. Where was the accent from before? Rough and low-born.

She'd have recognized *that* accent anywhere.

This man spoke like his betters. Was she going mad, perhaps? Was her desperation and shock so prescient that she'd summoned a memory and layered it over reality?

"Prudence, you answer him," her father barked.

"I-I was waiting for Father to gather me for the ceremony," she recounted, wanting to appease him. *Needing* to explain. It was so important he didn't think she had anything to do with this. No one would *really* believe that she would commit murder, would they? "There was a knock on my door and a note pushed under," she continued. "The note was from George." She pointed at the dead man at her feet and immediately wished she hadn't looked down.

Oh God. She'd thought the wedding was the worst thing that would happen to her today. She'd never been so wrong in her life.

How did so much blood belong in one body? How would she ever forget the sight of it? She doubted she could even look at her own veins the same way.

"Look at me," the inspector ordered. "What did the note say?"

"That he had to see me. That he had to apologize."

"Apologize," he echoed. "Had you reason to be angry with the Earl of Sutherland?"

Her brow furrowed and she cast an accusatory look at him. "You *know* I did."

"How would *he* know?" her father demanded. "You've never been introduced."

A glint of warning frosted the inspector's eyes impossibly colder. *Don't.* It warned. *Don't ruin us both.*

"I meant..." Pru turned to her father. "Y-you did. I told you George was unfaithful, and you insisted I marry him regardless."

Her father, a powerful man with the build of a baker who enjoyed his own work, put up his hands against Morley's attention. Such large hands for such fine white gloves. "It was little more than wild oats," he defended George. "And Prudence has always been a romantic, fanciful creature. I wasn't about to see her future ruined by rumor."

"It *wasn't* rumor," she argued, even though everything inside of herself told her not to. "Everyone knows George had bastards. He conducted a very public affair with Lady Jessica Morton. And yet you insisted I invite her to the wedding."

Why was she having this discussion covered in blood? When all she wanted to do was flee. Or fling herself into the inspector's arms.

She knew how strong they were. How capable they'd be of carrying the weight threatening to drag her beneath the surface of an ocean of despair and desperation.

She had to tell him—

"And so, you came to meet him before the ceremony," the Chief Inspector prompted very gently, as if he were talking to a child. "You came to receive his apology. Then what? What did he say to make you angry?"

She shook her head with such vehemence her eyes couldn't keep up. The beautiful Chief Inspector became a golden blur. "*Nothing!* He said nothing. I opened the door and he was... like this." She gestured to George's body, unable to look down again. "Blood poured everywhere, the knife was already in his neck. He was rolling on the floor trying to pull it out, so I ran to him and tried to help. I was thinking if he took it out, it would bleed that much more. That maybe he should keep it in. I was trying to hold it."

"Nonsense, you'd put it there!" her brother-in-law accused, jabbing his finger toward her. William's features were purple with rage, his thinning ashen hair stuck out in disarray. He wasn't a large man, but he was tall, imposing. And not for the first time, Pru wanted to shrink away from him.

How did Honoria stand him?

"I was *trying* to *stop* the bleeding." She turned to Morley, beseeching him. "I know it was silly, I don't know why I thought I could. But I had to try, didn't I? He was *dying*. And finally, he dislodged the knife and blood sprayed…" She held out her arms to show him. "And he was gone."

"That's not what it looked like when I came in," William hissed through his disorganized teeth. "She was pushing the knife into his struggling body. He was thrashing about and she was sliding it into his neck."

"I never!"

"If the Earl took the knife out of his own neck, how did you come to be holding it?" The Chief Inspector held his hand up against further comment from William while he assessed her from deep set narrowed eyes.

His suspicion lancing through her like a spear thrown by an Olympian.

Don't you remember me? she wanted to ask him. In the middle of this lake of blood. All she wanted was to go to him. He had to understand why—

"Honoria told me you hated him," William continued after an embarrassingly wet sniff. Was he crying? Of course he was, his best friend had just been killed.

Shouldn't *she* be crying? She felt tears somewhere, a threat to her distant future when she wasn't so numb. So cold and confused.

William continued his relentless assault. "She told me that you wept yourself to sleep last night at the thought of being his wife."

Yes, she'd wept plenty over the past few months. Perhaps she was empty now. Honoria had been right, but why had she told her husband? Why did it seem like her sister continuously betrayed her?

Prudence shook her head again, fearing she looked like a lunatic. "I don't *know*. I must have taken it from him. But, I didn't do this. I didn't kill him. I needed him! If I had the will or the stomach for murder, I would have poisoned him. I would have been clever. I certainly wouldn't have waited for my *wedding day*. I wouldn't have gotten all this blood on my dress..."

"Your dress is the least of your problems, you conniving bitch!" William lunged forward and Morley caught him.

"That's enough out of you." Morley's voice was hard as he flattened his forearm against William's neck and shoved him against the wall. He jabbed his finger within a breath of William's eye. "You leave this room and walk one door over to the right. There, you will *sit* and *wait* for me, do I make myself clear?"

William nodded, his anger turning to fear in the face of such authority.

That dealt with, Morley turned to her father. "Sir, I understand this is delicate, that the suspect is your daughter, but you're aware you'll have to be excused from this room, as you cannot be an impartial part of this inquest or this arrest."

Arrest? He was going to arrest her?

Her father ran a trembling hand through his shock of white hair. "I'm going for our solicitor."

Morley nodded. "I think that's best."

Her father's shaking hand followed the length of his beard to his sternum. "For the sake of our department, Morley. Our reputation. If you take her to the Yard, I want it done quietly, do you hear me? I will not be humiliated more than needs be. Her innocence will be proven quickly enough."

Tears finally pricked her eyes. Her father. Her stern, distant, self-aggrandizing father believed her at least. Believed *in* her.

Morley glared over at her, but this time his gaze lifted no further than the blood on her pearlescent gown. "That remains to be seen."

Pru wanted to bury her head in her hands and cry. She almost did. But remembered the blood in time. She might have lost what was left of her wits if she'd smeared it on her face.

Morley stepped to her father and put a hand on his elbow. "She'll be taken quietly. You have my word. You should inform the guests of the death, but not the murder... none of the details need be made public. And I think you'll need to control your son-in-law."

"Honoria will see to that," her father stated with absolute faith.

Honoria controlled everything she possibly could.

Her father turned to Pru and she locked eyes with the man she'd desperately tried to please her entire life.

And she saw what broke her heart.

Doubt.

He might claim to believe her, but he didn't in his heart.

"What am I going to tell your mother?"

He left before she could answer, taking the hand-wringing reverend with him.

And they were alone.

Pru looked down, locking her knees to keep from going to him. From prostrating herself in front of this stranger.

So much blood.

She'd been so proud of this dress. She'd loved it.

And now... it was all she could do not to rip the blasted thing off and throw it in the fireplace.

They stared at each other for a silent eternity, and when she could bear it no longer, she took a step forward.

"Prudence Goode," he stated blandly. "I'm arresting you under the suspicion of the murder of George Hamby-Forsyth, Earl of Sutherland."

"It's *you*. I know it's you. I've been looking everywhere since that night—"

"I told you to leave him," he said furiously, stabbing a finger at the body of her would-be husband. "I *ordered* you that night, and here you are."

"I know." Her miserable heart shriveled away from him.

"Did you do it?" he asked, his eyes snapping with constrained anger. "Did you kill him?"

"No! I just told you what happened. He was already—"

He held a hand up, turning half away as if he couldn't stand to look at her before he gathered himself and faced her with a greater sense of calm.

"Tell me the truth," he said with more restraint. "And this could be one more secret between us. Tell me now and I'll do everything in my power to keep you from the gallows..."

Pru stared at him incredulously. *He didn't believe her.* He truly didn't think she was innocent. Her heart dropped like a stone. This man... this stranger who knew her more intimately than anyone in the world. This dream lover who'd treated her with more care than anyone in her life...

He thought she was a murderer.

"I won't go to the gallows," she said stoically. "I don't need your help."

"Like hell—"

"They won't hang a woman in my condition." Her hand went to her waist. *This* had been her secret. Not the murder.

His mouth opened soundlessly, and his fists curled shut as he stared at her for a multitude of shocked moments. "You're...pregnant?"

"Yes," she whispered. "And the child is yours."

CHAPTER 6

*M*orley retreated to his office on the third floor of Scotland Yard and stared at nothing for the space of an entire hour. His mind churned almost as sickeningly as his stomach.

Disbelief warred with distrust over acres of despair within him. And within that bleak, vast landscape a tiny pinprick of light pierced him.

A child? *His* child?

Had he ever dared to hope for such a miracle?

Did he believe her…about any of it?

How often had he fantasized about finding her? This goddess he'd met in the night. How many times had he wondered if he'd passed beneath her window without even knowing?

And, once again, she'd exploded into his life.

Covered in blood. Quite probably a murderer. And carrying a baby…

Christ, could this situation get any worse?

A sound drew his attention to the door, and Morley looked up to see the most vicious, notorious pirate since Blackbeard saunter in with his hat tilted at a jaunty angle.

The man had come up with him in the East End as

Dorian Blackwell, but a brush with death and a bout of amnesia had shucked the identity from him. Since they'd parted after Caroline's death, he had been christened The Rook on his pirate ship, but had recently married and subsequently shucked his murderous moniker for a brand-new one. Ashton Weatherstoke, the erstwhile Earl of Southbourne.

Known to his friends simply as *Ash*.

"Can you believe that wedding?" Ash tugged at the collar he wore impossibly high to cover the scars left by the lye meant to dissolve his body in the mass grave he'd crawled out of twenty odd years ago.

Morley stood to shake his hand, grateful for a friendly face on this, the rottenest moment of his adult life. They'd come so far from their days as street rats together, but some things never changed, like the man's impossible sardonic wit.

"I wasn't aware you were invited," Morley said. "I didn't see you there."

Ash smirked. "Oh, I was and declined the boring invitation, but it's all over London in the space of three hours. An Earl falling over dead at his own wedding? Whispers of foul play? What a bloody debacle, eh, Cutter?"

Morley lunged past his friend and slammed his door closed, whirling on the unfashionably tanned and brawny man who wore a smart suit as loosely as his devil-may-care smirk.

"I told you never to call me that," he snarled.

The smile widened to that of a shark's. "It's your name, isn't it?" He held up his hands against the onslaught of irritation burning from Morley's glare. "I'm sorry, I've tried, but I can't call you *Carlton* with a straight face." These last words were strained through a chuckle as if to elucidate his point.

"Call me Morley, then, everyone else does." He re-

79

turned to his desk to straighten the papers he'd upset in his haste, arranging them into tidy piles. One in need of signatures. One in need of written correspondence. One in need of dissemination to his clerk as signatures and replies had already been made.

Amidst all the chaos, he needed order. He needed it to think. To decide what to do next.

He needed to control the outcome.

What he *didn't* need was interruptions, even in the form of just-discovered long-lost best mates with murderous reputations of their own.

"Debacle," he muttered. "Doesn't even begin to describe what happened this morning." Looking up, he leaned on his desk with both fists, too agitated to sit down. What word could he possibly use? Catastrophe? Disaster? Nothing seemed quite strong enough.

Three stories below where they stood, a lone woman was locked in a secret cell.

A murderer? A mother?

His lover.

What to do with her was his only pressing concern.

"Is there a reason for your visit, Dorian?" he asked shortly.

"I told *you* never to call me *that*," the pirate sent him a black look that might have had a lesser man begging his pardon. Or his mercy.

Both of which he famously lacked.

"It's your name, isn't it?" Morley shot back the man's own words.

"Touché." Hard, obsidian eyes softened by scant degrees as Ash wandered about his spacious office. He read the commendations on the walls, looked at his certificate of knighthood, his army medals, a broken bayonet, a bullet that had been dug out of his thigh in Afghanistan displayed in a shadow box made by his regiment.

Catalogues of a life they were supposed to have lived together. A life that was stolen from them by the vagaries of fate.

The black eyes softened to something more filial and familiar. "Speaking of the man who took my name when I was presumed dead, Dorian is about to join us for a chat."

"Come the fuck again?" Morley straightened. "The Blackheart of Ben More, King of the London Underworld is coming here? To my *office in the middle of the day?*" His jaw locked against the rest of the sentence, hissing the last of these through clenched teeth.

"Former King of the so on and so forth. He's reformed, remember?"

"Allegedly," Morley muttered.

Ash waved him off. "It's a central location for us to meet, and we've information for you and Detective Inspector Argent to investigate in both your *vocational capacities.*" He bucked his brows rather meaningfully.

Morley rubbed at the tension tightening at the base of his neck. "The last time the Blackheart of Ben More was in these walls, I tied him to a chair and beat him within an inch of his life."

"That isn't *exactly* how I remember it." As if summoned by his title, the subject of their conversation let himself into Morley's office with nary a knock and left the door wide open behind him as he stopped abreast of Ash, his very own doppelganger.

Morley's fingers still itched to throttle the man often. Or, like now, punch the vaguely superior expression from his features and blacken the obsidian eye that wasn't covered by the eyepatch.

But alas, he could not. Morley and the so-called Blackheart of Ben More had established a truce recently—well, a ceasefire—for the sake of the man they both called brother.

The real Dorian Blackwell—now Ash—and an orphan named Dougan Mackenzie had been locked in Newgate Prison together as boys. Because of their similar looks, black hair, and dark-as-the-devil eyes, they'd been christened the Blackheart Brothers in Newgate, and the infamous moniker had followed them through a menagerie of miseries and misdeeds.

Upon Dorian's supposed death in prison, Dougan Mackenzie, who was serving a life sentence for the murder of a pedophile, assumed Dorian Blackwell's identity and release date.

He lived as Dorian Blackwell for two decades, as the reigning King of the London Underworld, whilst the real Dorian, having crawled out of a mass grave with no memory, lived as the Rook, King of the High Seas.

However, when Ash reclaimed his memory, he saw no great need to reclaim his name from his good friend, as his life with Lorelai Weatherstoke was the epitome of his happy ending.

When all was said and done, both Ash and Dorian decided to live with names they'd adopted instead of the ones they'd been born with.

Only Morley and Argent were the wiser. And all the more befuddled for it.

However, since Morley also lived under an assumed name, he could hardly cast aspersions.

People in glass houses and all that.

Dorian strode up alongside Ash with his hands resting comfortably in his pockets. He bumped the pirate with his elbow in a show of camaraderie. An extraordinary thing, as Dorian famously hated to be touched by all but his wife, Farah.

Though the Blackheart Brothers looked much alike as young men, time had separated them somewhat. Standing side by side as they were, it was easy to tell them apart. Ash wore his hair close-cropped, and his skin was swarthy and weathered by years at sea. The grooves branching from his eyes and the brackets of his mouth were carved deeper into features more savage than Dorian's pale, satirical visage.

Despite his eyepatch, Dorian remained as handsome as the very devil. He displayed more spirit and mirth than his piratical counterpart, wore his hair down to his collar, and outweighed Ash by perhaps half a stone.

"Here's trouble," Dorian greeted Argent with a slap to the shoulder as the amber-haired man strode in holding a coffee and a paper.

Argent cast his previous employer a congenial nod. *He* at least, turned to shut the door behind him, cutting their conclave of reprobates off from an increasingly curious detective branch.

"Christ, almighty," Morley said by way of salutation. "I've no time for trouble if you've brought it to my doorstep. Not today."

"Well, considering the exsanguinated Earl you've cooling in your morgue, I'd say we've arrived in the nick of time," Ash went to the window and opened the drapes onto Whitehall Place, uncovering an unfettered view of the spires of Parliament. "We'd meant to discuss Commissioner Goode with you after the wedding, but it seems that needs must."

Morley's lips compressed. "What about him?"

"Something is rotten in the State of Denmark," Dorian quoted significantly. "And the closer we come to the Yard, the more it stinks to high heaven."

"Out with it, both of you," Morley barked. "I don't have time for your cryptic dramatics today."

"No time for corruption in your own department?" Ash's black brow arched, and he speared Morley with a meaningful look.

"We've information that the ironically named 'Goode' needs a bit of moral direction," Dorian informed him with no small amount of smugness. "Who did we think of but your august self, Morley? This place is your life and your wife, and the shadows of justice your mistress. Goode's the perfect man to ruin, especially for your career. You could rise and take his place."

Morley shook his head, rejecting the very idea. On today of all days? Could he not escape the name Goode? "Why would I do such a thing? What have you heard?"

Ash turned from the window. The light reflected off the lye burn scars that crawled up his neck and clawed at his jaw. When he spoke, it was with a great deal less inflection than his more demonstrative counterpart. "Goode's nobility was built hundreds of years ago on the import of lumber to our little island, but I have it on good authority that his shipping company is smuggling more than just wood. There's a plant being hailed in the Americas as the new drug of the century."

"The coca plant," Morley nodded. "I've heard of it. It's not exactly illegal to ship it here, and it's widely used therapeutically."

Dorian made a disgusted noise. "It is illegal if the substance isn't declared at customs, and if it's not being delivered to doctors, but instead distributed to obsessed ghouls by coppers who are little better than bookies handing out beatings if they're not paid on time."

Morley looked from Dorian's one good eye, to Ash, and then to Argent, who studied the dark-haired men intently from where he held up the far wall with his leaning shoulders. "You're *sure* of this?" he asked.

Ash nodded. "I'm certain the plants are coming from his ships. Though where it's being refined into cocaine, I couldn't tell you."

"And *I'm* certain the drug is being leaked onto the

streets by your officers," Dorian insisted. "In the poor and rich boroughs alike."

"How certain?" Morley pressed.

"As sure as we are that you've nothing to do with it," Ash said. "And we've all the evidence you need to open up further investigation. However, since this man is your only superior, and you've no quiet way to investigate your own officers, I'd suggest the Knight of Shadows conduct the inquiry."

The Knight of Shadows. Did he want to be the sort of man who policed his own?

Was he truly so ignorant about what the Commissioner might be doing behind his back?

Morley stared at the three men who stood in front of his desk. Three men who'd once been three boys beaten down by the very laws that were supposed to protect them. They'd forged a bond together as teens in Newgate Prison that nothing on this earth could pull asunder.

Morley's own path had taken him on an entirely different road. A road that became a line between them. A line as tangible as the desk behind which he stood.

Alone.

They'd always stand together, those three. And no matter how much they trusted him, Morley never saw the insides of those prison walls and would thereby forever stay on the outside of their coterie.

On the other side of the line.

He'd been fine with that because his life had become one of order and regimentation where theirs were chaos and anarchy.

Cutter had followed the laws of the streets once.

But Carlton could not. He didn't exist without boundaries. He wanted the boundaries drawn in no uncertain terms so he could see exactly which parameters he was supposed to work within. He was a man forged in the meat grinder of war and then polished by the police force.

Except lately, the lines had been blurred by the Knight of Shadows. And he'd leapt over one particular line so far, he couldn't see it anymore.

And the consequences were about to be cataclysmic.

He lowered himself into his high-backed leather chair. The legs of which no longer felt so dense and steady. As if he could topple from his throne at any time. "I hear what you're saying, and I agree that this demands further investigation. But...there is a complication in regards to me."

"Do tell." Dorian's eye sharpened, and he was instantly rapt. "You are a famously uncomplicated man."

Morley let that go for now. "I've become a bit..." He cast about for the right word. Embroiled? Consumed? Obsessed? Entangled? "*Involved* with Commissioner Goode's daughter."

Argent perked to that. "Which one? Doesn't he have several?"

Morley swallowed, knowing that once this was out in the open, he could never take it back. It would be painful to endure their reactions, but possibly worth it if they could help him see through his pall to a course of action.

"The one whose wedding was interrupted by a murder," he muttered.

"Swift work, Morley," Ash exclaimed. "That was only what, three *minutes* ago?"

"Hours—"

Ash didn't appear to listen. "She's not *technically* a widow, so you don't have to wait the requisite year—"

Morley interjected. "No, you idiot, it was before today. Three months before."

Dorian gave an exaggerated gasp and clutched at his lapels, adopting an overwrought conservative, blustery affect. "An *affair*, Morley? A Chief Inspector and a knight of the realm. How utterly reprehensible."

"Morally derelict, I dare say," Ash added with a lop-sided grin.

"Quite right," Dorian thumped him. "What *will* they think at church?"

Morley didn't even have it in him to rise to their japes as he buried his head in his hands. "It's worse than that, I'm afraid. I've locked her in one of the cells downstairs."

A protracted silence caused him to look up, but he didn't find the astonishment he'd expected.

In fact, these hard men with terrible reputations seemed to be fighting back almost proud smiles. "If I'm honest, Morley, a bit of kidnapping is no insurmount-able impediment," Ash shrugged. "Show us a man in this room who hasn't had to lock his lady-love in some form of prison before she'd consent to be his wife."

"It was a Scottish castle for me," Dorian said with no little nostalgia.

"I'll see your Scottish tower, and raise you a pirate ship," Ash bragged.

"Closet," the monosyllabic Argent added.

Each of them shared a chuckle and, not for the first time, Morley was hit by a wave of sympathy for their wives.

"What happened?" Ash asked Morley, after wiping his smile from his lips with the back of his hand.

Morley pressed two fingers to each temple and worked in circles. He was about to regret this, but he needed to confess. To purge the sin that'd been weighing on him for so many weeks.

Because it'd been so long since he'd been so lost.

"Have any of you heard of the Stags of St. James?"

Ash and Argent shook their heads, but Dorian nod-ded. "Noble women pay fortunes for their sexual services. Madame Regina, who runs my brothel, suggested we recruit a few from Henrietta Thistledown."

Morley cleared a gather of shame from his throat. "Well, I was out one night, just about three months ago..."

"Being a vigilante?" Dorain asked.

"*Investigating*," he corrected.

"No one else investigates with a mask, but do go on."

Once again, he let that go. "My *investigation* of some murdered men took me to Miss Henrietta's, where they'd worked as stags. I was in the garden and Miss Goode sort of...mistook me for..." He couldn't bring himself to say the bloody word.

Ash's mouth fell open. "*A prostitute?*"

"Is she blind?" Dorian's nose wrinkled as he raked him with a disbelieving glare.

Morley sat back in his chair, cursing himself for saying a damned word to any of them.

It was Argent who leaned forward, his expression fascinated. "And?"

"And...we..." Morley flicked his hand out in a gesture that could have meant anything.

"Holy fucking Christ, you didn't," Dorian shook his head as if begging him to deny it and hoping he wouldn't.

"I need to sit down." Argent groped for the chair across from his desk and settled his hulking frame into it.

"I need a drink." Ash went to the sideboard next to the door.

Dorian stayed where he was, staring at Morley. "*You* deflowered a Baron's daughter, no, a Commissioner's daughter—*your boss's daughter*—before her wedding and got *her* to pay *you* for it? Christ, Morley, I've misjudged you all this time. Color me bloody impressed."

"Don't," Morley warned.

"Oh, don't be cross." Dorian waved his leather-gloved hand at him. "I'm certain you did it *properly* and *thoroughly* as you do everything else and then made up for it with piles of guilt and self-flagellation and sleepless nights and all that rubbish."

Morley crossed his arms. "I'm not discussing this with you further." He never flagellated himself, bastard didn't know what he was talking about.

Ash stepped forward, a drink in hand. "Don't heed Dorian. Pearls before swine and all that."

Dorian feigned outrage. "Speak for yourself, *I'm* not the one rolling in the dirt with betrothed debutants."

They all looked at Morley and lost their battle with mirth.

"I didn't know who she was at the time," Morley explained darkly. "Or I'd never have touched her."

Ash came behind the desk where Morley sat, and put a glass in front of him. He leaned a hip on the edge and poured Morley a healthy snifter from his own decanter before patting him on the shoulder. "I, for one, am delighted," he said, encouraging him to drink. "You were living like a monk, and let's be honest, you never were very good with women."

"A monk?" Dorian scoffed. "I was worried he was a bloody eunuch."

"Or had a terrible predilection," Ash added.

"That wouldn't bother me so much," Argent cut in, declining a drink with a wave of his hand as he sipped his coffee. "I never trust a man without a dark side."

Dorian's shoulder leaned against the wall and he crossed one foot in front of the other, a cruel gleam in his dark eye. "All this time I worried you took no other lovers because you were still in love with my wife."

"*Enough.*" Morley tossed his whisky back and slammed the empty glass onto the table with a bang loud enough to be heard by the occupants of the floor below them.

For a man who didn't believe in miracles, he knew he was witnessing one now as they all blinked at him in blessed silence.

Wouldn't last long, he thought bitterly.

They'd been taciturn villains all, before their women had made them happy.

Happy men never seemed to tire of conversation.

Except Argent, who only spoke when words were absolutely required.

"So angry, Morley," Dorian tutted. "Struck a nerve?"

Ash tossed a disapproving look over his shoulder at Dorian. "A low blow, Dorian, even for you. We are all of us angry men. It is that anger that drives the best of us to succeed."

"*Au contraire, mon frère*," the Blackheart of Ben More twisted an imaginary villainous mustache, ever unrepentant. "Cunning. Cunning is how we do what needs done."

"This isn't a bloody lark, it's my *life*," Morley grit out from between clenched teeth. "She's seen me as the Knight of Shadows. We engaged in a scandalous affair for a night. And now she's down there having quite likely murdered her fiancé and desperate to tell anyone who would listen my secrets."

"Does she recognize you as the Knight of Shadows?" Argent speared him with a serious gaze.

Morley nodded, feeling distinctly defeated.

"There's more to this, isn't there," Argent stated dryly, narrowing his verdant eyes. "Something you're not telling us."

Morley's head snapped up. There was no way for Argent to know, but the bastard was an infuriating genius when it came to reading other people.

"Is she blackmailing you or something?" the taciturn detective inquired.

Morley shook his head. "Worse. She's claiming I impregnated her that night."

At that, all sense of joviality drained from the room as the enormity of the situation pressed the very air into something heavy and dark.

For all their differences, all four of them had something very much in common.

They'd grown up without paternal care. Their fathers had abandoned them at best and tried to murder them at worst.

"Do you have any reason to believe her?" Dorian asked. "Have you seen proof of her condition or is she simply desperate to save her neck?"

"She hired a prostitute," Ash said carefully. "So, there's the possibility the father of her child could have been any number of men."

Morley thought on that, and then violently rejected that notion, voicing the fear he'd had for some weeks now. "I'm not certain she'd ever truly had a lover before me."

All the men suddenly seemed uncomfortable, but it was Dorian who said, "Well... I mean... there's an uncomplicated way to tell."

"Not... the way we... Holy Christ I don't *know*." Morley buried his hands in his hair and pulled.

"I'm afraid to ask, and yet I find myself anxious to find out," Argent said as if this surprised him.

Morley sorely wished he could be anywhere else. He couldn't very well admit that he was so bloody ravenous that he might not have noticed the physical barrier of her virginity.

That her arms were so sweet. Her body so tight, yet welcoming. Her moans might have been pleasure or pain, but her words were nothing but encouraging.

91

He proceeded carefully. "She wasn't...experienced, but neither did I notice a... physical impediment. She wasn't the shy, wilting flower, obviously, she approached me. But, neither was she a vixen. She'd found out about the Earl of Sutherland's infidelity and was angry at his selfishness. She wanted a lover of her own."

He didn't want to give them more. To say how adorable she'd been. And so damnably desirable he'd been on the verge of orgasm the minute they'd kissed. He'd been beneath her skirts as he feasted her to completion and was unable to tell if she were shocked or expectant. Nervous or experienced.

And yet. He'd known it was her first climax. She'd left no doubt about that.

"She made it sound like her intended was a selfish lover," he defended himself to no one in particular at this point. "But I can't say for certain now that she knew this firsthand. And she never went back to Miss Henrietta's. I paid to be informed the moment she did. So the chances of her hiring another lover are slim."

Though, if he thought about it... she could entice any man with the crook of her finger.

"Why go through with marriage to the blighter, then, if he was unfaithful?" Ash wondered aloud.

"Strictly speaking, she didn't," Argent reminded them over his coffee cup. "She was found with her fingers around the hilt of the dagger that killed him."

"Red-handed, as it were." Morley huffed a sigh between his compressed lips. "Why would she do it? Why would she do *any* of it?"

Ash shrugged, as if it really was of little consequence. "It's not for us to understand the mysterious minds of women."

"Or people in general," Argent agreed.

"Perhaps she agreed to marry him because she didn't want her child to grow up a bastard," Dorian, the bastard born of a ruthless Marquess, put this to them without a hint of his earlier levity.

"It's a probability." Morley felt his lip lift above his teeth in a snarl. "Or she wanted my child to be the next Earl of Sutherland."

"Can you blame her?" Argent had a distinct gift for finding the practicalities in an emotionally charged situation. "This pregnancy makes her *less* likely to kill the man who would lift her out of this bind, not more. She'd have been a pariah to her family and society if the child had been born without the luxury of a name. It's extraordinary what women will give up for their children…" Argent trailed off, staring at the blank wall.

"Unless Sutherland found out and threatened to destroy her with the secret," Morley theorized.

"Cutter," Ash said the name written on no documents and spoken by no one in the world but the unlucky few who'd known him decades ago.

Their eyes met, and suddenly Ash wasn't a pirate king, or the Rook, but that black-eyed boy. The one with whom he roamed the streets and threw fists and stole food and created impossible futures.

"Congratulations, Cutter." Ash's lips lifted into the ghost of a smile, his dark eyes softening to something almost tender. "You're going to be a father."

The weight of that word knocked the wind from him. A *father*. He'd given up that dream years ago.

"What are you going to do about it?" Dorian, the besotted father of two children gave him perhaps the first look of commiseration he'd ever received from the man.

Morley stood and shouldered past them all, retrieving his jacket from where he'd hung it on the rack. "My job."

CHAPTER 7

"*I didn't* kill him."

It was the first thing the woman said when Morley descended the stairs to the private interrogation cell in the basement of Number Four Whitehall Place with a bucket of warm water and stringent soap.

Prudence. Her name was Prudence Goode. He knew that now.

This chamber had, decades past, been used for little better than inquisition-like torture. Though the walls had been cleaned and scrubbed by a million different char maids, Morley could still smell the blood. It hung like condemnation in the air, flavoring it metallic and spicing it with mold and despair. He'd given Dorian the famous beating here. He'd used it to hide traitors for the Home Office and other high-profile criminals.

In the middle of the grey stone, *she* stood like a soiled white lily unlucky enough to adorn a battlefield.

Rumpled and bloodstained.

A tug in his chest had him clearing his throat. She was so sweet to look upon. So lovely and small and concerningly pale.

He'd thought he'd met enough conniving criminals, both men and women, to not be moved by seemingly innocent features. And yet, here he was, fighting the knight-errant inside him that desired to sweep her away from all of this and lock her in a tower where she would be safe.

Where she would be *his*.

"A clean frock has been sent for," he told her, pulling a tri-legged stool from the corner to perch in front of the bench upon which she sat.

The manacles on her wrists weren't secured to anything, she could have moved around easily. But she remained still, pressing her hands into her belly, as if holding on to what was inside.

A motherly gesture to be sure.

He sat close enough to watch her every expression intently, but far enough not to crowd her.

Far enough not to reach out, as he absurdly ached to do.

She'd been astonishingly fair-skinned the night they'd met. But today, even the slash of pink beneath her cheekbones had disappeared. Her lips retained no color. She seemed thinner now, less robust and vivacious.

This room did that to a person.

So did murder.

When she looked up, he made another astonishing discovery. He'd thought her eyes dark like Dorian's or Ash's, but he'd been mistaken.

They were the color of the sky before night descended. A deep, soulful midnight blue.

They widened at him, drenched with misery and fear.

"I *didn't* kill him," she repeated, her voice husky with unshed tears and the cold of this place.

Morley had made a profession of being lied to and

could spot a crook with hound-like accuracy. It took him no time to suss out the merit of a man.

But women... What confounding creatures they were.

He read the truth on her open face. And it seemed so improbable. So unlikely.

That he now doubted his ability to interpret anything at all.

Morley set the bucket between them and remained quiet as he divested himself of his jacket and rolled his sleeves up his forearms. He placed a stool in front of her and crouched upon it. Next, he took the soaking cloth from the steaming water and scrubbed it with the sharp-smelling soap before reaching out, his palm up.

She stared at him for a long moment, the braid that had made a crown for her veil wilting dejectedly to one side. "Did you hear me?" she asked. "I said—"

"I heard you." He kept his hand extended until she slowly peeled her arms from the protection of her middle toward him. The blood on her hands was no longer fresh, and some of it had peeled away from the soft white flesh of her fingers. Elsewhere, it had dried into darker, less crimson colors.

He draped the warm, wet cloth over them both and let it soak away the evidence.

"There are reasons to kill, Miss Goode." His voice echoed softly from the stones around them, and he endeavored to keep his intonation gentle.

She blinked over at him and his heart wilted...or grew...he couldn't exactly tell. He'd forgotten he had one for so long that these tremors inside of his chest could have meant any number of things.

"Perhaps Sutherland hurt or molested you?" he prompted. "Threatened you or... or the child?" He swallowed. A child. *His* child.

He'd have killed the man himself, were that the case.

She shook her head violently. "He was a cad, a liar, and a rogue, but George was never physically cruel. Despite my anger, I didn't wish him dead."

"You *were* jealous." He took the soiled cloth and dipped it back into the bucket, before tending to only one hand, wiping between her small, elegant fingers and around her fingernails. It felt intimate, somehow, what he did for her. But he had no intention of that. He only wanted to be kind. "You were jealous enough to… to come to me that night. Perhaps that jealousy became hysteria after so long, a rage fed by the rigors of pregnancy."

She tried to jerk her hand out of his grip, but he held fast.

"You're seriously suggesting that I was hysterical enough on my wedding day to stab George with a relic in a church where I was certain to be found out?"

He pulled her forward, closer, capturing her gaze with his. "I'm trying to give you a defense."

"I don't *need* a defense," she said through her teeth. "I need someone to believe me. And do you know what else I need? A *husband.* I needed George's protection for the child you and I made together. Because you left me that night. You left me without even a *name.*"

Her accusation split him open like a blade. Left him raw and wounded.

Because she was right. Had she a way to contact him, she mightn't have had to stay betrothed to Sutherland.

"That is counted among the many misdeeds I committed that night," he acquiesced with a heavy breath as he released her one hand and reached for the other. For a moment, the only sounds in the dank room were the drops of water into the bucket and their uneven breaths.

"I know who you are." Her whispered words fractured around him, barraging him from all sides.

He looked up at her sharply.

Her eyes stayed locked on where the skin of her hand emerged from beneath the blood.

"I worked it out while I was reading the paper some weeks past. You were no Stag of St. James. You told me you were a shadow. In fact, I believe you are the Knight of Shadows."

"You're clever," was all he replied.

"I've been trying to figure all this time why the much-touted savior of the city, this moral vigilante with a reputation for protecting innocence, would relieve me of my own."

She still wouldn't look at him. And he didn't blame her.

Her narrow nostrils flared with breath, and the hand in his trembled.

She was afraid.

"I only accepted what you freely offered." It was the truth. Not a defense. He was a blackguard for doing so. A moral reprobate and a scoundrel and the worst kind of bastard. But he didn't steal her virginity. He didn't take her. He claimed the prize she handed him wrapped in such a lovely beribboned package. He'd given, too. He gave her pleasure. He gave her gentility and deference.

He gave her a child.

Shit.

"Under false pretenses." She finally speared him with a wounded, accusatory gaze. "You let me think pleasure was your vocation. Everything about you that night was a lie, even your voice, your accent. *God.* I dishonored myself with a man known to my father. Did you know who I was?"

"*No*," he stated firmly, dipping his cloth back into

the bucket and running it between her fingers. "You know we've never met, and you'll forgive me if I don't keep up on society weddings, even that of my superior."

"Then...why?"

Her question stilled his hand, and this time it was he that could not meet her gaze.

"Why did you make love to me?" she pressed.

He'd been asking himself the same question for weeks.

"I didn't make love to you, I fucked you. I did it because you asked me to." He'd done it because she'd possessed something few women did. An indefinable allure that made him forget anything resembling reason or thought of consequence.

He'd done it because he'd been hungry and desperate for so many things in his life, but no privation had torn at him with such strength until she'd offered herself as a banquet.

She flinched as though he slapped her, and he instantly regretted his harsh words. But he'd be damned if he'd take them back. If he'd allow her to think she had any kind of sexual thrall over him now. Or any power at all.

Because the precedent had to be set if this was going to work.

Morley remained silent. Waiting for her next move. He expected her to make demands. To use that night as blackmail and threaten to tell her father.

"I wanted so desperately to find you," she murmured, as if in disbelief. "And here you were all this time, a charlatan charading as a gentleman."

She didn't know the half of it.

"A gentleman is nothing *but* a charade," he said stiffly, returning to his vocation of scrubbing her hand.

"I beg your pardon?"

"The million rules a gentleman lives by, or ladies for

that matter, it's nothing but pretense, is it not? A construct to hide who we truly are. What we think. What we want. We are naught but artificial beasts."

"No..." Her little nose scrunched as if he'd stymied her. "Our rules of civility separate us from the beasts."

"Nonsense. The rules give us a pretty cage for our beasts to hide in. And let people like your lot put yourselves above the rest of humanity. It's a way to identify who thinks they are made better than others by happenstance of birth and rigorous training." He made a wry, bitter sound. "Well, any man can train himself. Just look at me."

"What do you mean?" She finally pulled her hand out of his grasp, the soap making her clean skin slippery.

He meant to show her exactly who he was. Exactly what she was about to get herself into. "I come from nothing. Lower than nothing. That accent you say was a farce, it is the one I was born with. I used to speak like any other street rat out there, and high-born folk would kick me in the gutters." He gestured to the wall, beyond which a bustling city scurried with unwanted children. "But I trained myself to act like them. To look and speak and dress like them. And now... I police them all. The entire city. And one of their own will be my wife."

She put her hands to her eyes. "Tell me you are not engaged."

He dropped the cloth into the bucket and stood. "Don't be obtuse, I obviously meant you."

"What? Absolutely not!"

An anger welled within him, one as ancient as he felt. The anger of every unwanted child. Every unrequited love. Every rejected, low-born git made to feel not good enough. "I don't see that you have a choice," he said in a slow, even tone. "If you're pregnant with my child. I will raise that child, and that's the end of it. In any case, it's the best way of getting you out of this predicament."

She sat on the cot with her hands in her lap, clenched and white-knuckled. "My father... he will never approve."

"Oh, he will now." Morley would make certain of it.

"But..." She held up the manacles surrounding her wrists.

"We'll get to that," Morley said darkly as he lifted the bucket of soiled water and stalked away from her.

One catastrophe at a time.

CHAPTER 8

*S*hackles came in many forms, Prudence decided. She was given a choice between two, and no matter which shackles she chose, they were until death.

They'd each left their marks on her body.

As she sat in her parlor—no, Morley's parlor—her fingers idly traced the disappearing circles of irritation on her wrists where she'd been cuffed earlier and hauled into a private arraignment in front of a judge who'd lifted her confinement. He'd done this only after the Chief Inspector had promised a staggering amount of cash for her surety before he drove her to the registrar to trade her cuffs for a ring.

Despite everything, it had been Morley who'd looked as if he were bound for the gallows. He'd stiffly spoken their vows and signed paperwork before ushering her to his astonishingly handsome terrace in Mayfair.

Where Prudence's family had been waiting.

Pru stared at the ring. The symbol of eternity. This day had been a bloody eternity.

They all had traded awkward conversation through an uncomfortable dinner where, thank heavens, her younger twin sisters, Felicity and Mercy, were sprightly enough at nineteen to chat incessantly when heavy silences threatened to descend.

After a sumptuous but abbreviated three courses, the ladies had been asked to withdraw to the parlor so the men could talk.

They'd been talking for entirely too long.

Prudence glared at the door. Her father and husband were discussing, nay, *deciding* her future somewhere beyond. Shouldn't she at least be there? Shouldn't she have a say?

A lump of dread had lodged within her throat, and try as she might, she could not swallow it.

She mustn't be surprised. When had she ever wielded power over her own life?

Especially when it came to marriage.

It wasn't as though Sutherland had been her first proposal. She'd offers from Barons, foreign leaders and dignitaries, a Viscount, and even an American magnate she'd liked once.

But her father had rebuffed them all, holding out for an offer that never seemed to come until, somehow, she'd found herself firmly on the shelf.

It was Honoria, herself, who'd long-ago suggested an alignment with George. Honoria's husband, William, was both besotted with and devoted to her. Woodhaven and Sutherland were great friends, and he very much wanted his best friend married to his wife's sister, even if he had to press the man into the arrangement.

George had so much as admitted it. "I never thought to have a wife. Sorry you'll be stuck with me, old thing, as I'm terribly certain I'll make a horrendous husband." He chucked her on the chin, and everyone had laughed as though life would be a lark.

But in reality, they'd been laughing at her. Poor Prudence. She'd be stuck at home while her husband spent her fortune on other women. He'd gamble everything away and she'd nothing to say about it.

But at least her child would have a name.

The irony of it all was, being a wife and mother was all Pru had ever desired. She'd no great need to be an accomplished and influential noble matron, nor a modern single woman with progressive sensibilities. She left that to women possessed of better and bolder minds than she.

Her hours were happily spent enjoying simple pleasures. Riding fine horses on beautiful days and reading fine books on dreary ones. Shopping with her sisters. Paying calls on friends. Attending interesting lectures, diverting theater productions, and breathtaking musical venues.

She didn't dream of an important life, just a happy one. One with a handsome man who loved her, and healthy children to do them credit and fill their lives with joy.

And now, it seemed, one mistake in a fairy garden precipitated a lifetime of misery, scandal, and, at least for the moment, immediate imprisonment in her husband's home until everything was decided by men who knew better.

It was enough to crush her.

"Did you hear me, Prudence?" Baroness Charlotte Goode's shrill question broke her of trying to stare through a solid door.

Pru put her fingers to her aching temples, suddenly overcome by exhaustion. "I'm sorry, Mother, what were you saying?"

Pursing her lips, Lady Goode clutched a dazzling shawl around her diminutive shoulders and shivered. "I was wondering at the dark fireplace, dear. One would worry if your new husband can afford to warm the house."

Considering the sum Morley had paid for her freedom without blinking, Pru very much doubted the man had trouble keeping the household. Though, there did seem to be an alarming lack of staff for such a grand, sizeable home.

"It's still warm, Mother," she said with a droll breath, doing her best not to roll her eyes.

"He likely didn't want us overheating, Mama," Felicity defended from where she perched on a delicate couch overlooking the lovely cobbled street. Even in the dim gaslights of the late evening, her coiffure glinted like spun gold.

Mercy, never one to sit still for long, handed her mother a glass. "Drink this sherry, it'll warm you."

The Baroness took the drink, her shrewd dark eyes touched everything from the golden sconces to the muted sage and cream furniture of the sparsely decorated parlor. "You'll have to engage my decorator, of course. You can't be expected to live in such barren conditions. The house is nearly empty and old enough to be decrepit. I mean, look at the panes in the windows, they're positively melting. And only three courses for your wedding meal? It's as if—"

"It's as if I were released from prison for murder only this morning to be saved by a man who would give me the protection of his position," Prudence said sharply, her voice elevating in octaves and decibels with each word. "It's as if he had scant hours to plot the entire affair and endless things to consider, the least of which are the courses of a *farcical* celebration."

Her mother gave an indignant gasp. "I thought we all agreed *not* to mention—"

"Oh, don't let's antagonize her, Mama." Mercy moved to Pru's side at once and sank next to her. She

KERRIGAN BYRNE

gathered up both her hands and kissed them. "Poor Pru, it's been an upsetting couple of days."

Prudence attempted to summon a wan smile for her younger sister and wasn't up to the task. Her nerves felt like they'd been stretched on the rack and were screaming for release.

Upsetting... the word couldn't touch a description for the last forty-eight hours.

"I rather like Sir Morley," Felicity remarked, daring a glass of sherry of her own. "He's so...well he's such a..." Her wide eyes narrowed as she searched for the right word, tapping her chin with a burgundy-gloved finger. "Well so many men are either elegant, or handsome, or extremely masculine, but the Chief Inspector somehow manages all three."

Pru blinked at her sister. Leave it to ever-romantic Felicity to describe her husband perfectly.

It was what had attracted her to him that night. He'd been a savage in a bespoke suit. A beast burdened by sartorial elegance. The dichotomy never ceased to fascinate her.

Mercy patted her hand. "And your new home is lovely, Pru. Everything is so fine and well-preserved."

"Indeed, our rooms in town look like closets in comparison," Felicity added encouragingly.

Mercy nodded. "People are paying large sums on the market for these spacious grand old places. I'll bet that chandelier is imported and at least a hundred years old."

"How many times do I have to tell you *not* to discuss money in public, Mercy?" their mother lamented. "And our rooms in town might not be so large, but they've a fashionable address."

"This is Mayfair, Mama, every address is fashionable," Felicity said with a droll sigh.

The twins shared a wince with Pru, who returned Mercy's fond squeeze.

She'd always admired young Mercy's enterprising wit and busy mind. It was as though her trains of thought were numerous and confounding as those running through Trafalgar station, and branched in just as many directions.

Whereas Felicity's notions were a bit less weighty and more idealistic, their mode of transport a hot-air balloon drifting upon the whims of a strong wind.

Either way, they were each darling girls dressed in gem-bright silks and forever the fair counterparts to Prudence and Honoria's dark looks and darker deeds.

Before she could reply, footsteps clomped down the hall before the parlor door burst open containing the storm cloud that was her father. The dark blue eyes they'd all inherited from him glinted with displeasure from his mottled features.

"We're going," he stated shortly.

They all stood.

"Is everything all right?" her mother queried anxiously.

The Baron pinned Prudence with a scathing look as he announced through his teeth, "Everything is settled."

Morley stood in the door looking both resolute and enigmatic. He watched the tableau with a vague disinterest. Removed from it all.

Remote.

Would she ever be able to reach him?

Felicity and Mercy embraced, kissed, and congratulated Pru, each wearing identical looks of pity and concern.

"We've left a trunk of your things for you from your wedding trousseau," Felicity said. "Come around for the rest when you can."

Her mother curtsied to Morley and her father

shook his hand, each of them maintaining the barest façade of civility.

Her husband's manners remained impeccable and his expression impenetrable. His spine straight and tall as he looked each of them right in the eye.

They left with barely a word for Prudence.

She swallowed as a lump of hurt lodged above that of the ever-present dread aching in her throat.

Would it ever be comfortable to breathe again?

Morley stood between her and the door, his wide back expanding with deep breaths, as if he were bracing himself for something unpleasant.

Like turning to inspect his unwanted wife.

The short-cropped hair at his nape did little to hide a red flush on his neck and a trickle of sweat that ran into the collar of his evening suit. It was the only indication that he even suffered an emotion or two.

When she could no longer stand it, Pru asked, "What happened between you and Father? How on earth did you get him to agree—?"

He finally turned, and it was all she could do not to take a step back, so abrupt was the movement. Military in its precision.

"You don't have to worry about that."

"This is my future, of course I must worry about it."

Rather than look at her, his stare remained fixed on a distant point down the hall. "It's settled to both of our satisfactions…or neither. Now, follow me," he said as he swept past her.

What about her satisfaction? she wanted to ask. *Didn't that matter at all anymore?*

The old Pru would have said something. But fear lurked in the Prudence who'd spent the night in a jail cell. One that feared that if she displeased this new husband of hers, he'd toss her right back in the cuffs.

She trailed him as he led her through a long hall

with stunning antique scroll paneling but devoid of portraiture or art.

"I'm glad you both agreed, I'm just bewildered is all," she rambled. "My father is a stubborn man...not easily convinced of anything. And the very fact that he suffered through dinner without making a scene is nothing less than miraculous."

"Suffered?" Morley's disdainful sniff echoed in the empty hall. "I'm certain it causes him no end of suffering that his newest son-in-law is beneath him socially. Sitting at my lowly table must have been a torment for you all. I commend you for containing your disappointment."

"No! Not at all," she rushed, before ceding the falsehood. Her father, and especially her mother, were devastated more by the loss of Sutherland's earldom than the man, himself. And to have him replaced with a man of the working class, even a knight, was little compensation. "What I mean to say is that we're attempting something highly irregular. It'll take a miracle for society not to discover that I married two days after my wedding to poor George was interrupted by his murder and that I gave birth not six or so months after—"

He paused, and she nearly ran into the back of him.

"I would take it as a kindness if we mentioned the former Earl of Sutherland as little as possible in this house." His chin touched his shoulder, but he didn't exactly look back at her. A chill had been added to his endlessly civil tenor. "If *ever*."

"Surely that's impossible while I'm still under suspicion." She stepped closer to him. Close enough to put her hand on his back if she wanted. "Is that how you convinced my father to be agreeable? By offering to protect me from—"

"Your father is being investigated by the Yard for

smuggling illicit substances into the country through his many shipping companies. He is aware of your pregnancy, and he concedes that marriage to me is the thing that could very well save your life and his reputation. If you want the honest truth, I resorted to little better than blackmail to gain his word and his silence." He paused. "Let's not pretend I have his blessing." He turned the corner at the end of the hall and began to conquer the stairway up to the second floor.

Pru stood there for a stunned moment. "Smuggling?" She roused herself and trotted after him, lifting her skirts to climb after him. "Are you the one conducting the investigation against him?"

"I cannot discuss it."

"Not even with me?"

At the top of the stairs he finally looked back to level a droll look down his sharp nose. His eyes were like two silver ingots glowing from the shadows covering the rest of his features.

"*Especially* with you."

He disappeared from the stairwell and Pru crested the steps to turn and chase him down the corridor.

"The green parlor downstairs is for your particular use." He both spoke and walked in short clips. "But I will leave the running of the house to you. Decorate and arrange it how you like. I've a cook, a maid of all work, and a footman, but I'm certain you'll require additional staff. Hire them at your leisure."

A naturally curious person, Prudence ached to open each of the doors they passed, but she didn't dare. "Surely you don't have my dowry yet," she remarked.

He stopped, having come to the end of the hall. "Surely *you* don't think I need it," he threw a perturbed glance over his shoulder. "I've quite enough to keep a wife. Even a high-born one. I should think that's evidenced by my estate."

She'd offended him. She hadn't meant to, but despite his very fine house in an expensive part of town, and the sum he'd forfeited for surety, she hadn't any true ideas what his finances were like. "I didn't mean to imply..."

"You needn't worry. Your dowry is yours to do with as you wish. I don't require it and I won't touch it." He said this like her money was diseased, before he swept open an arched door. "Your room."

Pru had to brush past him to step inside, and she hesitated to appreciate the scent of cedarwood and soap wafting from his warm, virile body. She prolonged a blink as she remembered that scent. Remembered burrowing her face into his neck and gasping in great lungs full of it.

Even now, it provoked her exhausted body into a state of unnatural awareness.

When she opened her eyes, she marveled.

This wasn't a simple chamber, but a veritable suite. She'd a wardrobe at home smaller than the gilded fireplace, and everything else was to scale.

Like the rest of the house, the room was devoid of extraneous furnishings. However, the bed was half again as big as anything she'd slept in and angled toward windows that stretched from the ceiling to the floor.

Unlike the antique, leaded panes of downstairs, these had been installed recently, and the whole of the vast city spread out beyond in a tableau of dazzling light and spires.

"Your trunks are at the foot of the bed," he informed her. "Until a lady's maid has been procured for you, Lucy, the maid of all work, will tend to your needs. Unfortunately, she is with her ailing uncle until tomorrow afternoon. So you might need to call upon—"

"It's all right. I'll manage." She turned around,

clasping her hands in front of her, doing her best not to look at the bed.

He seemed to be avoiding it as well.

Lord, how different this interaction was from the last night they'd spent together. Would they ever find that sort of warmth again? Would he ever look at her with that all-consuming heat threatening to turn her into a pile of ash and need?

She watched him stride around the outskirts of her room, inspecting the view as if he'd never seen it before. Avoiding her as if she carried the plague rather than his child.

Perhaps he needed his mask.

"If you pull on these cords, the heavy drapes will fall and block out the sunlight if you are prone to sleeping late." He demonstrated by tugging on a tasseled cord releasing one of the cobalt velvet panels. "This one next to it secures the drape back in place without needing to tie."

"How clever," she murmured.

"I thought so." His hands clasped behind his back in a regimental pose and they stood like that, staring at each other for longer than was comfortable.

It struck her in that moment how little she knew this man. How little she understood him.

He stood like a soldier, but wore white-tie finery. Just today he'd been a blackmailer *and* a bridegroom. He was a Chief Inspector. A vigilante. A knight. Her lover. A husband.

Her husband. One who had certain rights. One to which she had certain marital duties.

Despite herself. Despite everything, a little flutter of excitement spread through her belly.

"Well." Morley cleared his throat and skirted nearly the entire room to avoid her in a controlled dash for the door. "Good evening to you."

"Good evening?" She parroted his words back to him as a question. Wasn't this their wedding night? "Where are you going? That is...are you...coming back?"

He stopped in the doorframe, his wide shoulders heaving with a long breath before he slowly made an about-face to regard her with a strange and vigilant wariness. "Only a base creature would expect you submit to the marriage bed after such a traumatizing few days." His expression turned hesitant. "You don't know me very well, but I assure you, I am not a man who is prone to—the kind of behavior I demonstrated upon the night we met."

The realization that he was being considerate warmed Pru a little. "It seems that night was out of character for us both."

His eyes skittered away. "Yes. A hard-won lesson of our mutual folly."

Something about that statement tempted her to argue but she could find no words. "I appreciate your consideration, and you're correct. I don't know you at all..." Pru fiddled with her wedding ring as she took a tentative step forward, latching on to an idea. "Perhaps you could stay for a while. We could talk. We could... become acquainted. I don't relish the idea of being alo—"

He retreated a step to hers, shaking his head decisively. "I've work to do."

Pru frowned. "Work? You mean... as the Knight of Shadows?"

"Among other things." His features locked down and everything about him became as hard as granite, including his voice. "You do realize if you utter a word about the so-called Knight of Shadows, the house of cards I've managed to build around you will collapse

113

entirely. Any notions of ruining me will only lead to your own damnation."

Perhaps *this* was why he'd been so cold. So distant. He thought she might reveal his secrets to the world, thereby ruining his life. He hadn't cause to know otherwise, it wasn't as though they'd a relationship built on trust.

"I'd never," Pru vowed. "You have my word."

She tried not to let it hurt her feelings that her word didn't seem to allay him in the slightest. "Very good." He gave her a stiff nod that might have been a bow, and his weight shifted to take a step away.

"Wait!" she called, evoking the brackets of a deepening frown.

"What else is it, Miss Goode? I did not lie when I said I had duties to attend."

The irritation in his voice stung her sinuses with the threat of overwhelming emotion. She turned from him, grateful to have a reason. He'd called her Miss Goode, as if he'd forgotten that she'd taken his name.

"My buttons," she croaked huskily. "They're in the back and if I haven't a lady's maid… I can't reach them."

She waited in the silence with bated breath until, finally, the creak of the floorboards announced his approach.

Prudence tightened her fists in her skirts and forced herself to be still as his fingers found the top button of her plaid, high-necked gown and released it. Gooseflesh poured over her and a little tremor spilled down her spine as he was unable to avoid brushing the upswept hair at the nape of her neck.

She closed her eyes again, swamped with an overwhelming longing. Gods, she wanted him to hold her.

No, not exactly. Not *him*. Not this wary creature of starchy reticence and wary silence. But *him*. The Knight of Shadows. She'd never felt as safe and marvelous as she had in his arms. Clutched to him. Pinned beneath him. Clenched around him.

Was he gone from her forever?

Had he ever truly existed at all?

She listened for his breath, and realized he held it.

The buttons gave way beneath his deft motions and she couldn't seem to summon words until he'd made it below her shoulder blade. Then everything she was thinking burst out of her like a sneeze.

"It's only that I have so many questions and so many fears that I feel I will die if I don't know *something*. Can't you understand how that feels? Is my life in London over? My reputation ruined? Does everyone think me capable of murder? What about George's funeral, I'll be expected to attend, won't I? Unless everyone thinks I killed him, then... Oh God. And what about you? Everyone will think—"

"People will think what I tell them to think," he said in a voice only a fraction less even and measured than his hands upon her buttons. "Only a trusted few know of your arrest last night and even fewer your release. The reverend has been silenced. Honoria and William have been sent away. Your fiancé had blessed little in the way of family, and his earldom is passed to some distant Scottish cousin who is happy not to ask too many questions. As for my part, I'm investigating the matter thoroughly, though Argent is officially handling the murder inquest for the sake of records, and a more secretive man you've never met."

She'd have to take his word on that. "What about the press? An Earl dying at his own wedding is an enormous story. All the people in attendance... someone will figure out where I am and what we've done."

His sigh was a warm tickle on her neck. "For now, they're chasing Honoria and William across the continent, thinking you are absconded to Italy to grieve and escape the horror of it."

She chewed on the inside of her lip. "Even still... there's bound to be a scandal. The truth will come out eventually."

"What troubles you the most?" he asked disapprovingly, having undone enough of her buttons to make the bodice of her dress sag. "Scandal? Or the truth?"

"I fear the consequences of what we've done," she said, holding her bodice to her chest before turning to look at him. "I don't want to raise a child under such a shadow."

The brow he notched was a few shades darker than his fair hair, and Pru realized her error. He *was* a shadow. The Knight of Shadows, in fact.

"As a man who has braved many a scandal, I care not what is said behind silk fans." He waved her worries away. "You've a bedroom rather than a cell. And no one as of yet calling for your blood. Until the inquest is over, it's best you remain out of the public eye so that I might protect you as well as I can. Those are the only answers I can give you for now."

Bereft, shaky, and utterly exhausted, Prudence gathered the last bit of strength she had to square her shoulders and ask, "Promise me you'll search with everything you have. Promise me you'll look elsewhere than in your own house for the killer."

"I promise I will look where the investigation leads."

A desolate disappointment pressed upon her with a tangible weight, curling her shoulders forward as if they could keep his words from piercing her heart. "Do you believe me...husband? Do you believe that I am innocent?"

His gaze became intent, searching, and then frustratingly opaque. "I believe you were right when you said that the truth will come out."

Pru successfully fought off crumpling until he'd turned his back.

"Good night, Miss—" he paused then, catching himself this second time. "Good night."

When the door closed behind him, Prudence limped to the bed as if a herd of horses had trod on her feet, suddenly hurting everywhere.

She collapsed onto the counterpane and released the tears she'd been too numb to cry since this nightmare began. They broke upon her like the tide, threatening to pull her under their current of despair.

She should have wept for a dead man. For the loss of her parents' respect and her freedom. For the horror of her utter ruin and the fear of being unable to lift her head in society ever again.

But she wept, because her husband couldn't bring himself to say her name.

CHAPTER 9

*M*orley didn't think his wife was dangerous solely because he wanted her. She was dangerous because he wanted to believe her.

He emerged from the underground tunnels into Whitechapel, searching for trouble. Aching for it. His muscles rippled beneath his skin. Ready. Oh, so ready. He felt hot and cold all at once. He needed to hit something. To maim. To pound.

Fucking unfortunate word, that.

Also...relevant.

He'd wanted to pound into *her* everything he'd denied himself for the past three months. To thrust and thrust and thrust until he lost himself to the bliss he knew he'd find in her body.

What harm could it do now?

She'd almost seemed like she'd wanted it. Hadn't she? No. *No.* Surely, he'd imagined the expectation in her eyes.

The invitation.

Leaving her like that, with her dress half hanging off her shoulders, was one of the most difficult things he'd ever done. *God!* Just uncovering her neck to the top of her corset—the mere sight of her shoulder blades had driven him mad with lust.

For a stranger. For a possible murderer.

For his wife.

He was a beast on a short leash tonight. *His wedding night.* He'd used every ounce of civility he could feign on this difficult, exhausting day and now he could set free his wrath on the dregs of the city. Tonight, he was on the hunt for a singular criminal. A particular crime.

And he knew just where to find it.

He passed plenty of illegal acts. Bordellos, gambling hells, gin peddlers, thieves, and all sorts up to every kind of sin.

This was his genesis, and might very well be his end. This putrid place where the shadows were full of danger and the pallid streetlamps only illuminated unpleasant truths. He slid between them like a cat, avoiding detection as even desperate, waifish fiends and daring prostitutes shrank from his shade.

He heard the name whispered behind his back upon occasion.

Is that him? The Knight of Shadows?

The police beat was easy to avoid, he'd been doing it for decades. He knew their routes, and their times.

Hell, he knew most of their names.

What he needed to discover, was which ones sold cocaine to the innocent and weak.

The deeper he drove himself into the squalid darkness of Dorset Street, the more layers of himself peeled away. He shucked off Carlton Morley. His stringent mannerisms and his staunch courteousness. He even yearned to be rid of the ridiculous mask and moniker of the vigilante.

Tonight, he felt like someone else. Someone he thought he'd buried long ago.

Cutter.

As he lurked through the thoroughfares he'd once owned as Cutter 'Deadeye' Morley, he felt a piece of his puzzle click into place.

For three bloody months he'd been turning a problem over in his mind, chewing it with as much success as he would a rock. Breaking against it. Grinding himself down.

Who was the man who'd made the ballocks decision to fuck a stranger in a garden?

Carlton Morley? Or the Knight of Shadows?

He'd needed to come here to find the answer.

It all made perfect sense now. He'd been so visceral that night. So raw and filled with every emotion he'd never allowed himself. Anger and lust and need and pain. He'd been so fucking hungry. Hungry for a kind of sustenance he'd never had.

He'd been...

Cutter.

Cutter had fucked her because he wanted to. Because she was a bit of beauty and warmth he'd never allowed himself. The thief who'd never had parents to speak of, who'd learned his morals from whores and cutpurses. Who'd committed murder for the sake of revenge.

And reveled in it.

He covered up the murder in his past, and if he found out that she'd been the woman to stick that dagger into the Earl of Sutherland's throat...he'd be tempted to cover that up too.

Because despite everything she may or may not be... he still wanted her.

Could she sense it, somehow?

Was it because they had killing in common? Like begets like, after all, and if Prudence Goode was the woman he feared she was, had she selected him because her dark soul recognized his?

Even as the suspicion lanced him with horror, his gut violently rejected it. She was a stranger, an enigma to him, but his instinct was to believe her.

To trust her!

Trust was not an emotion with which he was familiar.

What did he know about her, really? That she was both bold and amenable. Her eyes were kind and her mouth wicked. She'd a temper, but was as levelheaded as anyone could expect under the circumstances. She succumbed to logic just as easily as lust.

She might have killed a man in cold blood.

What sort of mother would a woman like that make?

A rueful sound echoed off the damp walls of a dank alley he all but slithered down. The irony of his hypocrisy both irritated and amused him.

The father of this child was Cutter fucking Morley.

And that was both why he'd married her and why he hadn't touched her. No matter how her shape enticed him. Regardless of how the memories of her creamy thighs and silken intimate flesh tormented him. Despite the urge he had to throw caution to the wind and plunge his hands into her luxuriant hair and trail his mouth over every delectable inch of her sampling summer berries and soft flesh...

His leather gloves creaked against the tightening of his fists.

He. Couldn't. Touch. Her. Not until he found out if she'd *innocent* blood on her hands.

There were reasons to kill. He kept reminding her of that because *if* she was found to be guilty, he wanted —he needed—a reason to save her.

Because the life inside her womb *was* innocent. Pure and untainted by the ugliness of this world. Of these streets. And he'd be goddamned if he wouldn't do everything in his mortal power to keep it that way.

Six months. He had six months to investigate the death of Sutherland and the shipments of illicit substances sweeping the streets.

He felt like a man standing before a tryptic of mirrors, seeing a separate reflection in each. One, the methodical Chief Inspector. The next, a vengeful vigilante. And the third... a boy with a terrible secret and a broken heart.

To reconcile himself. He needed to shatter the third mirror.

Two shades broke from the lamplight of a rotten pub moving toward the alley in between, stealing his focus. Morley trailed them, melting from shadow to shadow like death, himself.

He moved when they moved. Waited when they waited, pressing himself against the corner of a building, listening to their excitement. Catching it with rampant kicks of his heart in his chest as the blue uniform of a London Metropolitan Policeman absorbed the light as he strode toward them, waving a walking stick.

This was what he'd come to see. An exchange of illicit substances. This... was where his trail to the very source began.

Morley waited for the men to pass the Copper his money. He waited until they checked the purity of the substance he handed back to them. He waited until they damned themselves.

Moving slowly, he cracked his fingers and reveled in what was to come. Three criminals. One in his uniform wielding a nightstick.

There would be pain. And he needed the pain. To inflict it. To endure it. To escape.

Yes. He'd put an end to Cutter very soon. But first...

he'd use every weapon in his arsenal. He'd cut out the truth if he had to. The sooner the better.

Because as much as he trusted no one, he trusted himself least of all...

To keep his hands off his wife.

CHAPTER 10

If it was the last thing she ever did, Pru was going to get behind the two locked doors in her house.

She'd been staring at them for a week. Or, rather, they had been staring at her.

They'd a somewhat strange relationship now, she and the doors. They greeted her every day on the way down to breakfast, beckoning to her with their iron latches and symmetrical arches. A cream-colored obsession, they were, and if she didn't get behind them today, she'd give in to the madness waiting in the periphery of her thoughts. Threatening to engulf her and drag her to perdition.

She couldn't exactly say why it bothered her so much. Why she spent so long in front of them when there were so many diverting rooms to occupy her. The first floor alone contained the large drawing room, the dining room, and a morning room attached to the well-tended back gardens through which the modest stable and carriage house hunkered in a cozy stone corner. She'd found a small library, in which she rejoiced, connected to her spacious parlor on the second floor, along with a couple handsome unused guest rooms, and her husband's study.

The third story was where she slept, and only four doors graced the long hall. One was her bedroom and dressing room, obviously, and the other a washroom.

She needn't the deductive powers of a Scotland Yard detective to suss out that her husband slept behind one of the locked doors.

In theory, at least.

Nighttime was when her body reminded her she carried his child with bouts of vicious nausea. So, when she lay awake staring at the canopy, doing her best to contain the retching, she'd often hear the clip of his shoes on the floorboards as he returned home from occasional nocturnal adventures as the Knight of Shadows.

Pru would lie awake and listen to him putter about behind the locked doors. Sometimes it sounded as though he'd brought his enemies home to grapple with them in the middle of the night and she'd burn to know what he was about.

He'd be gone before she awoke.

She never saw him. They never spoke. But she knew her husband kept apprised of her. That the staff, meager as it was, updated him on her well-being.

After a particularly restless night where she'd vomited until the wee hours, she'd been presented an effervescent drink by the thin, birdlike cook at the lonely breakfast table.

"From the master," the woman had told her. "To settle your ills."

She'd not even been able to stomach her usual breakfast of toast that morning, but the moment the ginger ale had fizzed its way down her throat and spread relief in her belly, she'd thanked the stars for him.

The gesture, tiny as it was, had touched her.

He cared.

More likely about the baby rather than her, but even so. She wasn't surprised, per se. She remembered his deference the night they'd been lovers. The tempering of his strength. The tenderness of his touch. The attentiveness to her pleasure.

To dwell on it now would drive her deeper toward madness.

A tray had appeared in her parlor, and upon it she found little treasures almost every morning. A furniture catalogue. A card of information for a staff employment company. Clothing patterns and collections for infants from which she could order.

She'd never had to send for her things from her father's house, workmen had simply arrived and collected her. She'd gone to her parents' house in her husband's fine carriage, finding them conspicuously absent, and had gathered what belonged to her.

And a few things that didn't.

They'd moved and unpacked her entire life without her having to so much as lift a finger.

Chief Inspector Sir Carlton Morley did just about everything around the house...

Except sleep. Or eat. Or live.

She might as well reside in a crypt for all the interaction she had. Ester, Lucy, and the footman, Bart, were polite but disinclined to break the barrier between mistress of the house and staff, regardless of her clumsy attempts. They treated her with careful suspicion, and in the moments they weren't aware of her regard, open disapproval.

Mercy and Felicity had sent word that they were only allowed to call around once per week.

There'd been no word from Honoria. And Pru had not spoken to Amanda since that day in Hyde Park. All her other acquaintances assumed she'd escaped her despair to Italy.

But no. It was right here. Screaming at her through the silence and loneliness that pressed her down from all sides as she stood between two locked doors.

Dammit. She'd had enough.

Prudence waited until Ester had gone out to the market, and went below stairs to pilfer the master set of keys from their hook in the pantry. She'd done this before, on day three, and discovered that none of the master keys matched the locks for the two mysterious doors.

Morley probably kept them upon his person.

The master set did, however, grant her access to his office.

Out of respect for her husband, she'd not disturbed the room past a curious peek that day. What if he somehow discovered that she'd snooped? She'd no desire to incur his wrath.

Today she was past caring. She needed a diversion. She needed to *know*.

It took her an hour and a half of rifling through his office to find what she'd somehow suspected would be there. He was so tidy for a man, so orderly, so comprehensively methodical. If he thought of everything, then he'd keep in the house just exactly what she'd been searching for.

Spare keys.

They'd been tucked into a file of legal papers in a drawer marked "security."

Clever.

They burned her palm as she raced back up the stairs. Her heart trilled in her chest like a captured sparrow as she stood in front of both doors.

She selected the left one first. Inhaling a bracing

breath, she slid the key in the lock and turned it, un-latching the door.

Upon first glance she was disappointed. She hadn't really known what to expect, but in her more fanciful moments she might have conjured a lair befitting the so-called Knight of Shadows. Uniforms maybe. Weapons. Masks and the like.

Unsurprisingly, it was nothing more than an immaculate bedroom. Even the dust motes that'd danced across her open windows didn't seem to dare venture into his space. The bedclothes had not a wrinkle. The shaving implements gleamed in a row on the curio as if they'd been shined with the silver.

But the faint scent of shaving soap clung to the air as the opaque water in the bowl had yet to be refreshed. That and other aromas drew her deeper into the room as if she'd been summoned by a spell. Cedar and fresh linen.

And that masculine spice that was distinctively *him*.

The rustle of her skirts disrupted the almost mausoleum-like silence as she drifted to a high-backed chair where a dressing gown had been neatly draped but obviously discarded after use.

Lucy hadn't laundered it yet or changed the pitcher, which meant that Morley, the master of the house, had straightened his own bed and shined his own shaving accoutrements.

What a bemusing man.

Unable to stop herself, Prudence lifted the robe to her face and inhaled. Since her pregnancy, she seemed to have the nose of a bloodhound. She'd never forget the warm, wild scent of him. It taunted her now, surrounded by his things as she was.

It might be the only appetizing aroma she'd encountered for weeks.

Belatedly, she looked around the room and noticed

something amiss. The paper on the walls was decidedly feminine, little forget-me-nots wrapped in ribbons. There was no view on this side of the house, and the space was decidedly smaller than her chamber at the end of the hall.

Her sound of wonderment snagged the air as the robe slipped from her fingers back to the chair.

He'd surrendered the master suite to her. The room with the best view, the largest bed, and the most comfortable furnishings.

An awfully considerate gesture, for a man who couldn't bring himself to share a meal with her, let alone a conversation.

It first occurred to her to offer the gesture back to him. To tell him she didn't want it, that she'd take the smaller room so he could once again enjoy his own accommodations.

If he'd only come home.

She'd have to figure out how to offer without him finding out she'd snooped.

Heaving a morose sigh, Pru left and locked his room, burning with curiosity about the next door. She fumbled with the key twice before opening it, and when she finally managed, she stood in the doorway for several moments while tears stung behind her eyes.

The room was in disarray. A lovely chaos. The entrails of packing crates were strewn about their treasures as if the unpacking had been interrupted.

This was what her husband had been wrestling with the past few nights.

Floating inside, Prudence touched each one as if it were made of the most fragile glass.

A wicker cradle. An expensive-looking perambulator. Delicate furniture ready to store tiny things. Soft blankets and cushions. Cunning toys.

Her breath hitched as she stopped in front of a fine-crafted rocking chair. The piece, itself, was lovely but what had her transfixed was the simple little doll placed just so on the velvet cushion.

Pru couldn't say why she used infinite care to retrieve it. The doll was neither fragile nor costly. The body little more than soft fabric stuffed with batting and covered in a white eyelet lace dress. The round head fit in the palm of her hand, the face painted somewhat catawampus, and the hair comprised of soft strings of lose gold yarn tied with blue ribbons.

No, the doll wasn't at all extraordinary.

But the thought of the man she'd married. The intense, mercurial knight selecting it for this room... now that was... that was...rather a marvelous image.

Smoothing her fingers through the strings of yarn she wondered, what if their child bore his golden locks? Or the impossible silver-blue of his eyes?

Little butterflies erupted in her belly, this time not at all precipitating sickness. This person they'd created... would sleep here, God willing. Would fill this house with commotion, and maybe a little cheer.

Lord knew they all needed an injection of that.

As Prudence spun in a circle for a moment, taking in the soft butter yellows, muted pinks, and periwinkles of the room, some of the weight pressing upon her fell away. Morley might not be ready to be any kind of husband, but he was preparing to be a father.

And, it seemed to her, relishing the venture.

But, why lock this room away from her?

A dark thought landed in her stomach, crushing the butterflies beneath a stone. What if he meant to raise this child without her? What if—

A ruckus interrupted the stillness of the house. Doors shutting, heavy footsteps on the wood floors downstairs. The scurry from elsewhere as Lucy and Bart rushed to attention.

Of all the days for her husband to come home before tea!

Prudence abandoned the doll to its perch and flew out of the room, locking it behind her. She raced down the first flight of stairs, but it became instantly obvious that she wouldn't have time to return any of the keys. Masculine voices filtered closer to the base of the stairwell.

"Bloody traffic," Morley's growl echoed up to the second floor. "Has the Earl of Northwalk arrived yet?"

"Not yet, sir," Bart replied.

"Good. Bastard is just as insufferably punctual as I am, which means I have to make a point of being early."

Pru suppressed a little flutter of panic. An Earl? Coming here? Now?

Northwalk, the title itched at her memory. Something so familiar and yet, she was certain they ran in higher circles than her family.

"I finally abandoned my coach to jog here. The rain soaked through my jacket. If I've time, I'll go upstairs for another."

Panicking, Prudence shoved the keys behind a potted plant beneath a window, and did her very best to affect a glide as she descended the final stairs to the main floor, hoping to cut him off.

Conversation seized as both men looked up at her appearance.

Pru faltered halfway down.

Why did he have to be so unspeakably handsome?

Why did he have to be so categorically inaccessible?

A week's time had almost blunted the reality of his imposing, vital allure in her memory. She'd almost forgotten the very sight of him threatened to steal every breath from her lungs and every thought from her head.

Her husband's gaze swept over her. An arrested ex-

KERRIGAN BYRNE

pression tightened the casual one he'd been wearing for Bart, his eyes flaring with something intense and ephemeral.

Before she had cause to hope, his features shuttered with the immediacy of a shop locking down for a long absence.

Bart had only just taken his employer's hat and coat, draping the later damp garment over his arm. He turned and bowed to her low enough to show the round bald spot on his pate. "My lady," he addressed her diffidently.

"Good afternoon." She shook herself from her thrall and summoned what she hoped was a convincing smile. "I'd no idea it'd begun to rai—"

He'd already swept through to the corridor to hang his master's things, apparently feeling no great need to await her reply.

Pru battled with an acute misery that warred for sovereignty with shame. She was such an unwanted stranger here. This didn't feel like her house.

Nor did it feel like her life.

And the man at the foot of the stairs wore more of a mask now than he ever did as the Knight of Shadows.

He just looked at her with those alert, assessing eyes. She'd begun to feel that even his silence was an investigative technique. A weapon he used against her.

An effective weapon, at that.

Because she felt wounded. Bruised.

But then, everything about him was weaponized. The smooth, composed movements of his powerful limbs, hinting at a controlled brutality. The precisely cut layers of his hair, the perfectly pressed creases of his suit, and the carefully manicured elegance of his hands.

Hands that could manipulate just as much pain as pleasure from a person.

There were men who radiated menace, danger, or violence. But her husband hid all that and reserves of so much more behind the cool, placid lake of his façade.

He was the danger you never saw coming until it was too late.

"You're...home," she observed, cringing at the daft bloody obviousness of her statement.

He addressed her with a curt nod, his eyes breaking away from her for the first time, allowing her to breathe. "I was just informing Bart I've a meeting best conducted here rather than the office."

"An Earl, I heard."

His mouth twisted ruefully. "A courtesy title, but yes."

"Is there anything I can do to help?" She hoped she didn't sound as pathetically eager as she felt.

"Not especial—" he looked sharply toward the door and cursed under his breath, his expression turning pained.

Pru hurried down the remainder of the stairs. "What is it?"

"He didn't come alone." Agitated, he took three steps away from her and thrust his fingers through his hair, smoothing it back. "I'm in no bloody mood."

"Did he bring his solicitor?" Pru guessed, wondering if he meant to interrogate the man without one.

"Worse." A beleaguered breath hissed out of his throat. "He brought his wife."

Pru brightened at the prospect of female company. She was acquainted with very few Countesses and even if the woman were difficult, she likely couldn't hold a candle to Prudence's own mother.

"I'm quite finished," she declared. "I can entertain the Countess while you conduct your interview."

A frown pinched his brow. "Finished with what?"

"No," she laughed. "I've attended finishing school

133

with excellent marks. I know how to receive someone of her station."

"Oh." Surprisingly, his frown deepened. "Well that will be of little consequence to Farah."

An instinctive little needle of discomfort pricked her. Farah? Not Lady Northwalk?

The bell chimed and Bart materialized from behind them to answer.

Her husband faced the door with the grim determination a battle general might face an onslaught of marauders. "I suppose it would be cruel not to tell you that Farah used to work as a clerk at Scotland Yard. I've known her for nigh on a decade."

"Why would it be cruel to—?"

"Because Blackwell is certain to mention that I asked her to be my wife."

CHAPTER 11

"*C*arlton Morley, you unforgivable rogue!" An angelic beauty with a coronet of silver-blond ringlets swept into their grand entry in an energetic flounce of mauve silk. "When Dorian told me you'd taken a wife, and under which circumstances, I nearly collapsed."

Pru stood blinking at the uncommonly lovely woman in open-mouthed dismay as Morley stepped forward to receive her light kiss on the cheek.

They knew the circumstances of their marriage? All of them?

Even Miss Henrietta's garden?

"You forget I know better," Morley replied in a voice infused with a charm he'd never bothered to apply with Pru. "You've never fainted in your life."

The appearance of Farah's husband had Prudence forcing herself to unclench her fists. She'd have to accept his hand, and it wouldn't do to have her palms bleeding from where her nails had dug.

"This is my...wife, Prudence Good- er Morley." He said the word wife as if it tasted strange in his mouth. "Prudence, might I introduce Lady Farah Blackwell,

Countess Northwalk, and her husband, Dorian, the Earl."

"Technically my son is the Earl," Blackwell said. "I've titles enough, and I actually earned all of them."

Of course! Prudence recognized him now. This was Dorian Blackwell, the Blackheart of Ben More. Who could care to be an Earl when you were once the King of the London Underworld?

The man was monstrous large and dark as a fiend. Despite the eyepatch, his gaze was keen and rapt, as he assessed her with undue intensity.

Pru thought she saw something like a comprehending approval in his smirk.

"Lady Morley," Dorian Blackwell greeted as if he'd never before thought to utter those words together. He bent over her knuckles and pressed a kiss to the air above them, never touching the skin. "It's been the cause of much speculation between Farah and me as to what prompted Morley to so hastily take a wife." In an inappropriate show of public affection, he straightened to put his arm around his Countess, and rested his hand low on her waist just above her bustle as if it belonged there. "I think the mystery has been solved, my love."

Farah turned her saintly smile upon Prudence. "You're a beautiful woman on any day, Lady Morley, but in that lilac gown you're a vision. Utterly glowing with maternal beauty."

Glowing? Surely not. She'd been losing weight because of her inability to digest food. She was pale, wan, and her eyes sunken with dark circles beneath. She felt more like a shade than an actual person.

They were being kind, of course.

She had to pinch herself to stop gawking like an open-mouthed carp. "I-I thank you, my lady, my lord. What an honor to greet you both."

An honor, and a horror.

The Blackwells were a sight unto themselves. He, dark as a demon with a demonic air of handsome ferocity, and she his unfettered radiant counterpart. It was plain as day Dorian Blackwell adored his wife.

The question was, did Farah return his affections? Or did she still covet Morley?

How could she not? Blackwell was a compelling man, if not specifically handsome, and he'd an air of vital masculinity few possessed, however he was a shadow in Morley's golden presence.

At least where Pru was concerned.

She looked to Morley, who wore an expression of one in a dentist's lobby awaiting a particularly unpleasant procedure.

The question was what? Did he not want the woman who owned his heart to meet the woman who now lay claim to his name?

The very thought was like a punch to the ribs, taking the wind from her lungs as well as her sails.

She didn't know which would have been crueler, for him to tell her or not... she might have been tempted to like the Countess had she not known her husband had once desired her.

That he'd wished to share a home and children with her.

Had they kissed, she wondered.

Prudence had kissed a few men in her two seasons out, enough to know that kissing Morley was an experience that eclipsed all else.

"Carlton, allow me to purloin your wife whilst you and Dorian conduct your affairs. I'm dying to know her."

Carlton? Even Pru, herself, wasn't on such intimate terms with him. Moreover, every time she tried to pin the name upon him in her mind, it refused to stick.

137

"Lady Morley?" Farah Blackwell didn't wait for her husband's reply. "Let's retire to your preferred rooms."

"O-of course. This way, Lady Northwalk." She gestured toward the stairs to her second-floor parlor.

"You'll call me Farah, of course, all my friends do."

They weren't friends, but Prudence nodded as she turned to lead the Countess away. She moved as if quicksand sucked at her feet, a sense of doom washing over her as she climbed the staircase. This woman in her wake, would she be cruel or kind once they were alone?

Farah Blackwell knew who she was, and the circumstances of her marriage.

Did that mean her husband truly trusted these people? Or that their secret was already out and they were trying to control the damage?

Either way, brittle though she felt, she was determined to face this woman with dignity and aplomb befitting the Queen of England, let alone a knight's bride.

Farah couldn't have astonished her more the moment the parlor door had shut behind them. She turned and swept her up into a desperate, but gentle embrace and held her there.

"Oh, you poor dear, what a nightmare you've been through. When Dorian told me the extent of the situation, I haven't been able to sleep but for worrying over you." She pulled back for a moment just to look at her. "I hope you don't mind the intrusion of a stranger, but I just had to see for myself if you are all right. Knowing Carlton, he's bungled the entire thing, stashed you here, and thrown himself into his work."

Pru swallowed a lump of alternating emotions. Gratitude and jealously. "You certainly know my husband well."

A wry smile brought dimples to the woman's cheeks as Farah pulled her over by the rain-streaked window.

"I see you are aware of our former attachment," she said, her grey eyes soft with understanding. "Then you must know how short and dispassionate it was. And how very long ago. I mean, my lands, I was still in my twenties." She waved it all away. "Ancient history all but forgotten."

Pru wasn't certain what to say. She was tormented by the memories of her husband's very physical all-consuming passion. Was Farah being kind again? Or dishonest?

Or had they truly not suited?

"It's nothing, my lady, should I ring for some tea?"

"I'd rather you sit. I'm not certain how long we'll be staying, and I have a rather lot to say."

Carefully, Pru perched across from her on the emerald settee and gestured for her to go on.

Farah's manner was soft and somber as she leaned forward to say, "I worked as a clerk at Scotland Yard for a handful of years. I have known every sort of criminal, and my share of murderers, and I am convinced you are not one."

Pru let out a shaky breath. "How can you be so convinced?"

"Well it makes no sense, does it? A woman in your condition doing away with the one man who can provide her the protection of his name on her wedding day. Found with the dagger in her hands and no story of defense?" Farah tutted and shook her head. "Furthermore, I've lived with a man whose life was ruined when he was wrongfully accused. There's a very singular helpless fury in that. I sense it torments you, as well."

"I wish you'd convince my—" Prudence caught herself in time. "Well, everyone else."

Farah gave a short chuckle "They're men, darling. Adorable idiots to the last. I'm sorry to say but your methodical husband will take incontrovertible proof to

KERRIGAN BYRNE

convince him, but it seems to me that he's intent upon finding it."

Was he?

"Listen." Farah gathered up her hands. "I know you'll feel isolated in the coming months, and that I cannot abide. I want you to call upon me for support in regard to all things. Be it men, marriage, motherhood... or Morley. I worked for the man for years, I am aware of his faults and flaws as well as his heroic qualities, of which there are many. I've birthed two lovely, healthy children of my own and I've been through—well, not what you are—but enough that I feel I can be sympathetic to your plight."

Pru didn't know what to say, or even how to feel. It was all too wonderful. Too wonderful to be true?

"How...incredibly kind of you."

"Also, I hope you don't find me too forward, but I've secured you an appointment with my doctor who specializes in the care of expecting mothers. He's the absolute best in his field, and he works closely with a local midwife, where they both tend to you *and* rely on each other's expertise. I'd never trust my feminine health to anyone else. All of my nearest and dearest friends are patients."

A little glow bloomed in the cockles of Pru's heart. Here she'd been so ill. So afraid. So incredibly alone, and had all the time in the world to go mad with questions and anxieties over the impending arrival of a child.

She gave the hands around hers a responding squeeze. "Farah," she tested the name. "I thank you. Truly. Anytime you would like to be so forward, I heartily encourage you."

"Splendid!" the Countess beamed. "Next week you're to come with me to the Duchess of Trenwyth's

140

to meet with our Ladies' Aid Society. Let's see, Lorelai, Countess Southbourne will be there. Millie LeCour."

"The actress?" Pru marveled.

"Yes! She and her beau, Christopher Argent, live next to Trenwyth where Imogen, I mean, Her Grace, resides. Oh, Samantha and Mena are coming in from Scotland. You'll have to excuse Samantha, as she's American." Farah said this as if it explained everything. "The Countess of Cursing, we call her, but once you get to know her you will be as in love with her as we all are. Mena is a delight. Never will you find a warmer Marchioness. In fact, she'll likely adopt you as she can't have children and will certainly angle to be godmother to Morley's child, as she is to all of ours. Devotion is her exper—"

Pru pulled her hands away. So many names, so many titles. It was all so much. "I'm sorry, but I'm afraid I won't be able to attend. I…I'm supposed to be in hiding, for lack of a better term. Besides, surely you agree I don't *belong* in this society. I've no title nor prescience to bring. I'm the second-born daughter to a Baron, is all. I'm merely Chief Inspector Morley's wife."

For the first time, Farah's mouth compressed with displeasure as her eyes gleamed. "My dear, no one is *just* Morley's wife. He's had a hand in everyone's fate in that room. He's saved more than lives, he's saved souls. I mean, there isn't time to regale you here, but I feel that you should come so we can all tell you the sort of husband you're blessed with. Morley is and has always been a remarkable man. We've all speculated and even schemed to get him a wife. I'm unutterably glad he's found you."

Grief threatened to bubble over in her chest in the form of a sob. "If you know of our situation, then you know this is not a love match."

Farah suddenly became very serious. "May I call you Prudence?"

"Pru, please."

"Pru... you've done what I was certain no woman in the world could do."

"What's that?"

"You've distracted Carlton Morley from his unimpeachable principles. I think, in time, you'll come to know what a Sisyphean feat that was."

Pru shook her head, unable to understand.

Farah seemed to debate something internally, then said, "Morley and I had a working relationship for longer than five years, and a flirtatious companionship. It took him those five years to drum up the nerve to kiss me. You felled him in five minutes! You, my dear, are the temptation he needs. You will force some happiness upon him, I think, and it's the only way, as he will fight you tooth and nail. But he is the best of men, he deserves every happiness."

Prudence didn't allow herself to close her eyes, because every time she did, she saw her husband's lips on Farah Blackwell's.

And she desperately wanted to like the woman.

"Why didn't you marry him?" The question surprised Pru more than it did Farah, it seemed. "I mean, when he asked you. What made you refuse?"

Farah gave a nonchalant shrug, her expression rather wistful. "My heart always belonged to Dorian. It's as simple as that. He never had a chance. I never once regretted my decision, but I won't hide from you the fact that I will always be fond of Carlton. That I respect and admire him. Everyone does. Even my husband, who was once on the wrong side of the law. For all Carlton postures, he's an exceedingly fair and understanding man. He's not without his own past, you know."

That intrigued her. "What past?"

Serious conversation preceded boots as the men climbed the stairs, announcing their inevitable invasion of the parlor.

"I will leave that for him to tell you," Farah said mysteriously.

This time it was Prudence who reached out and clung to Farah's hand as if it were a lifeline. "I don't know that he will...I don't know him at all. I'm so lost. Please, if you have any information. Any insight...I..."

Farah regarded her indecisively. "I promised I will, and I shall impart to you everything I can. Come to us next week. You'll learn all that we know, I vow—"

It was Blackwell who barged in first. "What ho, wife? We've the unfortunate need to leave now to meet my brothers' train. I've brought the second carriage to contain either Ravencroft's shoulders or Gavin's ego. I'll allow them to fight over it."

Pru gawked at the man. If Blackwell thought Ravencroft large, the man must be a giant.

He bowed to Pru. "It was an unmitigated pleasure to meet you, Lady Morley. Please call upon us for the smallest thing."

"Thank you."

Farah gave her another impulsive hug before releasing her with a blustery noise. "The smallest thing. I *really* mean it."

They saw themselves out, and took a whirlwind with them.

Prudence watched her husband peer at the empty doorframe as though contemplating the emptiness he found there.

Did he also note the easy way Blackwell put his possessive hand on his wife's waist? How he walked in deference to her. His every muscle seeming attuned to her movements, her protection, her needs.

Did it make him envious? Or melancholy, like her.

Eventually, he flicked a glance at her as if surprised to still find her there.

"It was very kind of the Countess to come," she ventured. "She was...very solicitous. Gave me the name of a good doctor."

He gave the illusion of a nod. "Farah is a good woman," he said carefully.

As opposed to herself?

Pru stared at him, doing her best not to appreciate how the cut of his vest hugged his narrow waist, flattering the width of his chest and shoulders, the breadth of his back.

A back she'd once clung to in spasms of bliss.

Her fingers curled at the memory.

He was right *there*. So close to her. She could reach out to him and touch the body that'd once rode her like an untamed stallion, wild and rhythmic and powerful.

His lips had tasted the most secret parts of her. His eyes had burned with lust. His features softened with worship. Tightened with pleasure. Tortured with hunger.

And now?

Nothing. He was so remote. So empty. Bleak.

Where are you? She wanted to shout. To throw things. To rant and rave at him until he bloody cracked the mountain of ice between them. *Who are you? What have you done with my lover?*

He turned abruptly, as if he'd heard her silent screams. But the question in his eyes quickly flickered out, replaced by that infuriating civility.

"It's a chilly night," he said. "I've had a bath sent to your room."

So thoughtful. The ponce. "Thank you," she gritted out.

He nodded, looked as if he might say something else, and then thought the better of it. "Good evening."

He left her in her puddle of her own frustrated loneliness, possibly to pine for the woman who'd gotten away.

CHAPTER 12

*M*orley let himself into the nursery and shut the door, leaning against it for several breaths.

With all he had on his mind, one simple fact existed in the world, crowding out all others.

His wife bathed only paces away. She'd lowered that soft body into the steaming copper tub and slicked soap across creamy, unblemished, aristocratic skin. Her breasts would lift above the water as she washed her luxuriant hair. Her thighs would relax apart, her hands perhaps finding their way between them to...

The bundle he'd clutched in his hand crumpled beneath the clench of his fist, and the product inside provided a much-needed distraction.

He tore the package open with uncharacteristic lack of ceremony, and went to the rocking chair, crouching to place the intricately carved train engine next to the doll.

He fantasized about the train given locomotion by a chubby little hand. A boy, perhaps. But maybe a girl. He and Caroline had spent hours playing trains with some charity toys they'd found at the church once.

So long as he capitulated to Caroline's demand that

the conductors fell in love with the women they'd rescued from the marauding bandits, then she was a fair
hand at the battle, itself. Just as bloodthirsty as any
outlaw.

He touched the gold of the doll's hair and took a
moment to keenly miss the girl with whom he'd
shared a womb. She'd be an aunt now, probably a
mother, too. They'd each be forty in a year, or so he
thought. No one had ever told them their precise
birthday, but he'd pieced it together as well as he
could.

Caroline.

How different the landscape of so many lives would
be if she'd lived.

Morley might have still been a rifleman in the army,
but it was unlikely he would ever have considered the
beat at The London Metropolitan Police.

So many others would have carved a different story
in the book of fate if not for the choices he'd made.

Perhaps their lives were arguably better for the path
Caroline's death put him on, but what he never expressed to his friends was that, in his darkest moments,
he'd have taken it all away from them just to have her
back. To give her the chance at life. To leave him any
kind of family.

So he wouldn't have spent the past twenty odd years
so acutely alone.

Perhaps, he'd often reasoned, if she'd been there,
he'd not be so bloody broken.

He'd become the man he pretended to be. A
better man.

Today, this moment, was the first time he shrank
from that thought.

If it had all gone differently, he might have married
young. He might have even sired children.

But not *this* child.

Not whomever quickened within the womb of his lovely wife.

His hand went to his heart to contain an extra little thump at the thought.

Children were born every day. Thousands upon thousands of them. It was no great happening or miracle. But he couldn't shake the feeling his entire life had led up to this. *This* child.

If Caroline had lived, this child might never have come to be.

And, for the first time, while he still mourned her loss, he couldn't bring himself to wish as he had before.

Beset by a complicated amalgamation of regret and love, shame and anticipation, he pushed himself to his feet and set about tidying up the disorderly packing material in the nursery.

It seemed impossible that his wife's scent lingered even here, but he tasted it in the air. Berries. Sweetest in the late summer. She'd forever remind him of breakfast. His favorite meal until he'd feasted upon her—

Slamming a crate shut, he realized he couldn't be only a wall away from where she bathed without going mad. He retreated to his study, intent upon getting some work done.

By God. She was in here too. The walls might as well have been smeared with marmalade. She permeated every corner of his thoughts, and now there was nowhere in his house to escape her.

Slumping into his office chair he dropped his head onto his palm and rubbed at a blooming headache. God he was tired again. He'd not slept for longer than three hours for... well, he couldn't remember how long.

And it didn't seem that would change in the near future.

Blackwell and he had conceived of a plan to concentrate their investigative efforts on the Wapping docks. His interrogation of the crooked officer the other night had been the first link in a supply line of narcotics, and other smuggled goods, that was more twisted and dangerous than the web of the most venomous spider. Morley, or rather the Knight of Shadows, had been spinning his own webs, beating answers out of countless men. Throwing them to what police he'd known still operated aboveboard.

Or, in some of the cases where he'd been forced to defend himself... throwing their corpses into the river.

All fingers pointed to the Commissioner, Baron Clarence Goode.

His bloody father-in-law.

However, the shipments had dried up entirely. Abruptly, in fact. And because of this, crime wars brewed in the gambling dens and rookeries of the underworld, and Morley couldn't be certain the city was ready for what was about to hit it.

Or how many casualties the impact would leave behind.

Christ. He was just one man. Who could he trust to—?

A few heavy, staggering sounds reverberated on the ceiling above him before a great, thunderous crash drove him to his feet.

The master bedroom. *His wife!*

Feeling as though he'd been kicked in the chest by an unruly horse, he took the stairs three at a time, sprinting down the hall until he exploded through the door, shearing the latch.

His very shaken, very *nude* wife was attempting to pull herself into a sitting position from where she'd sprawled on her back, using a toppled marble table to stabilize her.

He lunged forward. "Don't move," he barked in the

same commanding voice he'd used on countless criminals.

She'd already frozen when he'd burst in, but his words had the opposite effect, sending her scrambling to find something with which to cover herself. "Oh, bother," she groaned. "I-I don't... I'm all right. I just need—need a towel. Please. *Please* go."

"Don't be foolish," he admonished as he hit his knees next to her, his hands hovering over the slick, lithe lines of her prone form, searching for injuries. "What the bloody hell happened?" he demanded. "Did you hit your head? Is anything broken? Can you move all your limbs? No, never mind, don't try to move. I'm calling for a doctor. Bart?" he bellowed. "Where the bloody hell is he? Did no one hear you fall hard enough to shake the house? *Bart!*"

"*No!*" She seized his shirt when he would have risen with one desperate claw, keeping the other arm ineffectually over her breasts. "I don't want anyone to see me!"

"If he sees you, I'll replace his eyes with hot coals. I'm calling him to send him for the doctor."

"I don't need a doctor. I am perfectly well, I simply—"

"You don't get to make that decision, a slip like this is serious, especially in your condition! Must you fall so bloody often? I order you to take more care with your footing!"

He put his hands on both her shoulders to keep her still as she tried again to sit up. His grip slid as her still-slippery limbs flailed in a wild attempt to fight him off.

After a few slick and ineffectual endeavors, he succeeded in pinning her arms at her sides, leaving her gleaming body completely bared to him.

He resolutely examined *only* her eyes, as he leaned above her. They held no indication of the clouds one noted with a head wound. In fact, they sparked with dark azure tempests that would make Calypso proud.

"I didn't slip, exactly," she protested with a mulish expression.

"No? Then tell me how, *exactly*, you came to be on the floor."

Long, dark lashes swept down over damp cheeks flushed with heat. "I... finished my bath, stood, and stepped out of the tub to reach for the towel. By the time I had one foot on the ground I was overwhelmed by extreme vertigo and thought to steady myself on the table." A confused frown pinched between her brow as she looked over at the fallen furniture . "I must have fainted, because the next thing I knew I was on my back staring up at the ceiling."

"I suspect you're truly addled if you think *anything* you just imparted to me makes me feel a modicum of comfort," he gritted through his teeth. "You and the child *must* be all right; do you understand me? You lie here. I will get a doctor. And he will examine you thoroughly. That is the end of this ridiculous discussion."

He would have said more, but all the words had compressed the air out of his lungs, and he couldn't seem to fill them. His hands trembled where they shackled her arms and the legs he knelt on felt too unsteady to hold their position for long.

It had been *years* since his body showed such obvious signs of terror. Maybe since his very first battle when bullets missed him so narrowly, he could *hear* them sing by his ear.

Lord, but she was a weakness.

Instead of arguing, she lifted her palms to his chest, this time in careful conciliation. Her expression softened, warmed, and something pooled in her eyes that evoked inappropriate memories of the last time he'd held her beneath him.

"I'm not being reckless, you know. I often feel faint after a hot bath, and because our child is possessed of a finicky appetite, I haven't been eating as I should. Certainly, that's the cause of this spell." Her lovely features gathered into a twist of self-effacing mortification. "I dare say I crumpled rather than fell, and landed on my back, not my stomach."

His heart kicked beneath her hand, and he grappled with fierce and foreign emotion that stole his ability to speak.

"Is it your aim for the doctor to examine me in a shivering, naked puddle on the floor?" she asked with an arch of her brow.

Morley's jaw slammed shut. Now was *not* the time to notice her nudity. This was quite possibly a medical crisis.

He refused to glance down at her breasts.

He glanced.

He refused to look.

He looked.

Well he refused to appreciate.

Goddammit.

Lunging to his feet, he snatched the towel from the stand and returned to her, averting his eyes as he covered the more scandalous parts of her before crouching down again. "I'm going to carry you to the bed," he warned.

"I'm quite capable of—ooph!"

He scooped her from the floor and hauled her against his chest as her bare legs dangled over his arm. The towel covered the front of her, but there was nothing between her skin and his hands as he hauled her to the bed and sat her down gingerly.

"Sir?" Bart called from the end of the hall. "What's happened?"

Morley released her and strode to the door to keep

the footman from venturing into the room and seeing anything he ought not to.

Likely saving the footman's life.

"My wife has fainted and taken a fall; I need you to send for the doctor."

Bart's eyes went round with worry in his moonlike face. "Right away, sir." He scurried back in the other direction.

Morley shut the door, and when he turned around, his knees nearly buckled from beneath him at the sight of his wife levered over her chest of drawers, her arm frantically fishing within.

She still clutched a towel to the front of her, but she currently faced away from him. Revealing. Everything.

Morley's mouth went dry as lust punched him low in the belly with such savagery, he felt slightly ill. His body responded violently to a sight he'd never forget.

Her ripe bare arse and thighs created a perfect heart shape to frame the shadow of the cove between her legs.

Sweet Christ just when he didn't think he'd anything left in him to break.

Snatching up a nightdress, she straightened and pulled it over her head and down her body, all the while still flailing to find the openings for the arms and neck.

He went to her in swift strides. The moment he put his hands on her, she stilled, allowing him to guide her arms into their sleeves and unbutton the high collar enough to permit her dark head to pop through.

Something about helping her into her gown settled him, as well. His breaths calmed, though his cock did not, but he no longer felt as if his heart tried to escape by way of his throat.

She reached up to push the tangles of her hair away

from her face, but he beat her to it, smoothing the damp tendrils from her cheeks and elegant neck.

She regarded him with a lost, rather unsure expression that tugged at his heart.

"For future reference, you're being neither prudent nor good," he said in a voice suddenly made of silk.

Her lip quirked. "For future reference, my name has always been a lamentable irony."

She attempted a good-humored smile, but it never took. She only succeeded in looking exhausted and alluring, and very young.

Too young for him, probably.

Good Lord, he didn't even know his wife's age. He knew next to nothing about her. Her health. Her skills, her strengths, her flaws. Her life before this.

Before him.

Though he'd had her in a garden, he'd never even seen her naked before tonight.

Certainly, he'd fantasized about it to an obsessive degree, but nothing had been able to prepare him for the perfection of her. Generous breasts, dramatic curves, and an arse so delectable he ached to—

"You really should be lying down," he said with brusque efficiency, closing the door firmly on those thoughts.

Her face fell. "I needed to dry and dress. I'm not about to meet the doctor in the altogether, am I? Also, my hair will dry in clumps of snarls if I don't brush it."

He gently but firmly steered her toward the bed. "I will tend to you."

She kept any remonstration to herself as she allowed him to tuck the bedclothes around her lap. Her eyes tracked him as he retrieved her silver hairbrush from her vanity and brought it to her. "Allow me to—"

She snatched the brush from him. "No need, I've a tender head and it takes a delicate touch."

Better she do it, then. His hands still shook, and his emotions seemed to be taking wild, pendulum-like swings. His feelings for her, he realized, were not gentle. But ardent.

Violent even.

It was why he stayed away. Something volatile hung in the air whenever she was near, and volatility wasn't something he allowed himself.

Lord, but it felt as though he were an abandoned tangle of yarn only just discovered by a sharp-nailed woman intent upon unraveling him.

Morley perched on the foot of the bed, bending his knee so he could face her. "Do you still feel ill?" he asked as she began to run the brush through her damp hair, starting at the ends and working her way up.

"I haven't been for a few days beyond mild bouts of nausea." She flicked him a shy look from beneath her lashes. "Thank you for the ginger ale. I've been sipping it when I feel poorly."

He shifted uncomfortably. "Yes. Well. I read about it somewhere."

He'd read anything he could get his hands on, actually. Books on pregnancy and childbirth. Doctor's pamphlets and periodicals. Everything. If he was going to be a father, he'd be the most knowledgeable father in the kingdom.

She fell into a contemplative silence, her entire being focused on the task of her hair.

Morley watched her alertly, examining her for signs of… well, of anything out of the ordinary. Not that he exactly knew what to look for. Bleeding, he supposed. Another loss of consciousness. Confusion. Pain.

Charming little mannerisms became apparent under such close scrutiny. She'd one very expressive left eyebrow, while the right one never so much as arched. Her left hand was the dominant one, as well.

She'd a freckle beneath her right eye. Just the one. And a little scar behind her jaw on the right side. She slept in a great deal of ruffles.

And when she brushed her hair, she laced her fingers through the section to test for snarls in very rhythmic, graceful gestures.

The inky swath draped over the shoulder of her white nightgown, waving in places and framing her face with little tendrils that beckoned to be touched.

Lord she was lovely.

And she was his.

He'd never seen her like this. Even pale and fresh-scrubbed, damp and unadorned, she remained a beacon of beauty. The kind of siren that would dash a man like him on the rocks.

And still, he'd go willingly.

A strange, unidentifiable emotion stole over him. Not peace, exactly, never that, but a loose-limbed mesmerism he would akin to that of a cobra being charmed by a clever instrument. He couldn't look away. Nothing else existed. Just the woman in his bed and the gentle motions of her grooming. The air was warm and moist from her bath, and he breathed in the summer scent of her soap as his heart slowed and his lids grew heavy.

They sat in silence for a moment, or maybe an eternity, him content to do little else but drink in the sight of her.

"Do you still love her?"

The question manifested in the air between them, surely, as he'd barely noticed her lips move.

Morley started a little, sitting up straighter, uncertain if he heard her correctly as his mind had been quite pleasantly—extraordinarily—empty. "Pardon?"

She kept her gaze firmly focused on the gathering sheen of her smooth, glossy, untangled hair. And yet

156

she kept brushing. "The Countess, Farah, do you love her still?"

"No." The promptness of his answer surprised even him.

She flicked him a fleeting glance. "You can tell me without fear of reprisal," she urged. "I'm in no position to cast aspersions, and I can't imagine you lived like a monk before we—before our nuptials."

The irony was he'd done exactly that for some time now. He'd a few wild years during and after the war but...if one was to describe his romantic exploits of late.

Monk was apropos.

Until her.

"I hold Farah in high esteem," he answered. "But that is all."

"She returns your esteem." An inscrutable emotion darkened her features for a moment, and she abandoned her brush to the nightstand with a sigh.

"I don't know if I ever loved her." Morley couldn't tell what compelled him to explain, but the words escaped him in a torrent of truth. "I was of the opinion that she and I suited, is all. We worked easily together, and we enjoyed each other's company. We attended events and she liked to eat at the same establishments I do. I thought..." He'd thought she'd fill this empty house with something other than silence. He'd wanted someone to come home to. To share a life and all the beautiful, terrible things therein. "I thought love might grow between us. She's a good woman. Someone I'd grown to trust, respect, and admire."

The wobble of her chin belied her hard-won stoicism and she nodded slowly as if she did her best to digest his words.

"Unlike me."

I never wanted her like I want you.

157

He almost said it. The words tripped to the edge of his lips like a reckless man about to jump to his death. Farah was never a danger to him, but neither had she been a joy. He'd desired her, as she was lovely, and he was a man. But she'd never tempted him anywhere close to the line he'd leapt over for Prudence. He'd never ached in her absence nor did he fear the power she had over him.

For there was none.

Whereas now…

"Was your meeting with Blackwell about me?" she queried, her gaze pinched and worried as it finally met his.

"You know I can't discuss—"

"You can't discuss what? My case? My life? You realize this is my innocence to prove and if I knew what was happening, I might have a chance to help."

"It simply isn't—"

"How would you fare, husband, under similar conditions? Locked in this infernal house with nothing to do but worry about the future. Treated like everyone's terrible secret. It's cruel." Her voice became ragged on the last words, and her eyes shimmered with unshed tears.

Morley had felt pity in his life. Shame, regret, sympathy. But not this strange amalgamation of all of it.

"You're not a prisoner here," he soothed. "But it's safer for you if you're out of sight until things…settle. I thought we agreed it's the right thing."

She made a noise of irritation and scrubbed at her eyes to erase a forthcoming storm.

Hesitantly, Morley reached out and placed his hand on her ankle over the counterpane. Her bones were so delicate, so small beneath his hands.

"I sympathize," was all he could think to say. "In your circumstances I'd likely go mad."

She blinked at him, and her face relaxed a bit, some of the frustration draining into acceptance. "Then... why must I be left in the dark?"

"Because that is where I need you," he answered more vehemently than he'd meant to.

At her pained flinch, the explanation burst from him like a geyser. "Don't you understand? I cannot stand to be in the same room with you—*wait*." He held up his hand against her unspoken pain as her eyes went owl round. "That is, I cannot be in your presence *and* possessed of my wits at the same time. You're like...a tune in my head I cannot rid myself of. A torrent, or a whirlwind, spinning me until I cannot see my way forward. I can't have that now. I need to be objective. Unemotional."

"Unemotional?" she echoed slowly.

"Especially when the stakes are so high. When I want—" He caught himself just in time.

To see that she'd stopped breathing, her stare rapt and absorbed.

He'd said too much.

"When you want what?" she whispered.

"I meant to say...when the outcome has such a monumental effect on the life and future of everyone." He slid closer toward her and she moved her legs to give him room. Leaning forward, his hand drifted toward her until it fit over her abdomen. "Of the three of us."

She covered his hand with her own, and Morley suddenly found himself a prisoner.

His shackles silk rather than steel.

Even through her nightgown and the bedclothes, he could fell that her firm stomach had a barely discernable curve to it.

They each let out an identical breath, wondering at the life beneath their hands.

"Somehow I'm going to prove to you that I'm innocent," she declared with the resolution of a royal. "If I do that, would I be worthy of you then?"

Awash in a tide of foreign and frustrating sentimentality, Morley pulled away from her, unable to stand the intimacy and not take it further. "This isn't about that."

"It is to me."

He threaded his fingers through his hair, yearning to believe her. If only so he wouldn't have to face the dark part of him whispering that her innocence mattered not.

That he'd fall for her, regardless.

"Please, let's not talk of this now. I'm too...where in God's name is the doctor?"

"I assure you, I'm well. The table took the hardest tumble, I all but glided to the floor."

He turned his back on her, going behind the screen to lift the table back to its position. The furniture was a heavy piece, the top pure marble.

Gads, what if she'd pulled it over on top of her?

Suddenly he was very aware how dangerous a home could be to a woman and child.

"You don't have to stay, you know," she said, arranging the covers in a prim display. "It's dark. You may go about your...your work as the Knight of Shadows."

He took the watch chain from his vest and checked it. "There's no chance of me leaving tonight."

"I don't know how many times I have to tell you, there's hardly a reason to fret," she insisted.

"Oh? And from what distinguished institution did you get your medical degree, Doctor Morley?" He scowled at her. "I just found my *wife* crumpled on the floor; if that's not a time to fret, I can think of none better. So you will submit to an examination or—"

"Or what?" she asked around a wry smile. "You'll have me thrown in jail?"

That surprised a sharp snort of mirth from him. "Don't tempt me."

A red-faced Bart arrived with the doctor, a beakish gentleman with a gentle manner, interrupting further conversation between them.

Morley hovered as his wife was examined, palpated, and interrogated all in time for the doctor to declare that she and the child were likely in little to no danger of miscarriage. After advice was given and a draught administered, Morley left his wife's side long enough to pay the man and walk him out.

He stopped to fortify himself with several scorching swallows of Ravencroft Scotch before returning to her room.

Only to find her sleeping peacefully.

Her dark hair flared on the pillow, shining like a phantom halo of ebony around her delicate features. Her hand was draped next to her cheek, relaxed into a little cup, as if he might give her something precious.

A stark pang of yearning pierced him as the smooth side of his bed beckoned to him. Here she was, a strange and seductive fantasy sleeping the sleep of the innocent.

And she was his.

A dark desire welled within him with such ferocity he shuddered with it. He wanted to own her. To claim her, body and soul. To plant himself inside of her and pleasure her until she was mindless, until she was boneless, replete with satisfaction.

He wanted to feed her from his hands. To nourish her and the life within. He wanted to buy her things to adorn her loveliness. Gems and ribbons, silk and precious metals. A storm of errant whims and desires swirled and eddied within him until he felt as though his flesh could no longer contain the strength of it.

He. Wanted. Her.

KERRIGAN BYRNE

He wanted…everything.

"Don't tempt me," he whispered once more.

He'd meant it in jest before, but now it was a plea.

She was nothing but a temptation. One he couldn't resist for much longer. One that could bring his entire world down upon him.

And still he'd use the last of his bloody, broken remains to shelter her.

CHAPTER 13

*L*ess than a handful of days later, it'd taken Prudence and Mercy the better part of three hours to comb over their father's study, library, and personal belongings before they had finally stumbled upon the documents she'd been searching for.

Mercy was the perfect partner to rely upon for this assignment. She was fleet-footed, quick-witted, and always up for an adventure. Or, as she'd dubbed their vocation, a *caper*, a word she'd claimed to have purloined from the detective novels she was almost never without.

"Do you really feel like this will help clear your name, Pru?" Mercy worried. "I don't see what father's business could possibly have had to do with Sutherland's death."

"Probably nothing," Prudence agreed, carefully filing the papers away in a case. "But if I can provide my husband means with which to further his investigation into the illegal goods being smuggled into the city —to find the truth about father—I think it'll go a long way to establish trust between us."

Mercy sobered, a glimmer of doubt reaching through her eyes. "Pru...what if the truth is that our father is guilty? It would kill poor Mama. And...the rest of us would be ruined."

Prudence had abandoned the briefcase to gather her sister close. "Don't think I haven't thought of that," she soothed. "Our father is many things, but he is a principled, law-abiding man. I'm hoping the truth clears the Goode name. And, in the unlikely event my husband somehow uncovers his guilt..."

Mercy stepped away, smoothing her smart plaid frock and adjusting her hair. "Like Detective Inspector Aloysius Frost says in his fourth novel, *The Cheapside Strangler*, 'When the guilty escape justice, it is denied the innocent, as well.'" She wistfully locked the briefcase and handed it to her. "No matter how this plays out, Felicity and I will survive it. I mean...what's the worst that could happen? We're denied a season and end up as spinsters?" She shrugged. "Considering what you and Honoria are up against...I can't say either of us are aching to be wed."

Pru could have cried, but instead she kissed Mercy on the cheek and rushed to Number Four Whitehall Place.

She navigated the chaos of the infamous Scotland Yard with her briefcase clutched in hand, asking solicitous clerks, and a few gruff policemen, how to find the Chief Inspector's office.

Several minutes and four stories later, she stood in the hall adjacent him, admiring her husband at work.

Prudence felt rather like an explorer on a safari, watching a magnificent beast in his native habitat.

Unlike the holding cells and general rank pandemonium of the first and second floors—or the secrets in the basement, one of which she had recently been— men of all sorts and sizes crammed around desks here on the fourth. They filled the room with the bustle of the more intricate and intellectual side of crime enforcement.

Men with important titles retained the line of offices along the wall, and Morley's was the grandest.

He propped the door open to accommodate the tide of active lawmen marching about like worker ants. At the moment, he scanned documents of two uniformed officers standing at attention as if in front of a brigadier general. Oddly enough, he appeared more comfortable and casual than she'd ever seen him. His shirt brilliant white, and cravat tight as ever, but he'd shucked his jacket as a concession to comfort in the crowded and close air of the top floor.

Absorbed as he was, he didn't seem to notice the distress of the officers when he reached for his pen, crossed something out, and corrected it in the margin. The younger one, a brawny but baby-faced chap, blinked several times as if he might dissolve into tears as his comrade's shoulders slumped.

Prudence sympathized.

Another man in a somber suit and expensive hat barged into his office and Morley held up a finger, silencing him immediately without looking up.

Upon finishing, he signed the paperwork at the bottom and handed it back to the officers. "This was excellent. You're both to be commended."

The exaltation of the men brought a pleased smile to her lips as she took a moment to enjoy a triumph some might call trivial but was one she would give a limb for.

The approval of her husband.

Retrieving the papers, the officers nearly skipped out of his office and bowled her over as they turned the corner.

"Begging your pardon," the young one breathed, unable to contain his brilliant smile.

She nodded and pardoned him, genuinely happy for the lad as he marched away.

Her husband now conversed more discreetly with the new man who, she assumed, was a detective inspector as he wore no uniform.

She took the rare opportunity to study him in a candid moment.

Chief Inspector Sir Carlton Morley. This man was as different from the Knight of Shadows as chalk from cheese. He would never deign to rendezvous with a woman in a garden beneath the early summer night sky. Not this exemplar with a tidy desk, an army of officers, and sober, restrained manners. He was more machine than man. A cog that couldn't stop spinning lest the entire apparatus break down.

How strange that this was her spouse. This leader of men. This workhorse with a tireless back and fiendish reserves of strength and endurance.

Except. Did no one else note the grooves deepening in branches from his eyes, or the brackets of strain about his mouth? How could they not realize how isolated he was? How exhausted?

If he directed the force by day, and was a force unto himself at night... when did he rest? He'd no hobbies to speak of. He expressed no desires nor particular joys. She'd found nothing in their house to suggest any to her. No periodicals about riding or hounds. No cigars or much alcohol to speak of. Not even sporting outfits or antique weaponry.

His identity, both his identities, were dedicated to justice.

It was why the truth mattered so much to him. He'd devoted his life to it.

The conversation with his subordinate ended efficiently, and the detective was given his marching orders.

The veritable giant of a man glanced down at where she hovered just beyond the doorway as he left, and his astonishing russet mustache parted in a yellow-toothed smile filled with appreciative charm.

"Can I 'elp you, miss?"

She smoothed her hand down the front of her cobalt silk gown and touched her glove to the absurd little cap that sat atop her coiffure. "I'm next in line for the Chief Inspector, I believe."

"Lucky 'im," The detective gave a cheeky wink and swept his arm toward the door.

It was in that moment she noticed the floor had become much quieter than before as she felt more than a few speculative gazes following her.

This didn't exactly surprise her, as she was the only woman in sight.

Bobbing a quick curtsy, she stepped into the doorway.

Morley didn't seem to register who she was at first glance, but then he started in his chair as he gaped back up at her.

She imagined a ripple of pleasure in the liquid blue of his eyes before a frown furrowed his brow and deepened the grooves beside his mouth.

No. The glaciers of his gaze made it astoundingly clear he was distinctly displeased to find her here.

Both hands splayed on his desk as if he had to keep an eye on them. "Prudence. What are you doing here? Did you come through the front?"

Right. While he was an asset to her, she was only a liability to him. But she worked so hard to change that and had to bring the fruit of her labors straightaway.

Hurrying into his office, she took one of the leather chairs in front of his desk without being offered. "I found something, and I couldn't wait a moment longer to give it to you," she revealed, unable to contain her enthusiasm as she handed him the briefcase she'd been clutching. "The registers from my father's shipping company. Well, one of the triplicate copies on carbon paper. You're looking for evidence of smuggling, are you not? I believe, if you cross-reference it with the shipping records from the docks you'll find what you need to condemn or exonerate—"

He held up a hand for her silence, and something in the gesture drove her heart to jump into her stomach as he regarded her as one would a troubling puzzle.

"You realize..." he hesitated. "Prudence, where did you get these?"

"From the safe in his study," she said. "Felicity came out with me this morning to attend an appointment and then Mercy helped to search—"

"Have you considered what would happen if your father is convicted of a crime?" he flicked a careful look to his office door, but it seemed no one lurked close enough to listen. "If he is guilty, he'll be thrown in prison. Are you ready to facilitate that?"

Prudence had felt the weight of that since the moment he'd informed her of his suspicions toward her family. "My father is in a position of power, and I'd not have him exploit that at the expense of the health of the people he's sworn to protect. These documents have the ability to exonerate him just as easily as condemn him. I'm ready to facilitate you finding the truth, as soon as possible."

She'd the suspicion his silence was more intense than contemplative as he considered the briefcase for a protracted moment before spearing her with a look so full of possible meaning, her heart leapt from her stomach to her throat.

"If he is guilty..." she preempted his response. "Might you have mercy on him for the sake of my sisters?"

His lips compressed into a tight line. "The law is justice, and justice doesn't often reside with mercy."

"Yes, but...you have made yourself more than the law, have you not? You conduct half your life in darkness."

Again, he checked the open door, his jaw tightening as he tilted his head in a warning gesture. "Let's not discuss that here."

"I'm not asking you to overlook a crime," she said with a furtive lean toward him. "Only to allow my sisters and my mother to retain their money and property should he be sent away." She pressed her hands together in a supplicant gesture. "I'm asking you to show them the mercy you've shown me."

"You're different," he said with a terse annunciation.

"Why?"

"You know why." He shoved back from the desk and stood. "Besides, that sort of decision would be up to a judge." Pacing the length of the window behind him he glared at the briefcase. "I didn't know you were going to your father's house today. You shouldn't have procured this, it's too dangerous. What if you'd been caught?"

"No one else was home." She wrinkled her nose. "My father isn't the most scrupulous of men, but he wouldn't hurt me."

"You don't know what men will do when threatened," he lectured. "And you can't understand how you've complicated things. To procure evidence like this, I must go through the proper channels. If anything is to hold up in court then—"

She stood also, his reaction to her gesture crushing any exuberance she'd felt. "*You* forget I've been a Commissioner's daughter for as long as I can remember. Why do you think I didn't bring you the original copies? Surely you could come up with a reason for a warrant, and then procure the real thing."

At that, he froze, regarding her as if he'd never seen her before. "Yes. I suppose I could." His gaze warmed to something that looked like admiration as he drifted around his desk. "Forgive me..." He paused, suddenly distracted as his notice drifted over her, lingering at the swells of her breasts hugged by her fine high-necked gown, the curves of her hips accentuated by gathers of silk.

She'd dressed for him. To please him. And she found a giddy satisfaction that her endeavor had been successful.

"You didn't have to bring them all this way," he said in a voice roughened with a darker, more primitive emotion. "This isn't an agreeable atmosphere for you. You could have given it to me at home."

She shrugged and looked around curiously. "I wasn't worried about being recognized, as I've never been here before, and I was already in town at the doctor's so—"

"The doctor?" He tensed. "Are you all right? Is the child—did something happen? You sit and rest." He grasped her shoulders and pressed her back into the chair before striding to the doorframe. "Dunleavy, get my wife something to drink, and if it's that swill that passes for tea on the sideboard, I'll demote you."

Prudence twisted in her chair in time to see the lumbering man with the red mustache pop his head around the doorjamb to gape at her. "That was...I mean...you've a wife?"

One look at the wrath on his boss's face, and the big man scampered away, reminding her of a dog needing to find purchase on a smooth marble floor.

Prudence stood again. "Nothing is amiss. I had an

appointment with Lady Northwalk's doctor and mid-wife, that's all."

"Yes, but *why*?" he demanded, his muscles bunched with agitation.

"Well, it is common to be checked by doctors regularly when in my condition."

His lips twisted with grim approbation. "You didn't *inform* me of any appointment you had with a doctor."

"Why would I? Men don't usually bother with such matters."

"When have I ever given you the impression I'm like most other men?"

"Here you are, Mrs. Morley! I found you some of the good stuff fresh-brewed by that fancy ponce DI Calhoun." Dunleavy appeared with a clattering porcelain tea set on a tray that looked patently ridiculous in his mallet-sized hands. He walked like a man on a tightrope, his tongue out in concentration. "Swiped it right out from under 'is nose afore he had a chance to taste it."

"I don't mean to conscript someone's tea," Pru protested.

"'E were right chuffed when I told him who it were for."

"It's Lady Morley," her husband corrected with a sharp edge as he relieved the man of his tray and set it on the edge of his desk before pouring her a cup.

"Right, right, and a fine lady you are!" Dunleavy looked back and forth from her to his boss with a smile so wide it shoved his apple cheeks so high his eyes half closed. "Sir and Lady Morley, as I live and breathe! 'Andsomest couple in the whole of the city, I'd wager. I don't know why we always just assumed ya were a bachelor, din't we, Sampson?"

A little fellow poked his head around the mountain

of a man, his checkered wool suit hanging on him like it would a spindle of limbs.

"We always just assumed," he agreed in a voice as reedy as he was.

"No wonder the Chief Inspector din't tell us of ya, my lady," Dunleavy went on, swiping off his hat. "You're much too young and beautiful for the likes of 'im, in'nt ya?"

"You're too kind. I'm Prudence Morley, it's a thorough pleasure to meet you both." She extended her hand to them, receiving their deferential accolades as she enjoyed using her new surname in her introduction more than she'd expected.

Suddenly the two of them were three, and then four, the company in the office multiplying exponentially until Prudence felt as if she'd been introduced to every detective, sergeant, constable, and clerk on the entire floor.

Unsurprisingly, no one recognized her as Prudence Goode. Her picture never made it next to George's in the papers, as she wasn't high enough in rank to be a socialite nor low enough to be in their social class. Nor would these working men have aught to do with her father who held his offices in a separate government building.

To them, she was Prudence Morley, and her pedigree meant nothing past the man at her side. Didn't bother her one bit.

"Your husband's been keeping you secret, all to himself," a stout man of dusky complexion tattled.

She lifted her brows across at Morley, who seemed to be grappling with the storm of his temper before he allowed himself to speak.

"Should I be offended?" she queried with a mischievous smirk.

"Not at all!" Dunleavy hurried to his defense. "He's a

jealous man, I think. Didn't want the likes of us 'round the likes of you, can't say's we blame 'im."

"Oh," she drew out the word playfully. "A bunch of scoundrels, I see."

"He keeps us in line, don't you, Guv?" Sampson prodded Morley with a boney elbow.

"Not very well, apparently," her husband grumped. "Don't you lot have work to do?"

She put a hand on Dunleavey's arm, noting that more of the men crowded around the office, unable to squeeze themselves in, but wanting a look. "Tell me, Mr. Dunleavy, is my husband a monstrous, iron-fisted curmudgeon?"

"Naw," Dunleavy blushed and bristled his whiskers in a shy gesture. "He's as fair as they come."

"Fairest iron-fist in the land," someone called from the back. "Now convince 'im we need a raise, Lady Morley."

And uproarious laugh swept through the gathering, and she couldn't help but be swept along with it in their joviality.

"You've a husband to be proud of, but you already know that, don't you?" Sampson beamed.

She couldn't help but study him, enjoying his rare moment of discomfiture. "Of course. He's a paragon."

His expression shifted from irate to rueful as he held her gaze. One might almost believe them a couple now...sharing secrets with their eyes.

"Still holds the record on murder nabs, if you don't mind me saying," another crowed.

"I don't at all mind!" She glowed at them. "You know Carlton, he's such an enigma. Not at all prone to bragging. I want to hear everything."

Despite his protestations, she was inundated by his praise. Did she know he'd shot a man threatening his own mother at greater than fifty paces? He'd not only nabbed the thief of the Wordston Emerald, but recovered the gem and returned it to his owner. He heroically pulled fourteen men out of the rubble when the Fenians bombed the Yard some years ago. If they were to be believed, he'd had single-handedly reformed the Blackheart of Ben More.

"All right, that's quite enough out of you lot!" Morley shouldered past his men to widen the door in a not-so-subtle invitation to leave. His skin darkened to crimson at the collar and the color began to creep into his cheeks. "Lady Morley was just departing. She needs her rest."

Never had she seen such a crowd deflate so rapidly.

"You'll visit us again?" Dunleavy asked.

"Of course."

"Can't believe you kept 'er such a mystery, Chief Inspector. Next, you'll be telling us you 'ave an entire brood we've never met."

"Not yet." Unable to contain her smile, Pru placed a hand on her stomach as it still maintained the illusion of slender beneath her corset. "But I've been to see the doctor today, and he's confident that before spring..."

The men gasped and crowed, chuffed, and chuckled with enough enthusiasm to do any cadre of grandmothers proud. They took her hands and kissed them, and many of them moved to give Morley a grand slap on the back or an energetic handshake in congratulations of his virility.

Prudence couldn't remember the last time she'd enjoyed herself so thoroughly. There were words one didn't say in the aristocracy. Things one didn't even express. Babies were announced on paper and then hinted at as a "happy event" or "new addition" until the woman went into confinement. Isolated as if her pregnancy was a shame.

But not so here. She was celebrated. And so was the father-to-be.

She looked over at him, suddenly overwhelmed with something that very much felt like joy.

His thunderous expression had morphed to more thunderstruck than anything. As if he'd stepped into some world adjacent to the one in which he usually resided, and couldn't make heads nor tails of it. He accepted the shakes and slaps and hearty compliments, looking around uncomfortably as if he didn't know where to put them.

One thing became instantly, and heartbreakingly clear to Pru. Her husband's subordinates didn't just venerate and admire him…

They loved him.

Because he was a good man and a great leader. Someone who not just commanded respect but deserved it. He put wrong things right every day. He took care of so many details at home, she was certain he was just as thorough in his business, if not more so. No task was too menial or too difficult. He did what must be done without compunction or even complaint.

Prudence knew enough about the world of men to realize that was a very extraordinary thing.

A virtue to respect. A man to venerate.

He shredded his own soul and sacrificed his own health and happiness for countless Londoners who would never even know to whom they should be grateful.

How many women had the honor of sharing the life of a great man? A man who would leave his mark on the world and not have to sing his own praises because others did so. How many could claim to be honored to walk next to her husband?

To share a child with him.

She had to blink away a misting of emotion as the wonderment flowed through her.

Morley's forehead furrowed in concern as he caught her overwrought expression and was at her side in a moment, gripping her elbow to support her. "I'll walk you out," he murmured before addressing the room at large. "And I don't want to see anyone on this floor. You're either on the streets hard at work, or on your way home for the evening, is that clear?"

The men hopped to obey him, but not without jibes and whispers and merriment.

Morley pulled her off to the left toward the door to the back stairs. "I am your husband," he hissed.

"Yes..." was her slow reply. "That's been quite established."

He turned her to face him. "You mustn't keep important things like this from me."

Her eyes worked from side to side, searching for his meaning. "Like...like what?"

"You went to the bloody doctor, Prudence," he said in an exasperated whisper, drawing her through a hidden door and into an alcove full of dusty boxes. "I should have been there!"

Oh, they were picking up where they'd left off. "I-I didn't think you'd want to."

He sent her a bruised look as he resumed his pacing. "What...what sort of monster do you think I am?"

"The male sort of monster. Men never attend these things. It's up to the purview of the mother to—"

"If there is medical news about my wife and child, I'll bloody well be the first to know it." He rubbed at his forehead and then flung his hand out as if hurling away stress. "I will never understand aristocrats. The distance squeamish men keep from their families for the sake of propriety. It's patently ridiculous."

She let out a short sound. "I could not be more astonished at you."

"What do you mean?"

"You are either being obtuse or cruel," she accused. "Which is it?"

"Cruel? I've been nothing but deferential to you."

"I don't want your deference. I want you. Home. We've been married a fortnight and I've set eyes upon you perhaps thrice in all that time. You maintain a distance that surpasses the very idea of propriety. When in the past two weeks would I have possibly had the chance to tell you about this appointment?"

His shoulders fell a little and his chin dipped, reminding her of a chastised boy.

"You could have...left me a note," he muttered.

"A note, he says!" She gestured to the boxes as if they'd still an audience. "Is that what our lives are going to be? The polite passing of notes?" She extracted an imaginary pen from her bodice and dabbed it on her tongue. "Dear Carlton," she began. "Or should I call you Mr. Morley? Yes, I believe I should, that's more proper." She drew two strikes through her imaginary note. "I know we have not seen each other in several months, but I'm leaving this note to inform you that I've gone into my labors with our child. Please attend at your earliest convenience. All my kindest regards, Prudence Agatha Morley."

She shot him a glare as she signed her imaginary name with a flourish.

"You've quite made your point." He crossed his arms and leaned against the windowsill. "Your middle name is Agatha?"

"Argh!" She threw up her hands before reaching for the door, intent upon leaving.

He gripped her arm, whirling her around. "This is *me*, Prudence," he growled. "This is who I am. Paperwork and late nights. Responsibility and distance, this is—"

She stepped closer to him, her face lifted in challenge. "You're *wrong*. That isn't you, at all."

"You don't know the first thing—"

"You forget, husband, I've met you already. That night in the garden."

His eyes flared that quicksilver spark. "*That* was not me. That was—"

"If you say *a mistake*, I will slap you." She raised her hand in warning. "You were more yourself that night than I think you'd been in some time before, and *certainly* since. You were stripped of all this stalwart artifice. Bare and vulnerable. And yes, dark and angry." Her hand landed on his cheek, but only with caressing care. "And you needed me just as much as I needed you. And I think...I think you still do."

His chest expanded with short, rapid breaths as he held himself as straight and taut as a marble statue. His jaw, however, leaned slightly into her hand like a beast searching for comfort.

"You were so wonderful with me on my very first night," she remembered. "So gentle."

"Not bloody gentle enough," he bemoaned.

"You were perfect. *We* were perfect."

He regarded her warily. "Are we...not in the middle of a row?"

Her breath hitched with amusement. Farah was right, men were adorable idiots.

"I'm your *wife*, Carlton." She'd never called him that before. Not to his face. "For better or worse, our fates are tied together. I might not be what you envisioned, but...I'm *here*." She glided closer, until her breasts pressed against his chest, her body molding to his. "It's permissible to need me. To want me. If we have nothing else, we have *that* night. We have *this* child. And this…attraction between us. One that might, in time dare I hope, turn to affection?"

She lifted on to the tips of her toes to glide a soft kiss against his jaw.

"Prudence," he growled.

"You're so tired. So *tense*." She pulled his head closer, whispering her breath over his neck, allowing her suggestions to glide into his ear. "Let me ease you, husband," she urged. "Further than that. Let me *please* you. After all you've done for me—"

His head whipped back. "I'd never expect—not as payment—"

"I know," her fingers caressed the close-cropped down of fine hair at his nape, urging him back toward her. Aching for his kiss. "That is why I offer. I want you, husband. Through everything, that's never changed. Given the chance, I would make a myriad of different choices over the past three months, but not that one. I cannot bring myself to regret giving myself to you… having you…does that make me unforgivably wicked in your eyes?"

"No." She sensed the tempest within him, the battle of his dual nature, and identified the precise moment one of the factions beat back the other.

With a foul curse, he closed his hand around her wrist and pulled her after him as he veritably slammed open the door to their alcove, and another to the stairwell. He silently marched her down one flight of stairs, through two more doors in another chaotic office full of typewriters and noise, and then veered her into a long, deserted hallway.

She trotted to keep up as he swept her to the end of the hall and shouldered open an old door swollen with disuse. In an incredible dance of fluid motion, he tugged her inside, firmly shut the door, threw the lock, and pulled her into his arms to crush his mouth to hers.

179

All pretense of the civilized Chief Inspector melted away beneath the heat exploding between them. His hands were suddenly everywhere. His lips were no longer compressed into their tight, laconic lines. They molded to hers with a wild, wet consummation that surpassed anything she'd ever imagined.

He'd once again succumbed to the starving, carnal beast that lurked inside him. One locked away in a cavern so deep it was as if he attempted to bury it forever.

But anyone knew that a predator denied sustenance became the most dangerous of creatures. Prudence realized that she somehow possessed the key to the dungeon where he kept that beast.

And she'd hoped that once she'd let it lose, it would devour her.

True to his nature, he didn't let her down.

Her body melted against and around him while he kissed her as if he could make up for every absent night and every empty morning. Beneath the fervency of his embrace, a heart-rending sweetness existed. A sort of awestruck marvel that moved her to the very marrow of her bones.

This was something he couldn't express with words, she understood. Not yet.

Perhaps not ever.

Though there was no chance of him releasing her, she still clung to him, her fingers digging into the convex muscles of his back, reveling in the mounds of strength she found there.

His tongue didn't wait for invitation, sweeping into her mouth in drugging, silken strokes. He moaned against her lips and she breathed it in, relishing the honest pleasure in the sound.

The ragged need.

He crowded her backwards, never breaking the seal

of their kiss. His hands cinched her waist and lifted her onto a desk, or a table, she couldn't be sure. Only once he'd secured her there, did he allow his restless lips to venture elsewhere. He dragged them across her cheek, rooting into the sensitive hollow of her throat, nipping at the soft lobe of her ear as he pressed her knees open to fill the space with his hips.

This was how he would have her next, she realized. Here. Now.

He was going to take her again. To consummate their marriage.

In the scant moment she was allowed to absorb her dim surroundings, she identified the skeletons of shelves and boxes as some sort of ill-used storage room lit only by a grimy window.

Something about the illicitness of their setting sent excitement and anticipation surging through her. The only sound in the room was the rasp of her dress as he gathered it up in desperate fistfuls, and the tiny explosions of their rapid breaths.

She was frustrated by the layers of his clothing, as well. Whatever clay composed him, the very essence of him called to her. Arrested her every sense. She wanted to see him. To score his skin. To smell and touch and taste.

His rough hands snagged on her stockings as he pressed forward, urging her legs further apart to accommodate him. His fingers were both strong and gentle as they charted her inner thigh. Breathing seemed to become more of a struggle for him as he found the edges of her stockings and her garters.

When he tugged at the ribbon on her drawers, the curse he emitted drew fire from her blood and a flood from her loins. The desperate, crude word from lips such as his was indescribably erotic as it vibrated against her skin.

His fingers grazed her heat, producing a gasp between them. Prudence clawed at his shoulders and the short layers at his nape as he found the soft, turgid flesh already swollen and damp with desire.

"Yes," the word escaped on a jagged breath and her body moved sinuously, her hips curling forward, seeking the forbidden pleasure of his intimate caress.

He angled back just enough to look down at her. His face half exposed to the grey light, and half in darkness. The dangerous glint in his eye caused her to catch her breath before the slick movement of his fingers forced her to release it on a whimpering plea.

He watched her like a man witnessing a miracle or mapping the very cosmos, his features a mask of reverent awe and blasphemous lust.

"So wet," he breathed, his thumb circling the aperture of aching flesh above her opening.

She couldn't answer.

He didn't need her to.

As he evoked thrills of molten pleasure in her womb with the relentless pressure of his thumb, his finger slid through the ruffles of flesh protecting the entrance to her body, probing gently before sliding inside.

The electric delight of the intrusion drew from her throat a desperate sound she'd not known herself humanly capable of making.

"So tight," he ground out as though in agony.

She wanted to say something. To entice and encourage him. To praise and plead with him. But every time she opened her mouth, only a mewl or a moan would escape as she suffered instant and excruciating rapture at the mercy of his clever fingers.

He covered her mouth with his, swallowing the sounds as her pleasure intensified into a surge of throbbing beats as wild as primitive drums. Her hands clawed at him, her thighs clenched as spasms of bliss assaulted her, driving against her like the unrelenting waves of a violent storm. She was helpless to do anything but ride his hand, emitting strangled sobs, as her release drenched his fingers.

She was too pleasured to be scandalized by their wickedness. Too captive of her passions to be worried about discovery. She existed only in this moment. In this place where he dismantled the woman she was and rebuilt someone new. A creature of desire and darkness, suffused with only one need.

Him. This. *Them.*

He didn't bring her down gently this time, didn't take the time to soothe or distract her with drugging, lavish kisses, or to croon sweet words against her flushed skin. His hand left her only for a moment as his hips levered away.

And then it was there. Thick and hot and pulsing.

The crown of his cock brushed her sex and she bloomed like a garden of summer roses. She'd yet to regain her breath before he thrust forward, filling her with a sensation so infinitely wonderful, it unstitched her at her very core.

The sound he made could not have been less human. It was both dark and divine. Tormented and victorious.

Through the haze of frenzy and desire, Prudence recognized this for what it was. Her husband was claiming her. Possessing her with demanding aggression and fierce, primal need.

Finally.

He paused only at the hilt, grinding his hips to hers as if testing her depths. Even stretched to the limits of her physical capacity, Prudence welcomed every inch of him. Wishing she could take him deeper, that they could truly meld into one.

The moment lasted but the space of a breath before

instinct seized them both. She quivered with delight as he withdrew and filled her again and again with relentless, almost vicious, thrusts. His eyes were glazed pools of silver and shadow. His jaw clenched. His body a bunched, lithe machine of muscle, wrath, and unspent passion.

He was the most beautiful thing she'd ever seen.

"Again," he commanded tightly.

She shook her head, unable to express her lack of comprehension verbally.

His hand plunged beneath her skirts, stroking her where their bodies joined until it found the source of her intimate bliss once more. "I want to feel you... around me. Coming. Clenching..." His thrusts deepened, his muscles straining tighter as he thrummed at her with slick, masterful motions. "I...need..."

Without preamble, Prudence shattered into shards of pleasure. She flew apart, her soul rending from a body unused to and unready for such pure, electrifying ecstasy. Her head fell back on her shoulders, exposing her neck. He latched onto it like a fiend, laving and sucking and nipping at the tender flesh there until his own body suffused with a paroxysm of wracking shudders. He buried himself inside her as he climaxed, coating her womb with warm jets of his seed. His body locked inside her as wave after wave seemed to curl his spine, drawing raw, low, harsh sounds from somewhere deeper than his chest.

Perhaps, from his soul.

Eventually, his forehead fell against hers, and they stayed like that for an eternity, sharing breath and heat and a relieved sort of peace that had eluded them for months.

Sex with him was nothing like she remembered, and everything she'd wanted.

Perhaps it was different every time.

Oh, she hoped so...was it wicked of her to want to do it again when he remained inside of her?

Smoothing a featherlight caress down the soft cotton shirt covering his arms, she gave him an affectionate nudge with her nose.

That was all the encouragement he needed to gather her closer, lowering his head to kiss and kiss and kiss her until she thought she was in danger of another swoon. He took his tender time with her now, his lips pulling and tugging at hers. Exploring and soothing, nibbling and sampling as he allowed her to caress his jaw, the intricate fibers of his finely tailored vest, and wrap around to the silken panel on the back.

"One of these days," she whispered, "we'll make love in a bed."

He released a breathy sound of mirth, but still seemed unable to summon words.

Heartened, she nuzzled him. "Do you know what I think?" she asked rhetorically. "I think, if we tried a little, that we could make a go at love."

He pulled back from her. Out of her.

Prudence wanted to cry, to clutch at him, to plead with him not to retreat back behind his damnable façade. What had she been thinking speaking her mind out loud? She should have known better than to ruin the moment with sentiment. Not with a heart as fortified as his.

This had been her lifelong problem. She was never just happy with what people deigned to allow her.

She always demanded more.

His expression became guarded as he swiftly rearranged himself and righted her as well. "If I've learned anything from watching the successful relationships in my life, it's that love takes trust. And that, we do not yet have."

Though his words stung, she had to accept the veracity of them. "Friendship then… comradery at least?"

When he didn't reply immediately, she reached for him, feeling him slip through her fingers like the fine silt at the beach.

"This isn't nothing is it? It isn't empty." She tugged at him, needing him back against her, if only for a moment. "Because it doesn't feel empty to me."

When she worried he'd resist her, he didn't. He rested his temple against hers and took in a deep breath, as if he could lock the scent of her in his lungs. "This…isn't nothing," he ceded. "That is what makes it dangerous."

Pru did her best not to beam. It was something to him. She was something. Something she could work with. Could expand upon.

"Well…that's a start, isn't it?"

He nodded carefully. "You could say it's a start."

She kissed him and wriggled until he stepped back to help her down so she could smooth at her dress and hair. "Now that we've established that, I'll leave you to examine the evidence I've brought you. Perhaps if I can help you prove me innocent of murder, you'll think me worthy of your heart."

CHAPTER 14

*M*orley couldn't believe he was thinking of fucking his wife in church.

It wasn't even her fault. Quite the opposite, in fact.

She dressed as modest as a nun and adopted the visage of a saint for nobody's benefit as they occupied the front pew and no one but him could see her.

He'd not even had to mention that her Sunday best wouldn't do for a parish in Whitechapel. She'd emerged from her room wearing a gold and green striped high-necked morning gown that might have been the simplest in her trousseau. Her hair was pulled back into an uncomplicated braided knot and her hat and veil were suitably staid. Still she was the most superbly dressed woman in the congregation.

And the most desirable.

The sermon had nothing to do with the pleasures of the flesh, or the sins of seduction. Indeed, it was a rather sedate ecclesiastical exploration of personal generosity that'd set his libido to humming like the ceaseless vibrations of bumblebee wings. Not overshadowing things per se, but always there on the periphery, waiting to strike at the most inopportune time.

Perhaps that word, generosity, was the impetus for decidedly less room in his trousers.

If the last couple of days had taught him anything, it was that he'd a generous wife. One with a generous mouth, generous curves, and an adventurous spirit. Her appetite for food had returned with a surge and, along with it, other appetites demanded to be indulged.

He had only to reach for her and she was there, her arms winding around him with a tempting smile. She read his need like a sage, intuiting if he felt wild or languorous, deviant or tender. She denied him nothing and brought ideas of her own to their lovemaking that both astonished and thrilled him.

He looked over to where her gloved hands were folded primly in her lap over the placid tones of her skirt.

Last night those hands had been miraculously wicked. She'd insisted upon undressing him in the lamplight of her chamber. Purred with appreciation as she explored every inch of his skin with her elegant, wandering fingers. Her rather innocent delight gave way to illicit desire, and by the time she'd made her way below his waist he'd been nothing but a cauldron of boiling lust, his nerves in absolute anarchy. She'd requested to stroke him to completion, as she was curious about the male sexual experience and couldn't concentrate on it when she was also being pleasured.

A request he would have been an imbecile to deny.

He'd returned the favor, of course, his sense of gratitude and chivalry not allowing him to stop until she'd shuddered with exhaustion and begged him for mercy.

God, how he'd enjoyed their play, but he hadn't actually been inside her last night.

He missed her.

He'd missed her when he'd left her bed to prowl her father's warehouses at the docks. He'd missed her when he'd fallen into his own bed after only removing his jacket and shoes.

He missed her now, even as she sat next to him, her arm rubbing his occasionally, creating sparks between them he was surprised other parishioners couldn't see.

This was what he'd feared all along.

Attachment. Sentiment. Bloody befuddlement.

Before he'd discovered the truth.

As the organ played the closing hymn and her clear, sweet voice mingled with that of the congregation, Morley sat quietly, chewing on his thoughts. Pondering his misgivings rather than any forms of grace.

At first, when he'd thought her a weakness simply because his body responded to her, the situation still seemed somehow manageable. Now, he didn't just want her.

He...*liked* her. Dash it all.

As they stood in the back of the line waiting to file out of the church, she slipped her arm through his and tilted her head to gift him with a winsome smile.

She was like a spring garden against the grey stone. Vibrant and lush. Full of sunlight and sometimes rain. Always inviting, shamelessly flaunting her blossoming beauty, tempting him with pink petals of—

Goddamn and blast, could he not think about her naked for two bloody minutes?

Catching his scowl, she tugged at his arm and said, "Don't let's be grumpy, it's too beautiful a day."

"I'm not grumpy," he argued, grimacing at the ironic note of irritation in his voice.

"Hungry, then? I know I'm famished." She pressed a glove to her stomach, a gesture becoming more familiar the further along she became.

He wasn't particularly hungry, not for food, at any rate. But it suddenly became imperative that he provide her sustenance.

Over the past fortnight, his cook had given up on satisfying Prudence's increasingly obscure gastronomic whims. Which was just as well because his wife, being of the upper classes, had never much had the opportunity to sample London's culinary delights. Ladies were not allowed by some ballocks code of superior conduct to eat in public houses or dine at restaurants or clubs.

The working class, however, rarely shared such compunctions.

Morley found himself often hurrying home from Scotland Yard at the day's end, eager to garner a report of just what madcap craving would decide their supper. As soon as his carriage pulled into the mews, she'd sweep out in her pelisse and hat, and announce something like, "Your child is demanding salt. And onions, I think. Just mouthfuls of flavor and sauce."

"Onions, you say?"

"Mmhmm." She'd nodded rapturously. "And cracking large chunks of succulent meat."

"My child is an unapologetic carnivore?" he'd asked with a lifted brow.

She'd cocked her head and looked up to the side as if listening, before revealing. "Undetermined...I believe that last requirement is all mine."

That conversation had prompted him to drive her to Manwaring Street, where East Indian bazaars and spice markets magically unfurled with the dawn alongside eateries serving flavorful curries and savory meats and cheeses roasted in tandoori ovens.

They'd eaten with their hands, sprawled on cushions like ancient royalty whilst tucked away in a quarter of a city where they might have been any avant-garde couple. After, she'd insisted upon a constitutional back through the evening market where she'd purchased a pair of earrings and wildly impractical shoes.

The next night had called for cabbage and fish of all things, so he'd introduced her to Russian cuisine. The night after that, she'd given the rather innocuous request for lamb, however the precedent had been set. Morley had whisked her to a Greek establishment where lively men had danced to rousing music, delighting her to no end.

It alarmed him how much enjoyment he gleaned from these outings of theirs. How, for entire hours, he'd forget everything that threatened their future happiness and lose himself in nothing more extraordinary than a conversation.

His wife held little in the way of personal prejudices and was endlessly curious about, and appreciative of, the traditions and people he introduced her to. She'd a rare gift for observation, carefully and cannily picking out the subtleties and nuances of culture whilst doing her best to not offend. She never remarked upon the perceived class of the neighborhoods to which he'd taken her, nor did she make anyone she met feel like less than the most interesting person with which she'd ever held a conversation.

All of her attention was absorbed by whomever was speaking, and he noticed she'd the kind and genuine way about her that garnered them little extras of gratitude wherever they went.

It was why he'd dared to bring her to St. Dismas. Because this was the floor upon which he and Caroline had often slept in the winter. In the borough that'd whelped him and abandoned him.

He'd not been to the parish since before his wedding, and he knew Vicar Applewhite would be bereft he'd not been invited to the wedding.

They'd almost made their way down the aisle as the old blind priest stopped to bid every family a personal farewell, and to cover his anxiety, Morley leaned down to ask Prudence, "What does the little fiend crave for luncheon, I wonder?"

She made a pensive sound. "Do you remember three days ago when we sampled those sautéed Chinese noodles?" She swallowed before continuing, and he'd the notion she'd salivated.

"I do."

"Something *like* that, but not exactly that."

Instead of clarifying, he allowed her to work through the conundrum, having learned that she'd arrive at a specific flavor and texture eventually, and his job would then be to provide it.

"Butter," she finally announced. "There must be butter. And... maybe cheese."

"Pasta?"

Her mouth fell open and her eyes twinkled like sunlight on the South Sea. "Pasta," she breathed. "Ingenious suggestion."

"Angelo's on the Strand, it is," he decided, realizing that his own stomach grumbled emptily at the thought. "Francesco serves this white wine and butter dish with garlic and scallions—"

She grasped his arm with undue dramatics. "Cease tormenting me or I'll expire before we arrive."

He adopted a sly, teasing smile. "I suppose you don't want to hear about the fresh loaves of—"

"Morley?" Vicar Applewhite turned his face in their direction, the tufts of his hair sticking out in a riot of copper-grey as his grin unfurled a gather of teeth yellowed with age. "Morley, my boy, that you?"

Morley took the blindly offered hand and pressed an envelope into it. "Vicar," he said. "I'm sorry I'm late this month. There's extra in there. Just have Thomas count it out and he can take some home to Lettie and Harry, as I know they've likely covered expenses in my absence."

"You know them well." The envelope disappeared into voluminous robes with the swiftness that bordered on sleight of hand. "I'm sure you had good reason and...well, you're not beholden to our upkeep."

"You know I am," Morley murmured, very aware of how still his wife had become as she watched the exchange with interest. "But I do have reason. I'd like to introduce you to...my wife, Prudence Morley."

Out of sheer habit, she curtsied to the blind man. "How do you do, Vicar Applewhite? I was very moved by your words today."

The Vicar's features lit with an almost childlike radiance of unadulterated glee. "Oh my God! My happy day! I've had many prayers go unheeded, Lady Morley, and I'd given up on this rascal hitching himself to anyone ages ago." Before she could reply, he turned back to Carlton. "I heard we'd a new voice in the congregation. Like that of an angel. Pure and sweet and good. What a blessing. What a blessing! Praise be."

Disconcerted and embarrassed by the man's effusive emotion, Morley pressed his cold hand to the back of his heating neck. It'd become concerningly evident to him that his marital status—or lack thereof—had been more disturbing to those in his sphere than he'd ever have guessed. And among those who claimed to care for him, they unanimously approved of his selection of spouse.

"We'd stay and visit..." he began uncomfortably.

"No, no, I've tea with the Brintons as soon as they call around to collect me, but you must visit soon. You must tell me everything." He turned to Prudence, both hands reaching for her.

She took them in her gloved fingers, squeezing fondly as if they'd known each other for a lifetime.

"There always seems to be plenty of demons in this

world of ours. And not enough angels. I'm glad our Cutter's found his own."

Morley excused them and hurried her to the main thoroughfare, hoping she'd not caught the old man's slip of the tongue. He hired them a hackney, as he rarely brought his own carriage to this part of the city, and lifted her in, instructing the driver to deposit them at Angelo's.

She swayed silently on the overwrought springs of the cab as she subjected him to a thorough study before saying, "My sisters and I were raised by borderline zealots, as evidenced by our virtuous names. However, I wouldn't have thought you a religious man."

He looked out of the window at their dismal surroundings, hardening his heart against every over-thin waif or shifty-eyed reprobate. "I don't know that I am," he said honestly. "But others believe with such confounding fervency, don't they? I attend to observe them, I think. To learn what they love. Or what they fear. To watch the rapture on their faces and wonder what it must be like. To believe in something so vast. So absolute. To trust..." He broke off for a moment, returning his entire attentions on her. "To trust...in anything."

He found no condemnation in her, but an infinite sadness. "You do not go there to find grace? To find God?"

He made a caustic noise. "I've never understood the words. But, I think, I go there in case He might find me. If I'm standing in the right place. Maybe an answer to all this madness will fall on my head." He gestured to the city and the world beyond it.

To his surprise, a laugh bubbled from her, warming the moment. "Considering how much sinning we've been doing lately, you might do to fear a bolt of lightning instead."

In spite of himself, he chuckled along with her. "I'm not familiar with all credences and commandments but I'm fairly certain we've not been sinning since we married."

"I don't know," she said from beneath coy lashes. "It feels rather wicked to me."

If this had been his coach, he'd have gathered her to him and shown her the meaning of the word wicked.

"St. Dismas." She tested the name. "The penitent thief."

He shifted in his seat.

Smoothing at her skirts, she smiled to herself. "I confess I'd initially assumed you took me to this church so no one would recognize us, but now...I think I understand."

He shook his head, wishing he'd never taken her there at all. What had he been thinking? That he'd wanted to reveal the part of himself he blamed for her debauchment? Had he wanted to see if she'd hold a handkerchief to shield her nose against the stench of the wells and pumps he used to draw his drinking water from? If she'd shy away from the hard-working class and earnest people that lived in poverty alongside the criminal element?

If so, it was an unfair test. Although, one she'd passed with perfect marks.

"There's nothing to understand," he informed her with as much dispassion as he could. "I attend St. Dismas monthly. I'm their patron, you see. Applewhite shelters and tends to many of the hungry and naked children in this part of the city. One of the few true Christians I've ever known. I finance his mission to take some of Whitechapel's unwanted boys and help them find a direction. A trade. A means of survival."

"Because—"

"Because crime and violence are born of poverty

and cruelty," he explained. "The more means a man has to provide survival for himself and his kin, the less likely he is to succumb to vice or villainy."

"And because the Vicar once did the same for you?" Her gaze, as her assessment, was frank and open, and Morley wanted to shrink from it.

This was what he'd come here to tell her. Whom he'd come to introduce her to.

So why now did he hesitate?

Because he'd always had the upper hand in this relationship, he realized. It wasn't comfortable to give her something she could wield against him.

Across from him, the daylight slanted into slick iridescent blues glimmering from the absolute darkness of her hair. "You told me once that you'd grown up with the accent you used as the Knight of Shadows," she said. "The same accent the Vicar has, and everyone here."

"So I did."

"Farah mentioned you had secrets...and the Vicar, he called you Cutter."

His heart erupted into chaos as he watched her braid the strings of his past together without him saying a word.

"Is that your name? Cutter. Are you the penitent thief?"

He retreated back toward the window, watching as the years fell away between that time and this. A blond boy stood on a corner with his black-haired friend, assessing which pockets would be full. Which punters would be easily fleeced.

"It's who I was," he admitted reluctantly, staring into the hard, hard eyes of that boy in his past. Eyes that'd seen nothing but oppression and desperation, set into a face that only knew the touch of another human being as a quick box to the ears or a heavy punch to the face.

A body thinned with ever-present hunger and strengthened by hardship and labor.

Deadeye.

"I was a pickpocket and thief bound for a prison cell until one night…" He hesitated as the boy on the street corner lifted his finger to his cracked lips to hush him.

Don't tell her. Don't trust her.

But…what if she could understand where he'd come from? What he'd lost.

What he'd done.

What if his admission repulsed and terrified her? What if she told? She'd have the final secret. One that could rip his entire life to shreds and dump him right back into the gutter.

If he didn't hang for it.

"One night…the Vicar took me in and gave me a place to stay when I had none," he explained lamely, vaulting over the most important parts. "He was the one who nudged me to reinvent myself through documents I'd receive when joining Her Majesty's Regiment. And upon my return from war, he handed me the paper wherein there was an advertisement for men of my physical build and prowess to wear the uniform of the London Metropolitan Police." He sent her what he hoped was an unconvincing smile. "The rest, as they say, is history."

"That was truly wonderful of him," she murmured, extrapolating what she could from his vague memoir. "And so you repay him for his kindness with a monthly stipend?"

Morley seized upon the opportunity to distract her from the entire conversation.

"I give him the entirety of my salary as Chief Inspector," he revealed.

She visibly blanched, her mouth falling open as she gaped at him as if he'd ripped off his skin to reveal a demon. "But...but...how do you...?" Good breeding caused her to shy away from conversations about money. To know a man's work, even one's husband, might be considered vulgar. He pinpointed the moment she made peace with that vulgarity.

"I always wondered how you, even on a Chief Inspector's salary, could afford such a lofty address," she said. "Even my father has mentioned his government pay wouldn't cover food for our horses, let alone our houses. He's always implied our money comes from his land and shipping company."

His lips compressed ruefully. He was still looking into where exactly her father's wealth came from.

"Then...what about you, husband?" It was her turn to stare out the window. "If you were raised in these gutters and went straight from the army to the police, then how did you amass enough of a fortune to speak for me, without a need for my dowry? Dare I ask if you are a thief still? If the money you pay to the church is penance?"

"Actually," he said, becoming rather amused. "I suppose I did thieve a bit when making my fortune."

She did her best not to look appalled, and almost pulled it off. "You didn't!"

"Don't fret, I only stole information."

She leaned forward as if entranced. "Tell me."

"Once I was back from the army, I would be asked to go to exhibitions by my former regimental officers so they could place bets on me."

"What sort of exhibitions?"

"Shooting ones, mostly."

"Shooting ones? Why?"

He gave her the short answer. "Because I was a rifleman in corps."

Her eyes narrowed to slits as she tilted her delicate chin in assessment. "You must have been a rather incredible rifleman if you were asked to compete in exhibitions."

"Tolerably good."

"Oh come now, you'd have to be more than tolerable if they—"

"They called me *Deadeye*. It doesn't matter." He felt his neck heating again as he rushed past to avoid her comments or questions. "At one such event, I overheard my Captain discussing an investment scheme with an American by the name of Elijah Wolfe, a ruthless and unscrupulous miner who was drumming up funds to reopen his dying town's defunct iron mines. He was able to find no support whatsoever and I could smell his desperation. But despite all that, there was something about him…"

"Did you save a grateful noble from being fleeced by this unscrupulous American Wolfe?" she guessed.

He emitted a low sound of amusement. "I gave Eli everything I'd won on the exhibitions for a ten percent share. It was barely enough to keep his mine open for a month, let alone pay the workers."

Her eyes went round as saucers. "You made your fortune in iron?"

"No," he said wryly. "The mine is still defunct, as it only took a month to exhaust it. However, another mineral often resides where iron is found. A great deal less of it, worth a great deal more."

"Really?" she asked. "What is that?"

He caught her hand and gently squeezed the tip of her glove from the long middle finger, sliding the garment from her creamy skin. Holding up her knuckles, he kissed the ring on her finger.

"Gold."

CHAPTER 15

*P*rudence barely tasted her pasta. Instead she chewed on a puzzle, determined to uncover just what secret her husband was keeping from her.

She studied him across a private garden table behind what was possibly the most charming Italian café in the city, and contemplated everything he'd been in his exceptional life.

An urchin, a thief, a crack shot rifleman, an exhibitionist, a knighted war hero, an officer of the law, a vigilante, *and* a venture capitalist with interest in an American gold mine worth a fortune.

And, quite possibly, a liar.

Not about the gold, which was both startling, fascinating, and wonderful. But about what came before.

His childhood.

He'd left something out of that story, she was certain of it. As he'd spoken of his time at St. Dismas, she could feel him jumping over the graves of long-buried emotions, ripping up their headstones to pretend they'd never existed at all.

What a complicated man she'd married. Possessed of dichotomy between a heart capable of such unequaled valor, gallantry, and courage tied to a mind bedeviled by skepticism, enigma, and for lack of a gentler word, fear.

It was a word he would toss away and spit upon if she accused him of it. But if she boiled the amalgamation of his wariness, mysteriousness, and protectiveness down to a reduction as thick as the wonderful sauce anointing her pasta. She was certain she would find fear the main ingredient.

Not a fear of death or danger. His nocturnal vocation was evidence of uncommon bravery in the face of death.

So, what terrified this bold and daring knight? What drove him to hide himself, his past, in the shadows?

What had been done to him?

Or...what had he done?

"You're not eating," he prompted over a sip of his coffee. "If it's not to your taste, we can go elsewhere."

Jostled from her thoughts, Prudence picked up her utensils again and crafted herself an especially delicious bite. "No, it's marvelous. I was just lost in thought."

"Oh? About what?" He ate like he did everything else, she noticed, with correct and decisive efficiency. He'd been served a dish of pasta stuffed with meats, cheeses, and savory herbs in a voluminous red sauce, whereas she'd instantly selected the butter and white wine reduction over Capelli d'Angelo.

"I was thinking you're the one who needs to eat more," she said.

"I'm consuming a veritable mountain of food right now." He gestured to his plate. "In fact, if we keep this up, I'll need to have my trousers refitted."

Hardly. He was filling out a little, but the extra portions seemed to simply fuel the production of muscle rather than storing anywhere unsightly. "Yes, but, before I started prevailing upon you to take me to all these wondrous places, it was the perception around the house that because of your punishing schedule, you're woefully undernourished. Beyond that, you barely sleep."

She'd noted that in the past week his skin had gained a bit more color, and his cheeks filled from rather gaunt to merely sharp. He'd been eating better, but the smudges beneath his eyes remained, and the lines of constant strain, of ever-readiness, still etched into the chiseled handsomeness of his features.

His utensils stilled in his pasta and he stared down at the food with a queer little smile that vanished as quickly as it appeared. "I've heard officers complain for years about their wives nagging them to stay home more often. To take better care of their health."

She bristled a little until he graced her with a look so tender, she might have melted into a puddle beneath her chair.

"I always envied them." The glint in his eye dazzled her more than the sunlight fragmenting off the spray from the little garden fountain. Their round table was large enough to hold their meals, but only just, and it precipitated them sitting in such a way that their knees often brushed. An embarrassment of hyacinth, calendulas, and lilac blossoms cosseted them from the din of diners inside, creating a lavish, intimate oasis of their own in the middle of the world's largest city.

"Well, Lady Morley," he said around a circumspect bite of bread. "My lack of slumber is entirely your fault. Before you tempted me to your bed at all hours, I'll have you know I managed quite well to wedge sleep into my schedule."

"I suppose I shall lock you out of my bedchamber, then," she sighed as if it were a great shame. "If only because I care for your health."

He nudged her knee in challenge. "Don't you dare."

She laughed flirtatiously before a note of uncertainty pricked at her. "I know you live two very important lives but...would you possibly consider... devoting a few nights to staying at home?" she ventured.

You could sleep with me, she didn't say. Because he hadn't yet. He would leave her in the night, beholden to his self-proclaimed duties as the Knight of Shadows. Upon his return, he'd sleep in the room down the hall from her. Her breath trembled in her throat enough that she had to tug on the high neck of her gown. "I know I don't have the right to make undue demands, but once the baby comes—"

"Say no more." He reached over and caught at the hand still fluttering at her chest, caressing a gentle thumb over her knuckles. "I've been thinking the very same—"

"*Mi scusi, Signore Morley, mi scusi!*" The proprietor, Francesco, weighted down by a magnificent mustache, a round belly, and a Sunday newspaper labored over to their table. "*La carta. La carta! È così brutto. Non credo.*" He turned to her. "I do not believe."

A dawning frown overtook all semblance of her husband's good humor as he snatched the paper from the restaurateur and scanned it. Storms gathered in his eyes and thunder in his expression as he crushed it in his fist.

"Thank you, Francesco," he said, his teeth never separating as his lip curled into a silent snarl.

"Of course..." The man shot her a look of pity and scurried inside, not wanting to witness Pru's reaction to what she knew was going to happen. She wished she could follow him. Her heart became like a sparrow in a cage, flittering around her ribs as though searching for escape.

They'd drawn upon the luxury of luck for far too long. Eventually, the story would have to break. The truth was always going to come out, and with it a few lies as well, to flavor the story with delicious scandal.

She wanted to read it, but her eyes refused to focus. Not only did she blink back the threat of over-whelming tears, but also a creeping darkness at her periphery. She felt as though she'd been the victim of a blow to the head, and couldn't seem to shake the accompanying disorientation.

She caught the unmistakable word in the title of the article.

MURDER.

"What? What do they say? Do they think I—"

"It'll be all right," he soothed, instinctively tucking the paper behind him.

"Tell me what they wrote," she implored him.

He hesitated for a moment, before exhaling defeat. "It's been released to the press that Sutherland was stabbed and that you were in the room with him. The article mentions his past...infidelities and your possible reaction to them."

"They've given me a motive." She lifted her hand to her face, just to make sure she was still in possession of one, as it'd suddenly gone quite numb. "That can't be all," she fretted. "How did Mr. Francesco know to bring you the paper, does it mention our marriage?"

His features became ever more grim. "Thankfully, no."

"Then..."

He produced the paper and folded it so she could see. "Your portrait, I'm afraid."

"Oh, dear God." She looked down at the likeness, touched by a cold, cold horror. "What a rude sketch! It doesn't even look like me."

"Not perfectly, but enough that Francesco stitched it together."

"What am I going to do?" she cried, unable to stop

the words she didn't want to read from jumping out at her. "They've made me out to be a villainess. They've all but made the adjudicator's case for him."

"We're prepared for this," he said, attempting to calm her. "However, I think it's best we go home."

"But...I'm supposed to go to the Duchess of Tren-wyth's Ladies' Aid Society gathering with Farah today." She looked down at her plate of cooling pasta discon-solately. She wasn't finished, but she'd lost her appetite.

"I'd rather you didn't." He gave his lips and hands one last wipe with his linen before tossing it on the table. "The damned vulture who wrote this, and any other press, will be looking for you. It's best you stay out of the public eye for a bit, until we get this sorted."

"I see the logic in that," she said, her insides twisting with desperation. "Wouldn't that prove the journalist's point? I'll be hiding in disgrace. I'll look guilty."

Beyond that, she *couldn't* go back to the way it was before, back to only having their quiet staff and dust motes for company. Back to sheer silence and distance from the one man who'd begun to mean so much to her. "How close is this to getting sorted, would you say?"

She'd avoided pressing him about it too much. The past several almost carefree, passionate nights had her-alded a new epoch in their relationship, and she'd con-vinced herself that he'd all but forgotten about his suspicion. That he believed she didn't have blood on her hands.

That he was looking to exonerate her.

His face became a cool mask of careful emptiness. "I've a church full of suspects in Sutherland's case, and we're working through them as fast as we are able, starting with those closest at the time of the murder. Lord and Lady Woodhaven, your father, the Vicar, and spreading out from there. I'm even looking at Adrian McKendrick, the new Earl of Sutherland."

She nodded, scanning the paper again and again. "What about Father?"

"My searches of your father's warehouses and interests have borne some rather rotten fruit, I'm afraid," he admitted reluctantly, examining her for a reaction. "I've found registers of shipments from ports where the plant is believed to be indigenous. Shipments that bear Sutherland's name and signature. This intimates that your fiancé might have been in league with your father...and if that's the case, we'll need to add the Commissioner to the very short list of lead suspects in his murder."

"What?" She jerked entirely upright, dropping the paper into her food. "George wasn't a businessman, he thought trade and shipping were, frankly, beneath him."

"And so he certainly did," he agreed. "But impoverished nobility are being forced to consider all manner of desperate means whereby to buttress their dwindling fortunes. Could Sutherland have been one of them?"

Stymied, she shook her head. "I never thought to ask. But I had reason to believe he was after my dowry when I heard that he'd several illegitimate children to support."

"Disgraceful bastard," he said beneath his breath.

She knew they shouldn't speak ill of the dead, but she couldn't bring herself to disagree.

Do you really think he and my father were...dear God. This just keeps getting worse, doesn't it?" With trembling hands, she rescued the paper from her plate, and stared down at the words that damned her, possibly for the rest of her life. "How did they get this information?"

He shook his head. "I thought we'd plugged all possible leaks," he muttered. "The reverend, perhaps? He'd a jolt of conscience?"

"I suppose...but it's unlikely. Like you, my family have been patrons for years. He christened us all. What about anyone at the Yard? The judge? The registrar who married us?"

He made a fervent gesture in the negative. "I called in a bevy of favors that you wouldn't believe if I told you," he said. "They all knew that hellfire would be preferable to the wrath I'd rain down upon their heads if they spoke out."

"What about Honoria's husband, William?" she whispered. "He *loved* George and he was...was so *angry* with me. So certain I'd done it." A band reached around her chest and tugged, forcing a rather forceful exhale. The same pressure cinched at her head in a vise-like grip at her throbbing temples. "If William thinks I got away with murder, he might be using popular opinion to force your hand. To make me pay." She could say no more, her lungs had compressed the ability of breath completely away from her.

"Your bloody family," he gritted out, looking as if he might hurl the table in a fit of temper.

The dam she'd built to stem the current of her emotion crumbled, overwhelming her entire being with a desolate flood of emotion. As a last stopgap, she pressed both of her hands over her mouth to contain the cries, but she still couldn't seem to manage. They erupted from her as hot tears spilled in veritable rivers down her cheeks.

He was at her side in a moment. Gathering her to him in a bundle of bereft limbs and hiccupping sobs. His chest was hard and steady as the rock of Gibraltar as the tides of her pain broke upon it.

"I'm sorry, sweetheart," he crooned, his hands doing

a tender dance of comfort up and down her spine as he tucked her head beneath his chin. "There now. All will be well. You're not in any more danger than you were before. Not with me to protect you."

She clung to him, listening to his words as they rumbled in his chest, grasping onto them like a life preserver thrown to her before she drowned beneath her despair.

"There, darling." He pressed his mouth to her brow. "You weep as you like. I have you."

Yes. He had her. She was utterly his.

Could she claim the same tenure?

"I-I'm not weeping," she declared, as an order to herself to cease more than anything.

"Of course not, dear," he said solicitously.

"I mean. I d-don't ever," she said around hitches of breath. "I'm-I'm not a hysterical p-person. But I can't seem to s-stop. I—I—" She hiccupped loudly and could feel his smile against her hair.

"Sweetheart," he rumbled. "Not only are you going through what is likely the most difficult trial of your life, you're also with child." He pulled her back so he could look down at her with infinite tenderness, before brushing at her sodden cheeks with his thumb. "I should not have said that about your family," he repeated. "I was...aggravated by your distress, that's all."

"You've every right to curse them. I'm disenchanted with them as well. Here I thought them almost too righteous, and it turns out the entire lot could be crooked but for the twins." Her chin wobbled as a new wave of gloom assaulted her enough to push away from him. "God, how you must regret me. I've brought such chaos to your orderly life. Surely you wish we'd never—"

He caught her, pulling her back into the protective circle of his arms, this time having produced a handkerchief. "Stop it," he ordered against her temple as he pressed little kisses of consolation there. "Don't think like that."

"How can I not when—"

He distracted her by looping the handkerchief over his finger and tracing the corners of her mouth where the tears had run, then along her jaw, beside her nose, and gently across her cheeks. He feathered cool, wine-scented kisses across her swollen eyelids and against her heated forehead.

"Would it make you feel better to know my family would put yours to shame?" he asked, injecting a bit of levity into his voice.

She gave a delicate sniff, and then a heartier one. "A little," she admitted as he surrendered the handkerchief to her so she could blow her nose. "You've never spoken of your family," she realized, with no little amount of chagrin. She'd never inquired about them. "Where do they live?"

"They don't," he answered in an even, nonchalant tone that asked for no pity. "My mother died not long after our births, and my father drank himself to death a handful of years thereafter, but not before making life miserable for my sister and me."

She lifted her chin to look at him, finding his expression distorted by her watery confusion. "You have a sister?"

"I do. I...did. A twin. Caroline."

"A twin," she breathed, her heart softened by the way he'd said her name, and then skewered by the use of the past tense. She tried to imagine Mercy without Felicity—or vice versa—and her eyes threatened to summon a storm the likes of which they'd not yet seen. "Can you tell me...what happened to her?"

He looked down at her for a long time, and she met his gaze with silent encouragement. This was like the doors in their home. This was what he'd kept locked away from her, this pain shimmering in his eyes, radiating from his body and fragmenting his soul.

After an eternity, his lips parted and he revealed to her what she understood he'd not been prepared to impart in the carriage.

She stood in the circle of his arms as he took a sledgehammer to the shards of her already broken heart. He told her about two children shivering on the cold cobbles, stealing their food and necessary supplies. Of hoping his sister would marry his best mate. Of his desperation and disappointment when she'd turned to the profession of so many to provide for herself what he, an ignorant thief, could not.

He recounted the violent day of Caroline's death in vague and broken detail, though whether for her benefit or his, she couldn't be sure. His eyes remained dry. Distant. As if he recounted the horrible tale of someone else's sister's cruel murder.

Pru was a puddle of emotion again when he ran out of words. The story didn't even exactly seem over and yet he just…stopped abruptly.

Much like Caroline's life had, before it had truly begun.

This time, when she buried her face against his chest, she plunged her arms around his waist, holding him close to her, wishing to impart all the solace she possibly could.

He stood still for a moment, stiff and unsure, before heaving out a kept breath, and dropping his cheek to rest on her hair.

He relaxed against her, allowing her to take some of his weight as they propped each other up, creating a creature of more strength for the sharing of their collective burdens.

"To think," she said. "You could have drowned in

that pain. Could have let it own you. But you chose to rise, instead, to become this...this miraculous, extraordinary man—"

Abruptly, he drew back, lifting a finger to press against her lips lest she say anything kinder. His eyes were still shuttered, opaque with uncertainty bordering on anxiety. As if he still hadn't come to a decision. "I didn't tell you to gain your sympathy nor your admiration," he said before casting a furtive glance around the garden, finding only bees noisily eavesdropping on the last blossoms of lavender before autumn stole their bloom.

"I told you because I want you to know that...you're not the only one in this marriage with damning secrets."

Prudence shook her head, not understanding. "I have no secre—"

"I killed him." The confession hung in the air like a cold blade, waiting to slice them apart. "The man who hurt my sister, who looked into her eyes as they dulled and died. I found him, I cut his throat, and watched as his blood soaked my hands." He released her then, stepping away to show her his rough palms as if the stain remained. "He was a watchmaker, some nobody, who liked to hurt women. Girls. Who thought they deserved it." His voice broke for a moment, and he looked away, not in agony, but apparent disgust for a human he'd helped out of this world and into the next.

"Dorian was nabbed for theft that night, which provided me a getaway, and I showed up on Vicar Applewhite's doorstep. He granted me sanctuary. He washed the blood from my hands, much as I did for you the day I proposed."

"My God." Prudence stood as if her shoes had been welded to the cobbles. Her husband had just confessed a murder to her. The Chief Inspector of Scotland Yard.

He'd killed the man who'd raped and murdered his sister in cold blood.

So why wasn't she horrified? Or angry? Why did she still want to take him—and that grubby, starving adolescent he'd been—and rock him in her arms until she'd soothed away that pain? Confounded as she was by the truth, it took her a moment to process his next sentence.

"I revealed this to you as an olive branch," he said earnestly. "No, a commiseration. We're not so different, you and me. You see, revenge isn't only a human trait, but a universal one. Justice is our society's way to punish crimes, but when there is no justice, it's natural to seek vengeance—"

She jerked away from him so violently, his hands were still outstretched as she retreated a few steps to the corner of the garden.

"Yes, we *are* different," she insisted, her trembling intensifying again, but for an entirely different reason than before. "We are *absolutely* different."

He stared at her, his head cocked to the side in almost doglike befuddlement.

"You avenged your sister's death, and I do not think I condemn you for that. But I..." She clasped both her hands to her chest. "*I* did *not*. I'm innocent of any and all crimes but the one you and I perpetrated together in that garden."

She wanted to cry again, but, it seemed, she'd been wrung out of tears. Now, all she had left was a raw and open wound where her heart used to reside, one that ached and stung with every breath. "The fact that you still think I'm guilty is more disappointing than the condemnation of every paper and person in the whole of the empire. Don't you see?" She shook her head, knowing that, even now, her husband's mind, his heart, was closed to her. "I could face all this, every last individual I know and love turning their backs on me, if I could only hope that you believed me."

He stepped forward, reaching for her until she held up a hand against him.

"What I'm telling you, Prudence, is that it doesn't matter what I believe," he said fiercely, gesturing with fervent, sharp swipes of his hand. "It doesn't matter what happened in that room, I'm taking your side. Come what may, you have every tool at my disposal, every cent to my name, and every ounce of my power, influence, and expertise. I will get you out of this, you have my word."

"And I thank you for that, but does it not destroy you to do so? Should you not only take up my defense if I am worthy of it? You don't *know* that I'm innocent."

"And I don't bloody care!" he roared. "I'm telling you, dammit, that I would do anything for you. Do you understand? I would take responsibility on my own shoulders if I thought it would help. I would bring back the bastard and kill him, myself. I would commit perjury for you, Prudence, hell I'm afraid I'd commit murder if you asked me—"

"But I *wouldn't*. I. Would. Never!" She threw her arms up and turned away from him, pacing toward the fountain, wishing the sound of the water didn't bring up memories of the night they'd met. "All I ask, is that you find out who killed George and clear my name."

She felt him behind her, a looming shadow of conflicted torment. "Why are you angry?" he asked in a hoarse and ragged whisper.

"Because you don't trust me," she told the fountain, unable to look at him. "I'm sorry but you can't imagine how frustrating that is."

"Please," he beseeched her. "Try to understand, Prudence. I want you. I…am fond of you. Christ, you're the mother of my child and I believe we're building something of a life here. But in my line of work, it matters not what you believe. It matters what you can prove. The feelings I have for you would already influence the outcome of any investigation, and that's a liability I've decided to live with."

"How altruistic of you." With his every word, the wound in her heart began to stitch together. Not with a balming comfort, but with glacial sort of frigidity. She'd begun to erect her own fortifications, it seemed, so she didn't bleed out entirely right here in the middle of the midday meal.

And still he went on. "Try to appreciate the chance I took becoming your spouse. A woman I'd met only once in a reckless encounter. One with a knife in her hand and the blood of her would-be husband soaking her. Had we never met before. Had we not..." He trailed away with a brutal noise. "I have to look at the evidence, Prudence, and when it's all laid out in front of me, there is only one conclusion to be drawn from it."

"That I'm a murderer." She spun on him, her fists clenched at her sides. "Is that why you don't sleep in my bed? Why you lock the door to your rooms and to the nursery? To keep yourself safe from me, your mad, murderer of a wife?"

He made a helpless gesture as his eyes darted away. "Come now, that isn't fair. I can't rightly say..."

"Then wrongly say!" she spat. "You're afraid I might, what, sneak into your rooms and murder you in your sleep?"

"Not afraid, per se. I just felt it necessary to maintain a certain amount of distance."

"Ugh!" Picking up her skirts, she fled around the fountain, hurtling herself toward the door. It was all too much. The scandal, his revelations, confessions, hypocrisy, and concessions. Every emotion she'd ever named swirled within her until she felt as though she might detonate into a million plumes of volcanic ash. "I can't look at you."

His footsteps followed her. "Where do you think you are going?"

"To Trenwyth's."

"Wait." He seized her wrist, his grip careful but firm. "It's not safe. I thought we'd agreed you weren't—"

"You agreed!" She whirled on him, turning the full force of a mounting rage against him. "You've done nothing but make decisions for me since the beginning. And I've been so solicitous, haven't I? Because I needed to be grateful. Because I needed you to trust me. To help me. To save me. Because something awoke in me the night we met, and I fell a little in love with you then. The very moment I landed in your arms." She swiped at angry new tears as she twisted her wrist out of his grasp.

"But you've taught me that love is not possible without trust, and trust is not possible without proof, so..." She made a frustrated gesture before returning her hands to clench at her sides. "Here we are. I'm leaving now so you can be about your work. Go, Chief Inspector Carlton Morley, go find my measure."

"Prudence—" He lifted his hands, but she swept away from his reach.

"Don't," was all she said as she retreated through the door to escape in a hansom.

He didn't.

CHAPTER 16

I fell a little in love with you.

Her words haunted Morley as he followed Pru's hackney to the Duke of Trenwyth's spectacular white stone Belgravia mansion, and watched from a discreet distance as she went inside. They plagued him for several restless hours as he endeavored to focus on something, anything else. No amount of training, paperwork, reading, or investigation could silence the admission.

In love.

Every document he examined blurred beneath the image of the abysmal wells of pain in her eyes. The wounded expression that'd precipitated her anger. Wounds he'd carelessly, selfishly inflicted.

What a fool he'd been, having such a conversation after the disaster with the article. She was disconsolate, and he'd been awash in his own recollected grief and loss to handle that moment with the aplomb it had called for. He'd spoken in haste and had said every wrong thing he possibly could have.

If marriage had a dunce cap, he'd be in the corner for weeks, his nose against the wall.

Agitated, he attempted any number of pastimes,

wishing to calm the need to crawl out of his own skin. Crawl on his knees to her and beg her forgiveness.

He watched every minute go by, aching for her to return. Wishing she'd not sought comfort elsewhere, but also recognizing her need for a separation from him.

She was in one of the safest places in the city apart from home, among the wives of the most dangerous and protective men he could think of besides himself.

An eternal evening gave way to nightfall, and when he could stand it no longer, Morley punched his fists into the sleeves of his jacket, and struck out on foot toward Belgravia, keeping his eye on the traffic for her.

Trenwyth's imposing house was ablaze with light as Morley chanced to meet his prodigal best mate striding up the walk for, presumably, the same reason. To escort his Countess home.

Ash, Lord Southbourne, put his cane to his hat and saluted him with a piratical grin. "Look at us, Morley," he commiserated with a devilish tone. "As boys, did you ever in a million years dream we'd claim the West End as our neighborhood, casually fetching our high-born wives to take back to our manor houses to swive them like the common perverts we are?"

"Never in a million years." Morley couldn't even bring himself to pretend to enjoy the Earl of Southbourne's charismatic irreverence. He very much doubted this night would go in that direction with his own high-born wife.

He didn't merit it.

"I saw the papers today, Cutter," Ash said, sweeping him with an observant look bordering with as much filial concern as the shark-eyed pirate could muster. "How is she? How goes the investigation?"

Seeing no point in correcting the man regarding his

name, Morley lifted his hand to the back of his tense neck and squeezed, trying to summon an answer.

He was saved from doing so by the doors being nearly yanked from their hinges, revealing a frowning Farah Blackwell backlit by enough lanterns to give the impression of a heraldic halo of an archangel.

Apparently, one on the warpath.

"Carlton Morley, you incomparable *idiot*," she declared, planting her fists on the hips of her violet gown.

Morley winced. He might have known the women would rally against him.

It was what he deserved.

"Oh my," Ash turned to him, his dark brows crawling up his forehead in surprise, and no little amount of delight. "I'm dying to hear this."

"You told your pregnant wife you thought she might try to murder you in your sleep?" she nearly shrieked.

Ash gasped, pressing his hand to his chest. "Morley!"

Standing a few steps on the landing beneath where Farah seethed down at him, Morley squinted up, thinking that her words sounded a bit slurred and her eyes over bright.

"No!" he said reflexively, and then realized he was wrong. "That is, I didn't deny—"

"I have never been so disappointed in someone in my entire *life*," Farah scolded.

"I know your husband, Lady Blackwell," Ash jested. "I very much doubt that."

Emitting a cavernous sigh, Morley nodded, intent upon taking his lashes. "Invite me in, Farah, and I'll make amends."

"I think not!" she snapped. "You'll stand out there where you belong and explain yourself, or you'll turn right around and go home."

"But..." He looked to Ash for help, and found only

avid, ill-concealed enjoyment. "This isn't even your residence. Is Lady Trenwyth in there?"

She held out her hand against him with the judgement of St. Peter, himself. "You do not want to cross paths with the women in that house right now, Morley, as you are speaking to the only one who feels a modicum of compassion for you at the moment."

"Don't go in there, old boy," Ash said out of the side of his mouth. "There are plenty of banisters from which to lynch you. Best you run and change your name…again."

Shoulders slumping, Morley climbed the last few stairs to stand at least eye level with his accuser. "Let me preface this with the fact that I realize I handled the situation poorly."

"Understatement, but go on." Farah narrowed her eyes.

He turned to Ash. "Do you remember what Caroline looked like?"

The man's lashes swept down. "Yes, but I don't know what that has to do with—"

"Face like a fucking saint, she had," Morley pressed on. "Eyes wide enough to contain all the innocence in the entire world."

Ash's lip twitched at a fond memory. "Yes, and the brilliant girl could steal bacon from a bloodhound and get away with it."

"*Precisely.*" Morley turned back to Farah to elucidate. "My wife is the loveliest creature I may ever have the opportunity to envision in my lifetime. She's radiant and sweet-natured and wise and I enjoy nothing so much as her presence. But, doesn't that make for the perfect swindler? How can she ask me to trust her when I don't know her?"

Farah's brow crimped with concern as she contemplated his words. "You've lived with her for weeks. Surely you have *some* idea of her character now."

"Do we ever really know anyone?" he asked as defensiveness spilled over into ire. "I've arrested criminals who've been married for decades, to the absolute astonishment of their spouses. Besides, I'm not one of you idle rich with nothing better to do than lounge and travel and revel in each other. I'm kept rather busy tasked with the safety of the city and all, and then I've an entirely different vocation in the evenings. When have I possibly had the time—"

"Oh please," Ash snorted with distinctive derision. "I've killed men who've tried to feed me half the horseshit you just did, Morley."

"*Make* the time," Farah interjected firmly. "For both your sakes. Because I've met your wife all but twice and I'd take the stand to profess her innocence tomorrow. Not only that, but it's patently clear she might be the loneliest woman I have ever known."

Morley jerked, taken aback. "What do you mean?

Farah regarded him with rank skepticism. "Do I have to spell it out for you?"

"Pretend I'm an idiot."

A chortle erupted from the man at his side. "Why the need for pretense?"

Forgetting her indignation, or maybe just taking immense pity on him, Farah glided over and placed her hand on arms he hadn't realized he'd crossed.

"Morley, she's lost her entire family and reputation to this scandal. Her father might be a criminal. Her fiancé died in front of her. Her sisters are hardly allowed to speak to her. She was deceived by her best friend and her elder sister. And then... her *husband* abandons her in a strange home with nothing but stress to occupy her thoughts while she's pregnant with his child. A stranger's child. And a stranger you seem determined to remain. How can you make it impossible to get to know each other, and then punish her for it?"

Sufficiently chastised, he hung his head. "I always wanted to be a husband, but I think I waited so long because a part of me knew I'd mangle it."

"Oh, ballocks." In a rare show of the affection they once shared, Ash bumped his shoulder with his own. "You are the best of us, Morley. Always were. But you're prioritizing doing the right thing in front of being a good man, and thereby getting in your own way. That's all."

"She loves you, I think," Farah said.

Morley's head snapped up to catch her dimples appearing in a knowing smile. "I don't believe a woman can be as hurt by mere words unless she's opened her heart to that pain."

It was the second time the word had been uttered tonight. A word he never before dared to contemplate.

"And we loved her too," she finished, patting his arm. "I'm glad you came, now home to your wife. She's desperate to hear from you."

At her words he went instantly alert. "Go home? I'm here to *take* her home."

Doubt clouded Farah's soft grey eyes. "Morley...she left nigh an hour ago."

He seized her shoulders, panic landing like a stone in his gut, squeezing the blood from his veins. "An hour? Did you see her leave? Which way did she turn? Did she hire a hansom?"

"I confess I was busy with other details when she said goodbye." Anxiety crept into her eyes as well. "Do you have any reason to think she's in danger?"

He wanted to say no, but something didn't allow it. "She's fainted once already and what with the investigation into her father...the story in the papers today...I don't know. I sense peril."

Next to him, Ash's rangy frame tensed beneath his fine suit. "Those aren't instincts you should ignore, Cutter. Go back to your house, tear it apart, I'll look around here and we'll rally if she's not found immediately."

"I'll ask Dorian," Farah said, visibly shaken. "He disappeared some time ago; I think he's hiding with Trenwyth."

Morley clapped Ash on the shoulder before he launched himself from the landing and down the stairs to the road. He ran the mile home flat out with lung-bursting speed. He juked about pedestrians and dove behind and around carriages to the stunned approbation of many a driver.

He didn't care. Nothing mattered. He would tear the city apart. Hell, he'd burn it to the ground to find her. He'd dismantle every brick. Scorch every spire. Everything that'd ever mattered to him fell away in her absence, exposing exactly what she'd become to him in this short amount of time.

Did he fear for his unborn child? Of course, he did. But it was *her* name echoing in every footfall. Prudence. His wife. His woman.

As he rounded the corner to his own street, he allowed himself to slow at the sight of a familiar coach idling in front of the golden brick terraces. He felt the fear leach out of him with each panting breath when he found his wife standing on their porch, staring at him as if he were a wolf loose in the middle of town.

"Morley," Dorian Blackwell greeted him from the carriage window with the seemingly disembodied head and conceited smile of a Cheshire cat. "I've just spent the most entertaining hour with your lovely wife."

The adrenaline still surging through him mixed with a knee-weakening sense of relief as Morley tried to lock eyes with Prudence. Instead of allowing it, she gave him her back to let herself in the house, closing the door behind her with a fatal click.

Morley fell on Blackwell like a rabid dog. "Where the fuck have the two of you been for an hour? I just came from Trenwyth Place, where Farah is looking for you. If I didn't know how absolute your devotion to your wife is, I'd pull you out of that carriage and beat you to death for being alone with mine."

To his surprise, Blackwell's smile widened as he held up his hands. "Hardly alone, I conducted my sisters-in-law, Lady Ravencroft and Lady Thorne, to the Savoy where they are staying while in town from Scotland. I informed Farah thusly before we left."

The very plausible explanation stole the wind from his sails.

"Yes, well...she did not mark you."

"We'll blame that on her third glass of wine," Blackwell chuckled fondly.

Morley scowled, rippling with displeasure. "Why didn't you drop Prudence here first? This is rather out of your way."

"It was upon her request." Blackwell's one uncovered eye flicked a meaning-laden glance toward the ominously closed door. "If I'm honest, she wasn't in any great haste to go home."

Morley stood on his walk feeling like the war banner of a defeated army. Trampled. Torn asunder. And rather pointless anymore. He nodded his thanks to Blackwell, not feeling capable of forming kind words. "You might want to hurry back and tell Ash and your wife all is well," he muttered.

"Certainly." After a hesitation, Blackwell leaned out the window. "I know killers, Morley. I am one. You are one. We can sense each other, I think. Surely you already know she is not."

The moment when the truth collided inside of him

felt as though a thunderbolt had reached out of the sky and touched him. He suddenly knew what to do. He knew what to say.

Blackwell continued, "If you want my advice—"

"I don't." Morley pulled an abrupt about-face, and marched up the stairs to his home, hoping his wife hadn't locked him out for good.

CHAPTER 17

*P*rudence had known he'd follow her. That he'd have much to say. She didn't bother readying for bed as she felt no great need to confront him in a state of undress.

She felt vulnerable enough.

An acid taste crawled up the back of her throat, as she perched on the very edge of the mattress and laced her own fingers together in a painful clench at the sound of his footsteps coming down the hall.

She regretted how she'd acted before. Even after the Ladies' Aid Society had supported and encouraged her position...she still wished she'd have not lost her temper.

She hadn't exactly meant to tell the Ladies' Aid Society matrons her story, but Farah Blackwell had taken one look at her upon arrival and swept her into a circle of the warmest and most extraordinary women, who all demanded to know what was wrong so they could help.

Once she'd recounted everything in various shades of detail, Pru became surprised at just how eventful the past three or so months had been. No *wonder* she felt as deflated as a collapsed souffle. No wonder she'd been so unaccountably upset this afternoon.

Shame oiled her insides as she thought about the intimacy of the confession Morley had shared before their row. His sister was a protected and painful secret. His avenging of her death a susceptible concession for a man such as he.

He'd handed her the power to destroy him, and she'd whipped him with it.

After her ire had cooled...she'd had to admit he'd made some salient points. Even though the points skewered her through with injustice and agonizing distress.

She knew they needed to have a discussion, that she needed to make concessions just as much as he did. However, she couldn't bring herself to do it tonight. Not now, when she felt as though her entire being, both inside and out, was just one taut, brittle nerve flayed open and exposed.

Though she expected it, she still jumped at his gentle knock.

Closing her eyes against the dread, she silently pled. *Please, I can take no more. Not tonight.*

The door opened, and she knew she should stand and face him, that she should gather up her reserves of strength and determination, notch her chin high, and meet him will for strong will until they overcame their problem.

But, everything at the moment seemed as insurmountable as Mount Kilimanjaro. Producing tears would be a chore, let alone peeling herself off the bed.

She tensed as he neared, her eyes unable to lift above the carpet as she focused on steeling what was left of herself for this. For him.

He stood in front of her for a fraught and silent moment, and when she couldn't bring herself to lift her head, he did something that took her breath.

He knelt like a penitent on the carpet before her, reached out, and covered her clenched hands with his own. The contact thawed her frigid fingers, unleashing tendrils of warmth that radiated up her arms to ignite the tiniest glow of hope into her shivering heart.

"I'm going to tell you something, Prudence, and I don't require a response. In fact..." he hesitated. "It would be better if you just let me bungle through it, as we both know I will."

She swallowed in reply, staring down at his large hands. At once so masculine and elegant, so capable and so brutal.

His voice was paradoxically decisive and uncertain, but it lacked the harshness of before. It contained a hoarse note too tame for desperation and too bleak for nonchalance.

Composure, it seemed, eluded them both.

"Deceit has been a relentless part of my entire life," he began, dousing a bit of her hopes. Tempting her to curl in upon herself like a salted snail.

But she didn't move.

And he didn't stop.

"The only things I remember of my parents, are the lies they used to hurt each other with. When my father died, Caroline and I survived only through dishonest means. Everything we had could be taken by a craftier thief, a better con artist. It was the game we learned to play on the streets. After she...after I..." He broke off, filling his chest with an endless inhale as he pressed his thumbs into the grip of her fists as if he could likewise penetrate her closed heart.

Prudence relaxed her grip incrementally, doing her best to allow her insides to mirror the action. To open. To hear him.

"My parents never documented our birth, so I had no papers. I read the name Carlton off an advertisement for the Carlton Football Club posted on the building next to the military office where I joined up." He made a rueful noise, shaking his head at the younger man. "Another lie I told, one I thought would have no consequences because I fully intended to die in some hole on another continent somewhere. I never thought I'd live to see England again. Instead, I shot a swath through entire countries. Killing for an empire that fabricates falsehoods and misrepresentations to the world as if words like humanity and honor do not exist in the face of progress and expansion. And then..."

He turned her hands palm up to caress the delicate lines there with his thumbs as he continued. "I became a police officer, of all things. And I implore you to find me a vocation wherein someone is confronted with more deception. Not only do criminals lie to me for every kind of reason, but regular, frightened, generally honest people do as well, merely for what I am and the authority I wield. My subordinates consistently report errors and embellishments, and many of them, apparently, use the uniform for criminal enterprise."

He crept closer on his knees, powerful thighs bunching and straining against his trousers as he entreated her to hear him. "So much of my day-to-day life is spent unraveling untruths and investigating inaccuracies. I see them everywhere, and because of that, I think I've come to expect them from everyone."

"I understand," she murmured, as a sense of sympathy infiltrated her gloom. Such a life was not easy, such a mindset awfully arduous and burdensome. "You're telling me this is why you are unable to trust."

He gathered her hands to his chest as he brought their gazes even. Anchoring them against his pounding heart, he placed a fingertip beneath her jaw, nudging her to look up at him. Something shone in his gaze she'd never marked before. A gentle contrition. The glimmer of vulnerability. "Sweetheart. I'm telling you why I've been a fool. An unmitigated bastard. Prudence…I'm sorry."

She would have sworn her heart ceased beating if not for the thrumming in her ears. Had she heard him correctly? Or was she fantasizing this?

Had she fainted again?

Her gaze flew to his, searching for signs that she was truly going mad.

"You…don't have to—"

"I do," he insisted, his visage claimed by an emotion both desolate and resolute. "The truth is, I don't know you like a man should know his wife, but that is my failing, not yours. Beyond that, I think you are an honest person, possessed of integrity I've only ever pretended to have."

She stalled, blinking over at him in wonder. "You do?"

His features softened as he regarded her with such infinite tenderness, she felt as though it might melt her completely. "Yes. You're so open and vulnerable. You tell me everything you're thinking. You tell me what you want, and what you feel and what you know to be true. Hell, that very first night, your shocking candidness was the first thing that drew me to you. From the beginning of it all…I've been inclined to believe every word from your mouth."

The mouth he referred to fell open in abject incredulity. "Then…why?"

"Because everyone—literally *everyone* else—is a liar, including me, and with that, I have made my peace. But Prudence," he brushed his thumb up her jaw, his eyes touching her face everywhere, searching for something.

"You are the one person who can truly betray me, do you understand?"

She tilted her neck, pulling away from his distracting touch to shake her head with incomprehension.

"You're going to make me say it," he realized wryly, giving the impression of a boy squirming beneath a scolding adult's insistence he explain himself. The electric blue of his eyes disappeared as he hid his expression behind his lids. "You are the epitome of every desire or dream I've conceived of since before I can remember, and that is a very specific kind of torment. An unparalleled beauty, a superb lover, a woman of grace and kindness and intellect whom I can only respect and admire. A fantasy in the flesh, here in my house. With *my* name."

He lifted his empty hand to swipe it through his hair. "Christ, sometimes I have to just stand in the hall and stare at the door you sleep behind because I cannot believe my luck, my undeserved good fortune. You are *here*. You are real. And so is our child."

A sob escaped her. Not one adorned by tears, but disbelief. "But..." She didn't even know where to start. A part of her had awakened at his words, the part made of need and love and hope and happiness. "But...only this morning you thought that I—You said—"

"I know what I said." His jaw tightened before he continued, his brow crimping with earnest anguish. "Trust is not a word I understand. Faith is a foreign concept to me. Despite that, my instincts have screamed at me to trust you." His gaze cast down as his jaw worked over powerful emotion.

"And then that insidious voice inside of me warns that if I *did* believe you, and then discovered you lied? That you'd somehow swindled me, possibly the most incredulous man alive. Well...I've survived any number of disappointments, treacheries, and sorrows. But I don't see the way back from that. You could break me, Prudence, don't you see? It's why I've been pushing you so hard. Why I almost needed you to be guilty, so the terrible truth—if it was a truth—would be out. So it was safe to fall for you because you were just as dishonest as the entire world. Just as deceitful as me."

Prudence yearned to say so many things. To ask so many questions. To soothe him and set his churning mind at rest, but now that he'd begun, his torrent of words tumbled out in escape, like the freed captives of a heavily fortified prison.

Her hand stayed against his heart hammering beneath the hard muscle of his chest as he released his grip to tenderly cradle her face in his palms. The spark of warmth he'd ignited within her bloomed to an incandescent radiance, reanimating the spirit within her.

"I meant what I said earlier," he whispered, his gaze searching hers, beseeching her. "Even though I was being an inconsiderate ass when I said it. I don't care about scandal in the paper but for the fact that it distresses you. I'll send anyone to the devil before they hurt you. I am a knight. A man with a code. A warrior with a creed. I vow, from this moment onward to be *your* knight, wife. Someone who is honor bound to protect your name, your life, and your soul. I swear to you, that before this child is born, the world will know who did this. And they will know you didn't." His voice grew in fervency until he finished with the one thing she'd yearned to hear. "They will believe you, as I believe you."

His words eroded any thought of erecting barricades between them. Her next sob was filled with joy as she flung her arms around his neck, pulled him toward her body, and brought his lips down to receive her kiss.

The kiss that contained her heart.

She was lost. She'd been lost to him since the moment she'd tumbled into his lap. A fated fall, she realized, as if destiny had pushed her over.

And he'd caught her, as he ever would.

The moment tilted from overly emotional to intensely erotic in the space of an instant as he gathered her close and crawled up onto the bed, pulling her beneath him.

He was a remarkably self-contained man, her husband…until he wasn't.

His kisses began as soft as prayers and then built in power and demand as his grip on his own control became less tenuous. Hot glides of his tongue became deep, mating dances with her answering passions.

She melted beneath him, and he filled her spaces with the force of his ardor.

A voice inside urged her to let go of the brittle, desperate edge she'd been clinging to, realizing it was safe. She wouldn't fall. No, she'd join him here, to dance among the clouds.

His kiss contained so many things they'd still left unsaid. So many parts of his fractured being. He was at once the Knight of Shadows. A man possessed of unmerciful darkness, devouring her with breath-stealing intensity. And so, too, was he the Chief Inspector, assessing and observant as he brushed his lips across hers, creating delicious friction with his mouth, evoking an ache in her sex that demanded satisfaction.

And maybe the thief was here with her, threatening to steal her heart, even the parts of it she was still afraid to give. There was the sense of marvelous reverence in his touch, a bit of disbelief that belonged to the youth he'd been, the one unused to any kindness or affection.

Though she felt a fervency in him, he lingered over her mouth, kissing her with slow, languorous efficiency and tantalizing promise.

For the first time, he kissed her as if he should be doing nothing else. As if his mind was empty of naught but this moment. And the next. As if they were immortals who might go on kissing for a hundred years and never tire of it.

And, indeed, she wished it were so.

If ever there was a moment in need of prolonging, it was this one.

And yet…a pressure built within her that urged her legs apart so he could settle his big body between them. The barrel of his erection ground against her between the impediments of their clothing, and she was suddenly anxious to be rid of them.

She wanted all of his skin next to hers. All of his heat and his need and his sex.

As if reading her mind, he broke the kiss, lifting away from her only to tackle the placket of tiny buttons that stretched from her chin to her waist.

He made it to her clavicles before ripping the garment open, and lowering back to swallow her faint protestations with more distracting kisses.

"I'll buy you a dozen bodices," he whispered against her mouth. "If you only let me tear them from you each night."

Appeased, she let him unwrap her like a present, releasing this strap, undoing that ribbon, unclasping a hook. His mouth explored every inch he uncovered as if finding it for the first time.

Her chemise caught beneath her swollen, tender breasts as he dragged it up, and she felt them pop free with a little bounce before he swiped it over her head and tossed it somewhere on the floor.

"You are so beautiful," he groaned.

"So are you," she replied with breathless candor.

His smile was touched with chagrin as, instead of reaching for her breasts, he lifted his fingers to her hair, deftly searching the plait for pins, pulling them from a head she hadn't known was aching until the pressure had ceased.

He returned to kissing her with new depth and untried angles as his fingers wended through the braid, unspooling it softly until her hair fell in soft waves down her bare back.

Questing fingers slid up her spine, thrilling her to the core and mingling a shivering chill with the answering heat of need.

No longer willing to stay dormant, Prudence slid her arms around him, sinking her fingers into the heavy, lambent locks of his neatly trimmed hair before lowering them to tug at his collar.

His fingers lifted to help, and their hands tangled in a newfound haste to divest each other of the trappings of their garments.

Once they'd wrestled themselves naked, he climbed up her body like a cat, laying her back beneath him as he pressed a muscled thigh dusted with golden hair between her legs.

They spoke in smiles and sighs as she tested the taut ridges of muscle at his ribs, and down over his corrugated abdomen to reach for the hard and tender flesh below. She still marveled at how silky the skin of his sex was, pulled canvas tight and pulsing with blood and lust. It was hot velvet poured over steel, and she loved nothing more than the moment it fit inside her. As if he'd always been made for her. The key to her lock.

A apropos metaphor, as whenever he'd finished with her, she became quite unlatched. Undone. Open.

He began to chart a course with his lips down her body, pulling his sex from her grasp with a plaintive moan. A little moisture lingered on her fingertips, and she knew by now that meant his arousal had reached a peak. That he approached a point of no return.

His golden head bent over her breast to release a steaming breath against the puckered peak. He browsed at the nipple with only his lips, laved at it with a barely there lick of his tongue.

Moaning her encouragement, Pru squirmed beneath the attentions, not too far gone to be touched by his conscientiousness. Her breasts had been unabatingly tender before, and he was the kind of man who didn't forget that.

One who always cared about her pleasure and her comfort.

He didn't use his teeth until he nuzzled into the valley between them, nipping at the skin and then soothing it with a velvety lick.

In the light of the lamp on her dresser table, he became a silhouette of sin, his powerful body hunkered over hers as if protecting his next meal.

And a meal, she was certain to become.

He swiped his tongue across his lips, making them glisten before he dipped his head to press a butterfly-soft kiss to the delicate swell of her belly.

The sight of it touched her eyes with the burn of emotion to rival that of the heat of desire. It was him that put this child inside of her. This act. This bit of miracle of making allowed mere mortals, the culmination of which one might call a glimpse of divinity.

"Mine," he growled possessively. The tickle of his breath against her bare stomach set every hair on her body to vibrating in awareness. Her muscles coiled with need, and her knees fell further apart, inviting his kiss to the throbbing center of her.

Offering herself.

His hands smoothed up her taut thighs as he nuzzled into the soft, fleecy curls, inhaling deeply.

"Christ, you're perfect," he breathed against her sex, causing an intimate spasm of anticipation.

His tongue split her in one upward stroke.

He kissed her there as he'd done her mouth, with feverish ardor. His tongue slow and long, hot and hard as it tangled with the satin of her intimate flesh. Sliding forward, withdrawing, slipping in and about as she writhed beneath him.

Struggling to breathe, Pru reached for him, lacing her fingers in his hair as he nibbled and tugged with his lips, explored with his tongue as if he couldn't decide which part tasted the best.

And then he was there, at the tight, clenching opening of her body, delving against it, entering her in shallow thrusts that sensitized her so exceedingly, her hips came off the bed in a sinuous arch.

Unable to contain herself, she chased the pleasure of his mouth in lithe, supple movements. She trembled and strained, danced and bucked, until he was forced to seize her hips and pin her down, so he could thoroughly dismantle her by enclosing his mouth over the stiff, tender bud.

Euphoria suffused her in spasms of delight as the culmination of desire broke over her in wave after wet wave of release. She wanted to thank every pagan god of sex and sin, and she rather thought the rhythmic, ecstatic sounds she made might have paid sufficient tribute as he wrung from her a bliss she'd never before reached.

Only once he was certain she'd been sufficiently brought back to earth, did he leave her with one last naughty kiss before wiping the gloss of her from his mouth with the back of his hand.

His features were taut with a particular wickedness as he kneeled up between her parted thighs and gazed down at her exposed sex with the reverence of a man at the end of a grail quest.

Suddenly shy, she went to close her knees to hide

the still-pulsing flesh from his view. He stopped her by shaping his hand over her mons, stroking it gently, dipping inside to wet his fingers, then spreading her nectar on the jut of his sex.

He lifted to retrieve a pillow, and effortlessly maneuvered her to slide it beneath her hips, tilting them upward.

Leaning over her, he caught himself on his elbows as he slid the head of his shaft along the slick cleft, lodging against her entrance.

His eyes burned down into hers, as he fed her his cock inch after pulsing inch until he'd embedded himself so deep, she felt the stirrings of a new pleasure. Of a glory left untapped.

Something unfurled as he seated inside her. Something previously dormant and unaccountably sweet. They'd been lovers a handful of ecstatic times now, and each time had been incredible in its own right.

But this. This connection...it reached beyond the physical. She could feel his heartbeat, but in her own chest. The cavern of his loneliness and the space she took up inside it, making it smaller.

His gaze became incredulous, and he gasped out her name as if unsure of what was happening.

"I know," she whispered, drawing her hands down the splendor of his skin. "I feel it too."

The uneven struggle of his breathing called to her, and she twined her arms about him, pulling him in for a searing kiss. Tasting her pleasure on his lips. The essence of his skill and her unending desire for him.

Then he moved.

He set a deep, primal rhythm, angling into her with maddening proficiency. She felt the heavy weight of him inside her, against her, over and around her, cocooning her body with his.

Though her limbs felt liquid with the torpor that

followed such a consuming climax, she couldn't bring herself to remain still beneath him. She lifted her knees to his sides, wrapping her legs around his pistoning hips.

His cock touched something inside of her, eliciting an instant pleasure so keen, it bordered on pain. She arched toward it. Or maybe away, feeling as though he'd thrust a rod of lightning against her spine and the currents lifted her into thunderclouds where a storm shook her asunder.

She was dimly aware of his own breath catching before a sound ripped from him, something like a growl snagging on velvet as his muscles built upon themselves. Tightening. Trembling. Seizing. Before the warm rush of his release spread inside of her.

It took her a while to find her way back from the stars. Her husband, as was his way, took care of everything. He washed her, then himself, pausing at the lamp to turn down the light, melting the shadows down the walls until they were only encased in a dim amber glow.

He settled them both beneath the coverlet, resting his shoulders against a pile of pillows, and pulling her to lean back against his chest so he could rest his chin on her head and twine his arms around her. Big hands encased her tightening belly, and he idly stroked her as she lazed in the aftermath. Their limbs entwined and the fine down on his legs tickled her bottom, but she was too spent to care.

Prudence tuned to the aftershocks of their joining, the twitches and throbs of her body, the resonant beats of her heart. She loved the scent of them, the bloom of sweat and heat and come, subtle and alluring. Tempting and erotic.

He'd never held her like this before. He'd...never stayed.

Lanced with a sudden anxiety, she swallowed. "If you're going to leave, you'd better go now." She injected a teasing note into her voice. "I'll be cross if you wake me later."

"I would stay..." he hesitated. "If you'd have me."

"What about the Knight of Shadows?" she protested, angling her head to look up at him. "Doesn't he have somewhere to be?"

His hands coasted up her ribs and gently palmed the weights of her breasts, testing the thin, silky skin beneath. "He's exactly where he should be."

She relaxed against him, her heart swelling until it felt two times too large for its chamber. This was bliss. This moment. Were she a cat, she'd be purring.

"I'm going to be a better husband to you," he murmured, his voice full of self-approbation as he curled around her as if he could create a buffer of skin and muscle and blood from the rest of the world.

Nestling deeper against him, she turned to press a kiss to his jaw, feeling the tug of sleep against her lids. "You already are."

CHAPTER 18

*W*hat they needed was a honeymoon, Morley decided.

He'd eschewed the very idea at first—no—that wasn't right. He'd never even *entertained* the notion for obvious reasons.

But now…

Now he'd lost all ability to focus on his work.

Reports needed briefing, men required orders and permissions, warrants begged approval to go to the courts. He had half a dozen active crime scenes in this borough, alone, and an iron worker's strike waiting to happen right on London Bridge.

He signed the correct papers, assigned the appropriate investigators, listened as best he could to debriefings and such. But now, as he waded through reports, he realized he'd read the same paragraph going on fifteen times now.

He wanted to just send it all to the devil and climb back into bed with his wife.

He'd been late to work for the first time in fifteen years this morning, because he'd lost track of time just watching her sleep.

Though he usually kept the blinds pulled dark and

240

tight, Prudence preferred to sleep with them thrown open so she would appreciate the light as it played across the city, and wake to the sunshine beckoning her out of bed.

He balked at the idea, at first, but then he'd woken to the pillars of dawn painting the lavish dark waves of her hair with the beautiful iridescence of a raven's wing as it trailed across the white silk of the pillow. She might have been some mythical heroine of a fairy tale, locked away in a torpor spell, awaiting him to slay her dragons and kiss her awake.

He might have done it, too, if little smudges of shadow hadn't lurked beneath her fluttering eyes. Her breaths had been so soft and deep, her onyx lashes a stark contrast over cheeks paler than he liked.

Instead, he propped himself on his elbow and simply studied her in a rare, unguarded moment. It only seemed fair. She'd stripped him bare, laid him wide open and dangerously close to defenseless. The intimacy he felt forming between them, the bond that wove between his ribs and hers, stitching their ticking hearts together, was made of some stronger material than the steel and ice he'd encased around his heart.

Something magical, probably, if one believed in that sort of ridiculous thing.

Which he didn't.

And yet, when had he ever slept so well? When had he ever been on the precipice of such a sheer and infinite ledge, and felt so safe?

She really did sleep the sleep of the innocent. Even after all the wicked things they'd done together.

And the ones he still wanted to do.

Christ, they'd need weeks. Perhaps longer. Honeymoons made so much sense now.

He could take her to Antigua to swim in a warm ocean as blue as her eyes. Or maybe closer, somewhere continental? They could cosset themselves in the far north beneath ceilings of glass, watching the Northern Lights snap overhead as he made love to her on soft furs like a Viking lord. Or they could visit a Moroccan spice market or Turkish bazaar and sleep beneath lattices of flowing silk with air spiced with exotic blossoms.

He'd let her decide, of course. He didn't care.

For the first time in…maybe ever…the idea of doing a bit of nothing actually appealed to him. So long as it was with her. He would lounge like an Olympian, feeding his goddess any ambrosia she desired. Learning her, consuming her. Mind, body, and soul.

"Wherever your mind is, I want to be there too."

Morley jolted back to the present to see a smirking Christopher Argent lounging against his office doorframe.

"You're not invited," he said irritably.

"Ah." A sly understanding sparked in the man's clear eyes. "Speaking of your wife. A messenger boy came to deliver this. She's gone to her sister's to help pack some things."

Morley snatched it from his hand, his ire spilling over to impatience. "You read it?"

"It was on a card, not in an envelope," Argent remonstrated, not a man used to defending himself. "How could I help myself?"

"Unscrupulous cretin." Morley's words had no heat as he looked at his name scrawled in flawless feminine script.

Argent's shoulder lifted. "I've been called worse." He stalled, lifting his hand to his jaw to rub at some tension there. "Morley…the murder case you handed over to me some months back, the Stags of St. James…"

He looked up at the uncertain note in Argent's voice

before he'd been able to read the note. The Stags of St. James…a case growing colder by the day.

The very investigation that'd started this entire thing.

"What about it?"

Stoic features arranged themselves carefully, as if Argent knew he was treading on unstable ground. "I interviewed a man recently who intimated one of the Stags of St. James had regularly lain with a high-born, dark-haired beauty. He said she was a, and I quote, 'Good girl.'"

Good girl…as in…*Goode* girl?

Morley went very still, carefully examining the effect the information had on him.

It wasn't his Goode girl. He knew that. He trusted that. His wife had told him it had been a discussion between her friend and her elder sister that'd sent her looking for a stag in the first place.

"Prudence has a sister with dark hair," he said. "She's married, but could have used her maiden name for such purposes. She and her husband, William Mosby, the Viscount Woodhaven, were sent to Italy by the Baron."

Agent's brows made a slow decent as he pondered this. "How does a Baron send a Viscount to Italy, one wonders? Even if he is a son-in-law, I can't see a man like Woodhaven being easily told what to do."

"*Impoverished* Viscount," Morley clarified, rifling through some papers to find the slim file he'd made of Woodhaven on a whim. "Honoria's dowry and monthly upkeep is all that keeps them afloat, I've gathered."

"Honoria?" Argent echoed, his voice sharp as a blade in the close office. "If she's in Italy…how can your wife be meeting her at a row house in Gloucester Square?"

Morley's skin flushed hot, though his blood felt like

ice in his veins as he looked down to scan his wife's hastily scrawled message.

Darling,

My sister has sent a carriage and request for my help. It seems Honoria is ill-treated by William, and has decided to leave him. I'll be at her residence at Gloucester Square to help her pack and figure out a new temporary living situation. I don't imagine I'll be late for dinner, though I warn you we might have a third guest at, what I've come to view as, our rather sacred suppers. I apologize in advance.

Yours,

Prudence

His thumb brushed over the word *Darling* before he stood, buttoned his jacket, and retrieved his hat. A slick of unease oozed between his ribs and he knew in his gut that he needed to go to his wife.

Puzzled by the strength of the instinct over such a trivial note, he stopped to inform Argent. "Their stay on the continent wasn't supposed to be indefinite, however..." He rubbed at a queer weight lodged beneath his sternum. "Something's not right."

It was all he needed to say to receive a grim nod from Argent. "I'm accompanying you to Gloucester Square, obviously."

They arrived a miraculous half hour later, after galloping through the streets as if the whole of London was Rotten Row.

The house was handsome, but not what one would expect of a Viscount, and Morley could only imagine what a blowhard like Woodhaven thought of his diminished circumstances.

Morley unceremoniously shoved past a sputtering butler intent upon denying them entrance, and found Honoria in a dimly lit drawing room, squinting down at a book with a glass of wine in her hand.

It wasn't even half one in the afternoon.

Dark, raptor-keen eyes lifted, advertising that the woman was not yet in her cups.

"Chief Inspector," she greeted blithely before snapping the book closed and gathering the voluminous, cream-colored skirts of her dress to stand.

Morley was given to understand it was widely accepted that Honoria was the great beauty of the Goode daughters, but he couldn't bring himself to agree. There was a sharpness to the symmetry of her features that he'd never prefer to look upon. Too many pointed angles and dramatic lines. He much preferred his wife's pleasant, ethereal comeliness.

"Do come in. I haven't been able to properly meet dear Prudence's husband. Please," she gestured to a piece of furniture that must have been expensive half a century prior, "sit down and I'll ring for tea."

"Where is Prudence?" he queried, eschewing her civil offer. His hand couldn't seem to release the door latch. He wouldn't relax until he set eyes on his wife.

"Certainly not here." Her features were smooth and cool as tempered glass.

Morley's heart stalled. "Then where? Where did the carriage take her?"

The only outward sign of a response was the slight tilt of her head. "Are you telling me you have…lost my sister, Chief Inspector? Because I assure you the last place she would be likely to venture is this…woebegone house."

"If not lost." He shoved the card at her. "Then she's been taken."

"I'll search the house," Argent said, neglecting to ask for permission as he began opening every door down the hall of the first floor.

Honoria scanned the note two full times, her composure crumbling like the walls of an ancient fortress ruin. "Dear God." She covered her mouth as eyes brimming with moisture flew to his. "William forged this note. I swear it. If she is in one of our carriages then... he has her."

"Woodhaven," Morley said, feeling his muscles harden at the uttered name. He never liked the man's reaction to Prudence, but he'd dismissed it as the lunacy of grief. A brief investigation of him had him dismissing the man as a coddled milksop dining out on his family's ancient name. If he'd returned from Italy so soon, could he intend to take revenge on the woman he blamed for his best mate's death?

"He was so angry, about so many things," Honoria revealed in a horrified whisper. "But I didn't think he'd —" Unable to finish the thought, she rushed forward. "Please. Come with me. I might know where they are."

A cold blade of dread slid between his ribs, threatening his own poise. "Would he hurt her because of Sutherland?"

She caught her lips between her teeth as if biting them could hold back tears. "If I had to guess, it has something to do with me."

"What do you have to do with it?"

"My husband is an obsessive man, Chief Inspector," she said, revealing the shadows that haunted the façade of serenity as she stepped past him to reach for her shawl in the front entry. "He is vindictive and manipulative. The only thing that controls him, is his need to control me. His need to *make* me love him. Make me... God. You can't know what life with him is like."

"If he has touched a hair on Prudence's head, you won't have to worry about living with him anymore," Morley said darkly. "Where have they gone?"

"William told me he and some partners of one of his investment schemes had business at the Chariton's Dock in Southwark."

Morley didn't know the place. He thought he knew

every inch of this city, but that dock didn't even ring a bell.

"There's an old flour storage warehouse there. My father bought it years ago, but he's done nothing with it. I know William's been working out of it. I can show you where it is."

"How many men would he have with him?" Argent asked from where he glided down the hall. "Would these partners be armed, perchance?"

The question drew her eyes wide with panic, but she shook her head. "I-I don't know. I rarely mark my husband when he's discussing business. You have to understand, he's never had one of his ventures succeed." Her brows knit together. "But this one, it's been profitable. He's not been able to keep himself from throwing the income in my face but...I don't have the details."

"I'm going." Morley rushed back toward the door.

"So am I." Honoria dogged him down the steps and onto the front walk before he turned and seized her by the shoulders.

His grip gentled when he felt her tense and flinch.

"You're staying here," he fought to keep his voice gentle against the rising tide of his own urgency.

"She's my *sister*. Besides, you just said you don't know where it is."

Argent jogged down the stairs after them. "We might need backup if these associates are as shady as they are likely to be. I'll go for Dorian and Ash."

"Very good." Morley angled himself in the opposite direction, lamenting how much city lay between Southwark and Mayfair. "I'll meet you at the docks."

Argent stopped him with a hand on his arm. "Is that wise? To go alone?"

"I don't give a dusty fuck if it's wise," he growled. "It's what is happening."

The large man assessed him with that cold, cold gaze of his. "Are you good, Morley? Where is your rage?"

"What sort of question is that?" he asked impatiently.

"An important one," Argent insisted in that monotonous way of his. "Where is it? Because I can't see it. Is the fury deep or is it close to the surface? Can you make the decisions that have to be made? Because that is your wife and unborn child. What if you arrive to find the worst—?"

"Don't," Morley snarled, wrenching his arm away and shoving his finger in the assassin's brutal face. They stood like that for a moment, Morley's breath sawing in and out of his chest. "Just...*don't.*"

It didn't bear consideration. It would be the loss that shattered him completely.

Morley glanced at his reflection in the window. He didn't look like himself. Harsh. Mean. Drawn tight and locked down. His eyes gone flat.

Dead.

"I'm going to get my wife," he said. "You do what you will, I'll do what I must."

Argent nodded, leaving him with his departing words. "Wait for us, Morley. Don't let your fury endanger her life. I made that mistake once and Millie paid for it with blood."

Morley leapt onto his horse and reached down to pull Honoria up behind him.

"I didn't know she was with child," Honoria said into his ear. "Is it...George's?"

"It's mine," he growled, gathering up his reins. "Now, I'm going to ride like hell," he warned. "Can you hold on?"

"Like hell is the only way we Goode Girls ride," she said, her voice flinty with an admirable strength.

Morley spurred his horse out into the square, astonishing society matrons and bustling errand staff as he went.

Where *was* his rage? What emotion lived in him now?

Fury was often hot. A constant companion of masculine brutality he assumed every man carried within him.

But not now. *This* emotion was stark. Unutterably bleak. An icy chill that echoed through a vast yawning abyss opening in his chest. This was what caused men to summon demons and sacrifice virgins. This rage. This power. This need to crush and consume. This desperate hope to stop all things beyond his control if only to protect that which was most precious.

Men like Argent. They owned their darkness. They wore it on their skin. He'd always had to hide his behind a badge of gold. Or a black mask. He had to pretend the darkness wasn't there. Waiting. Breeding. Growing.

His was patient fury. A glowing ember of ever-present wrath.

And now, that fury was about to be unleashed.

CHAPTER 19

*P*rudence wondered if the fact that she carried a child made her more or less likely to survive her brother-in-law's madness.

It was the most awful thing she'd ever had to contemplate.

He'd shoved her in the corner of a long warehouse with a labyrinth of wooden crates haphazardly strewn about the moldy stone floor. Crates he and his four comrades were now frantically prying apart with crowbars, flinging the lids, and diving into as if they might contain the holy grail.

The afternoon was grey, but abundant windows filtered light into the two-story warehouse that was little more than an open floor free of landings or offices. One wide wooden gate would open right onto the docks where steam-powered boats unloaded their goods for storage and dissemination out of the wide bay facing Water Street. From the skeleton of a silo taking up nearly the entire street-side entrance and the strange, layered architecture of the roof, Prudence thought maybe this had once been a place to store grain or flour.

Impossible to tell now.

She'd suffered the bulk of her paralyzing panic in the carriage, where William had shoved a pistol in her face and screamed at the driver to ride on. Her saving grace was that he had done a horrible job of tying her wrists and ankles.

Thank God.

Taking advantage of their distraction, she worked frantically on the bonds. The ones at her hands were loosening, of that she had no doubt, she just had to keep at it.

It was the only thing that gave her hope. The one reason she kept a tenuous hold on her sanity.

Because once she was free, she'd have to figure out her next step...

How to get past five men with pistols tucked into vest holsters or waistbands when she had no weapon at all.

One thing at a time.

At least he wouldn't get away with it, she thought. If the worst happened...her husband would miss her at dinner, and he'd come looking. He'd *know* who had her.

Morley...a well of longing surged inside with such visceral desperation, it escaped on a sob.

William straightened from another fruitless search, slicking his thinning hair back from a sweating brow as he speared her with a pinched glare. A gentleman of leisure like him was unused to such strenuous exertion. Especially one as soft and bloated as he.

"Your fucking husband," he sniped, as if reading where her thoughts had just been lingering. "Gave the order for old Goode to send me abroad without so much as a by-your-leave. Just to save your narrow hide." Thin lips parted in a leer so chock-full of disgust, she could barely look at him. "What did he think, that I would take orders from him? A *nobody?*"

She wanted to tell him that her husband wasn't a

nobody. That he was more advantageous a spouse than a dozen viscounts or even a hundred dukes.

She held her temper, for the sake of her child.

"He thought you'd help your family in crisis," she said evenly, trying to keep him calm. "William, if this is about Geor—"

"*This family*, so uppity for such low rank." He shook his head and began to wedge his crowbar into the next waist-high crate. "I've done my part for this family, merely by elevating it from the slums of mediocrity."

He threw his body weight down on the crowbar and tipped the lid aside before wading into the shavings of protective packaging. "Why do they even allow Barons to keep titles, anyhow?" he said as though muttering to himself. "They're hardly needed these days, it's not the Middle Ages. And your father, debasing himself with this shipping venture to make his fortunes, only to remain so miserly with his stipends." His lip curled in disgust. "A tighter bankbook doesn't exist in Christendom. *Where is it!*" In a shocking explosion of temper, he pushed over an entire crate. Prudence cringed away as it splintered, spilling an array of silks that unspooled in a riot of color.

"What are you looking for?" she asked, hoping to keep him talking as the knot at her right hand *finally* gave enough for her to slip through it, rendering the other one useless.

Still, she kept her hands behind her back.

"Payment for the risk I took," he snarled. "Payback! I've a barge waiting at the end of the dock, and we'll be out to sea before we're missed with a crate full of cash."

"If this is about money…"

"Of course, it's about money!" he roared "Every bloody thing is about money these days. Birth and titles and blue blood mean nothing anymore in this churning, blasphemous machine that is our nation now. What happened to the nobility?"

She leveled him her coolest stare. "Are you acting nobly now, William?"

"Don't question me, you sanctimonious cow." He struck her with the back of his hand, wrenching her neck to the side. Pain singed her cheek and brought tears to her eyes.

An explosion shattered the very next moment.

Prudence managed to look back in time to see one of the men nearest a window drop to the crate he'd been bent over.

Missing the top of his head.

She covered her open mouth with both of her hands to contain the scream bubbling up from inside of her. It escaped as a raw, strangled sound.

Another crack resounded through the warehouse, shattering the window beside where a grizzled man reached for his weapon.

The bullet sheared through his neck.

Pandemonium erupted outside the warehouse as day laborers and dock workers scattered at the unmistakable sounds of a rifle.

Prudence was sorry for their fright, even as her chest expanded with elated, overjoyed relief.

He was here. Her Knight of Shadows.

He'd come for her.

William dropped the crowbar and drew his pistol as he and the two remaining men scrambled to find from which shadow the gunman fired.

"Don't fucking stand at the windows, you bloody imbeciles!" he screeched.

The hired thugs took longer than was wise to recover after the initial volley, and Morley was able to clip the wing of a third man before they scrambled to take cover behind the very crates they'd been searching.

A deafening barrage of bullets pinged everywhere from the floor to the few skylights above. Prudence dropped to her knees, covering her head with her hands as slivers of splintered wood rained down on her.

Eventually, they ran out.

Her heart skipped several beats in the eerie silence that followed.

Had they gotten him? Had they shot the man she loved? Her one hope at salvation?

Right when happiness was in their grasp?

The sound of glass breaking behind them stole their attention to the far end of the warehouse by the loading bay. One more man dropped to his death before the echoes of the gun blast finished rebounding in her head.

"William," she hissed, tucking her legs beneath her so she could loosen the rope around her boots. "Let me go now, or this will end very badly for you." Her foot popped free on the last syllable, roughening it with strain.

He opened the cylinder of his pistol and shoved his shaking hand in his vest pocket, extracting two bullets and angling them into the chambers. "Do you *really* think it's wise to threaten me?"

"I'm not threatening you, I'm warning you," she cried. "My husband was a long-distance rifleman in the army. He's going to shoot every man in this room. He's *going* to *kill* you."

"Not before I kill you."

Prudence spied the crowbar he'd dropped next to a container and lunged for it, hoping to get it before he had the chance to reload that gun.

He surged up, caught her by the hair, and wrenched her back against him, using her as a human shield.

The cold kiss of the pistol against her temple

matched the metallic taste of fear in her mouth.

"Either we both get out of this alive. Or neither of us will," he yelled to the unseen gunman before whispering to her. "Not that you deserve to live."

He dragged her so his back was against the stone wall, clutching her to his front with an arm locked around her neck.

Any tighter and she'd choke.

"I didn't kill George," she panted, both hands pulling at his arm to keep her throat from being compressed. "I swear. There's no reason to hurt me."

"I've known that all along, you idiot cunt. Who do you think plunged the knife through his neck?"

Shock sent Prudence's limbs completely slack.

It made sense. William had found her. He'd been so keen to point the finger at her.

Because it got him off, scot-free.

"He was…your—your closest friend!" she cried.

"The friend who fucked my wife." Hatred dropped like acid from his words.

"*What?*"

"Don't be too sore at Honoria," he said in a voice as dry as sawdust. "She had her scruples. When I told her I was going to set up a match between you and George, she protested most ferociously. Until finally I sussed out why. She was bending over for him at least three times a month. It disgusted and disturbed her, to think of her lover fucking her sister."

Prudence fought for breath, her panic flaring to a fever pitch as they neared the doors out to the docks. Honoria? And George? The betrayal of her sister sliced through her worse than any pain George might have caused her.

"I told her if you ever found out about them, I'd ruin you in a way she hadn't yet conceived of. And she knew me well enough to believe me."

"But, I've done nothing to you," Pru said in a broken voice.

He'd finally made it to the far corner of the warehouse, and he dared to peek up to see if he could open the door without a hand blowing off.

The air remained still but for the clamor outside. "All wars have collateral damage, I'm afraid." His voice echoed off the cold stone walls. "Besides, you deserve it now. That bloody husband of yours has been getting in my way. Confiscating my goods. Arresting my brokers and interrupting my supply chain all to clear your name."

"The cocaine," she realized aloud. "You were smuggling it in my father's ships?"

He let out a long-suffering sigh. "I care not for the stuff," he said. "I was going to boil the frog slowly, establish the vulgar shipments to smuggle in goods, make a tidy fortune. Then, tip off the police so the Baron would be arrested. George too, as I forged his name on the papers. And I'd walk away with your father's wealth as well."

"But you killed him instead? On our wedding day?"

He made a noise of derision. "Did you know, by the time you were to marry, George was actually besotted with you? That he was thinking of trying at being a decent man. That's when I knew, he didn't get to claim happiness. None of them get to. And I ended him. Now open the fucking door."

She reached out and fumbled with the latch, her fingers weak and cold from lack of blood. *Wait*, she paused. "None of whom?"

"The men my slag of a wife fucked beneath my own roof!" he roared.

Prudence froze. "The Stags of St. James," she whispered.

"Whores!" Panic and rage, it seemed, was making

him maniacal. "My wife paid *whores*. They defamed her. They turned her into a creature of vile lusts and tempted her to stray. Men like them, like George, cunning and handsome and charismatic."

"So you...murdered them?"

"If only to make *her* pay twice. Thrice, even. She had bruises where no one can see. She has wounds that will never heal. I made sure of it. But still she wouldn't keep to *my* bed. She didn't obey me. She didn't fear me! And so, she forced my hand. I've put every man who touched my wife into the ground. As a warning to her...she has no ground to run to, not even after we make our getaway. I'll come for her. I will—"

"Why not take me now?" The door swung open, and the gun ground into Prudence's head with devastating force.

At the sound of Honoria's voice, William cinched his arm so tight, little stars danced in Prudence's periphery as she fought for breath.

Honoria stood at the doorway draped in gingham and cream silk, her features almost serene in their perfection. Her beauty a beacon in the chaos of blood, bodies, and broken glass.

Prudence clawed at William's arm, trying to warn her sister, to scream her name.

Honoria only shook her head. "William. Is all this really necessary? Could you not have just taken me with you today, instead?"

"Honoria," he choked out, his hold slackening a little. "You came."

"Of course I did," she said with a coy roll of her eyes. "You're my husband. Do you think I would have let you get away?"

The sound he made was pure anguish and abject joy.

It disgusted Pru, who couldn't help but search the

doorway for another shadow. For the man who could come put an end to the horror.

He was here. He'd already leveled the entire field. But...where was he now? What could he do?

"Go, Honoria," Pru pleaded. "He's mad."

Her sister never broke eye contact with her husband. "He knows exactly what he's doing. He always does, don't you, husband?" She held a hand out, the elegant fingers steady and coaxing. "Now let us leave here, together."

"The money," he said, in the voice of a plaintive boy. "It's not in the blasted crate it was supposed to be in. I haven't found it yet."

"Because I seized it last night."

At the sound of Morley's seemingly disembodied voice, William cocked the pistol at Prudence's temple, drawing a shameful whimper from her.

No, Morley hadn't seized the money. He'd been with her all night. Why was he lying? Why would he upset the man with the gun to her head?

"Don't you dare, Inspector," William crowed. "I'm taking the boat and crossing the channel. These two are my tickets out of Blighty, do you understand?"

"That is where you're wrong," said the shadows. "You're not taking one more step."

"Or what, eh? Do you want me to paint the floor with her brains?"

"William, no," Honoria pleaded, her façade of composure cracking. "She's pregnant. I *know* you wouldn't kill a child."

"It seems I picked the wrong sister," a disgusted William hissed in her ear. "Honoria's dry and barren as the Sahara, and frigid as the Arctic."

"Only toward you," she said in a voice gone flat as death. "I made certain your seed never took root, but none of my other lovers found me cold."

William's entire body tensed, and for a moment, Prudence knew it was over. Time slowed to a fraction of its pace, and the greatest regret she could muster in her last moment was that she wouldn't get to see her beloved husband's face before the end.

A tear escaped her as she squeezed her eyes shut.

He jerked, and a shot detonated, the pain lancing the side of her head with a searing agony she'd not expected to feel before the end. Another shot blasted. And another.

The weight of his arm around her throat immediately released and she screamed in a long breath.

I'm...alive, was her first thought. But the pain...had she even been shot?

More puzzled than shocked, Pru opened her eyes in time to witness the immediate aftermath.

William's gun was no longer aimed at her head, but forward, before his hand went slack and the weapon clattered to the ground.

Honoria's eyes swung to hers and they held for a moment as the only sound Prudence could hear was the air screaming with one insufferable monosyllabic note.

The pain was only in her ear, because the pistol had discharged next to it.

A starburst of red appeared on Honoria's buttercream bodice right above her heart.

They both stared down at the bullet wound in her sister's chest as William's body slumped to the ground, a puddle of blood rushing beneath her boots.

Her husband had killed him, but not before William had taken a shot at his own wife.

Prudence's scream echoed from far away as she launched herself forward, hoping to catch her sister before the woman's buckling legs failed her.

CHAPTER 20

*D*orian Blackwell swooped inside, catching Honoria in his arms as she slumped forward.

Prudence panicked at the dire look he gave her as he lifted Honoria with a grunt and swept her from the warehouse, out onto the planked unloading dock.

Prudence scrambled after them, daylight blinding her as she seized her sister's hand and brought it to her cheek.

"Honoria! No. Oh, please. Can you hear me?" she cried as Blackwell gingerly settled her sister down flat on the planks of the dock and ripped her petticoats to create a bandage. He shoved it into Prudence's hands and guided her to press down on the bullet wound with brutal pressure.

"Keep this here," he ordered before he surged to his feet and left them. "Don't move."

Pru couldn't imagine how terrible the pain of a bullet was, but Honoria's eyes merely fluttered, her features draining from pale to a ghostly shade.

"Don't go. Don't go," Pru pleaded with her sister. "Not when you're finally safe. Finally rid of him."

Honoria's dark eyes opened and caught hers for a moment, flooded with some awful emotion she couldn't identify. Her lips moved, but the pressure and ringing in Prudence's ears still impeded her from hearing such breathy tones.

"I can't year you. Dammit. I can't hear you," she lamented.

Honoria's bloodless lips moved more deliberately, her porcelain features pinched with pain. "I'm sorry. I should have told you…I…was afraid…"

"Shh. Shh. Shh." Prudence wanted to smooth her hair, but she dared not let up on the pressure of her wound. "Honoria, I didn't know what he was. What he was doing to you. No wonder you strayed. I'm not angry about George. Please don't blame yourself. Just— Just be well."

"I love you," her sister murmured through her tears, and Prudence was glad to note enough of her hearing had returned that she could make out the words. "We don't say any of that, do we? We Goodes. But I do. I love you."

"I love you too," Pru said, tears leaking from the tip of her nose. "I will for a long time so don't start saying that like you mean goodbye."

"You are a wonderful sister. And I…I'm not…"

Prudence looked up at the almost-deserted docks, noting some brave souls began to push themselves away from the places behind which they'd taken shelter. "Send for an ambulance!" she shrieked at them.

"I've done one better," Dorian said, leading men back toward them. They set down two poles and spread a canvas material between them, presumably erecting a makeshift stretcher. "There's a sawbones not two streets over I've used for a decade to dig bullets out of men who don't want questions asked at hospitals."

"Absolutely not!"

Despite her near-hysteria, his features softened as he regarded her. "Lady Morley, I've seen a lot of wounds like this. It's unlikely to be fatal if we get her immediate care and cleaning. Allow me to—"

"I will allow you *nothing*," she threw her body over her sister's, bracing her weight on her hands. "You will get an ambulance and she will be taken to a hospital, not some underworld sawbones. I'll not have it!"

Blackwell made a sound of impatient consternation. "Where is your husband, I wonder?"

"He was *supposed* to wait for us." The man she recognized as Millie LeCour's husband, Argent, peered into the doorway and took stock of the significant carnage inside. "He didn't leave aught for us to do but clean up the corpses." If she didn't know better, she'd have thought he sounded plaintive.

As if he were looking forward to the violence.

"I suggest you get to it then." A voice from above drew their notice, and they all looked to the roof of the warehouse where Morley stood against the slate grey sky.

Of course. He hadn't been shooting in through the windows. At least not the ones on the ground floor. He'd somehow scaled the building to the second or third floors and shot down through the smaller portals above. He'd have had to navigate the sharp angle of the roof and steady himself on precarious perches to shoot from such angles at such distances into the dimness.

His skill was nothing short of miraculous.

Morley dropped his rifle down to Argent, and then deftly levered himself over the edge of the roof, controlling his drop with only the strength of his arms until his feet were far enough from the ground to drop into a crouch.

He scanned the area, his gaze skipping right over Prudence as he stood and adjusted his cravat that had gone only slightly askew through the entire ordeal.

"Morley," Blackwell held up his hands helplessly,

though he was no longer armed. "You know Conleith; he's more than an adequate surgeon."

"Titus Conleith?" Morley's sharp jaw hitched as he stalked toward them with the predatory grace of a jungle cat. "That Irish devil dug more bullets out of more soldiers than any man alive. He could do it blindfolded."

Prudence didn't budge, something inside her had snapped. "This is no battlefield surgeon's tent," she hissed. "This is my *sister* and—"

"Titus Conleith?" Honoria astonished them all by breathing out the name in a ragged sob. She clutched at Prudence with clawlike fingers. "Take me to him," she begged. "Take me to him, *now*. You must let them, Pru," she said, her eyes overflowing with desperate tears. "You must."

Pru peered down at her, trying to remember the last time she'd seen Honoria cry. "Are you certain?"

Honoria's eyes were wild and extra dark in a face drawing paler by the moment. "I—I need him. Please, Pru, let me up. Let them take me."

Scampering back, Prudence felt herself being lifted to her feet by strong arms and anchored to her husband's side as Blackwell and the men gingerly boosted her sister onto their makeshift stretcher and navigated the docks back toward the road.

"I should go with her," she fretted, her legs suddenly feeling like they'd lost their bones.

She'd never liked William. She'd never been very close to her sister; Honoria had always made it impossible. Was it any wonder she'd been so aloof? So alone. She'd been locked in a private hell inside her own home.

Married to a monster.

"You are going *nowhere*." Her husband still refused to look down at her, his mouth compressed into a tight hyphen as he sized up a few of the dock workers looking on in slack-jawed amazement.

"You," he ordered, pointing to a steely-eyed laborer in his fifties. "Go to M Division on Blackman Street. Ask for Sgt. Catesby and a contingent of men to secure the docks."

"Sir." The man touched his cap and hopped too, as men tended to do when Morley gave an order.

"Argent." He turned to where the heavy-built man in a sharp auburn suit was examining the rifle in his hands. "Send our men round to the Commissioner Goode's residence in case Viscount Woodhaven had any thugs making mischief there. Then, I want Detective Inspectors Sean O'Mara and Roman Rathbone to tear through any of the Baron's warehouses to find the missing crates with the contraband Woodhaven was looking for."

Argent gave a sardonic two-fingered salute and sauntered off.

"The rest of you, this dock is closed until further notice, clear off."

A few laborers, obviously unhappy about the loss of a day's wages, looked as if they'd argue. Others, perhaps the ones who'd witnessed Morley's capabilities on the roof, dragged them away without making eye contact.

Her husband was not a man in the habit of repeating himself.

That handled, he hauled Prudence with him as he strode for the river-side corner of the warehouse beyond which steam barges and various pleasure boats churned the river with their relentless traffic.

The moment they turned the corner, she gasped to find herself immediately trapped between a rock wall and a hard place—the hard place being her husband's body.

His hands were everywhere as a torrent of curses

spilled from his lips. "Jesus Christ, Prudence. Did he hurt you?"

His fingers searched her face as if he were a blind man, his thumb hovering over her cheek where William had struck her. His glacial eyes flared with unnerving intensity he visibly struggled to contain.

Drowning in the unspoken but not invisible tension between them, she opened her mouth to speak, but nothing emerged. No words came forth to express the sheer incalculable emotion sweeping through her in knee-weakening waves.

An emotion she could now identify but didn't have the courage to express.

"I'm—we're—all right," she finally assured in a voice much wobblier than she'd intended.

"Well, I'm bloody not!" he burst, pushing away from her to rake shaking hands through his hair. "Never," he said with a hostile glare. "Never will you put yourself in danger for the sake of another, is that clear?"

"But...she's my sister. Surely you can appreciate the importance of that. You put your life on the line for people every day." She kept her voice even, soft, appreciating the volatility simmering through the heavy musculature of his shoulders and arms, heaving his chest into swells of uneven breaths. "Every night," she added meaningfully.

"I'm well aware of my hypocrisy, Prudence," he snapped. "But it doesn't fucking matter. You can't—I won't bloody—God! I'm not built for this." He paced three steps away, and then returned as if ricocheting off an invisible wall.

His words lanced through her, and she went taut with fear, grateful for the wall behind her, holding her up. "For...for what?" she asked in a watery breath, wondering if everything was about to change.

If she was about to lose him.

265

"For loving you, goddammit," he said with an almost savage antipathy. "I have to fight the image of that bastard's gun against your temple every time I close my eyes. For the rest of my damnable life. I have to relive the agony of possibly losing you. Of losing both of you."

"Oh..." she breathed, her heart giving a few extra thumps.

"It'll drive me mad," he ranted. "This unholy, unhealthy need I have to bask in your presence. This possession—no—this *obsession*. How am I supposed to run London's entire police force when I'm so consumed by you?"

"I—"

He wasn't finished by half. "I'm tempted to haul you to work with me and throw you in the cell, just so I can be certain of your safety. What sort of lunatic does that make me? Do you think that I could have survived this had it turned out differently?" He gestured to himself with sharp, wild arms. "And all of this right after last night. Right when I have everything I want in my grasp, *everything*. If he'd have—" His voice broke and he covered it with a rough sort of growl. "I swear, I've never felt fear like that before, Prudence. I've had you for a blink of time in my life, and yet, I'd have eaten a bullet before facing the rest of my years without you." He turned to her, his face mottled and the tips of his ears red as he nigh trembled with unspent emotion. "Now," he demanded. "What do you have to say for yourself?"

Prudence wondered if he could see the radiance in her heart shining through her eyes. If he knew how every word of his dressing-down had fallen like a Byronic poem on her ears. She wondered if she could ever have anything to say that could mean so much, because all she could come up with was, "I—I love you, too."

He blinked, his features gone perfectly blank.

Then, he seized her in a lightning fast motion,

buried his hands in her dark hair, and slanted his mouth over hers, kissing her with a desperate ferocity.

Prudence surrendered to the kiss instantly. She understood now, what his coldness out on the docks had meant. The reason he wouldn't look at her.

He had to make sure everything was taken care of before the fissures in his composure cracked, and then shattered. He'd just killed five men with five bullets. He'd climbed a three-story warehouse and, stealthily as a cat, he'd put his deadeye to use.

When the warmth between them kindled into heat, he tore his mouth away, apparently aware of their surroundings.

He put his forehead on hers and they shared desperate breaths as he smoothed his hands down her arms to her waist, splaying his palms on her middle. "I shouldn't have admonished you," he admitted in a voice laced with regret. "Especially not after the trauma you've had. Christ, all I want is to wipe this day from your memory. To erase the bruise forming on your cheek. To coddle and cosset you. It's damned unsettling." His brow wrinkled with chagrin.

She nudged him with her nose. "I want to remember this day forever. I will look back on this as the day you saved my life and freed my sister from the clutches of an evil man." She smiled, winding her arms around his neck as she clutched him close. "I'll remember this as the day you said you loved me."

His arms stole around her, bringing her fully against him, as if he couldn't hold her close enough for his liking. "I promise you, Prudence, I'll say it every day for the rest of our lives together."

Though she was still weak-limbed from the panic and strain of her ordeal, she thrilled with a sense of fulfillment and belonging. As if his love strengthened her, lacing threads of steel in the silken feminine fabric of her being. Nothing would tear them apart. Not lies nor doubt. Not villains nor adversaries nor their own wounded hearts.

Drawing back, she looked up into his dear, dear face, and thought she might have seen something of the same sentiment lurking in the silver-blue brilliance of his gaze.

"Did you hear?" she asked, hope and pain catching in her throat. "Did you hear William confess to George's murder? To and the Stags of St. James?"

"I did, sweetheart." He flicked his gaze to the side, shadows reclaiming some of his brilliance. "I could grovel at your feet for a decade and it wouldn't assuage my guilt."

She reached up and traced the fine divot in his chin with a fingertip. "I would say it's not necessary," she shrugged. "But if groveling is what will placate your conscience, far be it for me to stop you."

He huffed the ghost of a chuckle against her hair as his arms tightened. "All right, my little minx of a wife... I'll admit I'm new to groveling. How does one go about it?"

She took a full minute to pretend to consider. Not to punish him, per se, but to enjoy the circle of his protective embrace. To feel their heartbeats synchronize as she pressed her head against his strong shoulder. To nest in the one place she'd truly felt alive. And at home.

From the first night she'd given herself to him, a stranger.

"I imagine foot rubs are excellent groveling techniques," she ventured.

"I imagine you're right."

"And long Sunday mornings in bed."

"Now," he tutted. "That's a reward, not a punishment."

"I suppose, groveling is neither of our strong suits." She buried a smile in his shirt. "I want to reward you."

"You are my greatest prize," he said, stiffening a little as the chaos of emergency sirens and the clattering of horse hooves against the planks shook the docks beneath their feet.

She pulled from his embrace with a weary sigh, drawing her hand down his arm to lace her fingers with his. "This life of yours, it will always be thus, I gather." She gestured to the warehouse full of chaos, the advancing lawmen, the curious milling crowds. "Whether you're the Chief Inspector or the Knight of Shadows."

His eyes glimmered with concern, a frown pinching his brow as he looked toward the approaching tide as if he would send them away. "You deserve more than—"

She turned him to face her. "If I'd have you promise me anything, it's this. I know you are a hero to many, but you are only husband to me. I will not be your mistress while the law is your wife, and your children will not be bastards. I cannot live in an empty house and sleep in an empty bed and love a man who has been drained empty by the demands of this city."

"I know," he said.

"That being said, I'm proud of what you do," she soothed. "Of who you are, and I'd not change that. I will send you out that door every day. But you must come home to me. I must hold you and love you and make love to you. You must eat properly, and rest appropriately, and find a bloody hobby, do you understand? Something that wastes time, but you enjoy for no reason."

His smile tilted over to a perplexed grimace. "A hobby?"

She just shook her head. "We'll have that row later."

He seemed to accept this with a Gallic sort of sobriety as he turned toward the streets. "I can send Farah and the ladies to come get you. You don't have to face all this."

The offer was tempting, but she shook her head, looping her arm through his. "We'll face it all together."

Just like they would everything from now on.

As a family.

*M*orley lounged in bed with his cheek against his wife's creamy shoulder, gazing down at the mountain of her belly. He was only half listening as she, stretched on her back and naked beneath the sheets, read a Knight of Shadows penny dreadful aloud, stopping to giggle at a particularly unbelievable passage.

This Knight of Shadows business was certainly getting out of hand, but luckily, he'd recruited a few promising men to take up the occasional mantle. It was interesting to hear the conflicting reports of criminals and civilians alike who'd a chance meeting. Sometimes he was average height, lean, fair haired and agile. Other times, a dark-skinned mountain of a man, able to meld with the shadows. He was a youth, or mature. Spoke with an exotic accent, an Irish one, or his own on Tuesdays and every other Friday.

He'd kept his word and it hadn't been difficult for a moment. Their quiet nights together soothed his soul and excited everything that made him a man.

They made ceaseless love in increasingly creative positions, as her stomach became an impediment. Then they'd talk, or laugh, or read until one of them, usually her, drifted to sleep.

Tonight, she seemed unusually restless and uncomfortable, so they'd mounted pillows beneath her knees and he'd promised to suffer while she amused herself with one of the new rash of novels written about his exploits.

Rain tapped on the windows, casting the shadows of rivulets upon the bed. The optical effect lulled him as did the lively rendition of his wife's voice.

"Oh, dear," she mocked. "The Knight of Shadows is about to sweep the damsel onto the rooftops and debauch her! Listen to this..."

He levered up, clasping his hands on both sides of her belly as if it had sprouted ears. "I beg you to spare innocent ears," he teased. "That can hardly be appropriate!"

She threw the book at him, missing on purpose. "Neither are the things you say when you're making love to me."

He cast her a chastised, wretched look. "Touché." Leaning down, he gathered the sheets away from her breast, and then swept them down her belly so he could lay his ear against it and close his eyes.

He loved to listen for the little one, and tonight a slight nudge pushed back against the pressure of his cheek.

His breath caught, and Pru's did, as well, her hand reaching down to sift and stroke the strands of his hair.

"I was thinking..." she murmured dreamily. "If one of them is a girl...we could name her Caroline. Or does that cause you pain?"

He opened his eyes, an ache bloomed in his chest both bitter and exquisitely sweet. "It hurts to remember, but it would be worse to forget," he told her honestly.

Honesty had become their default communication, and because of it, they flourished.

"Her loss has become a part of me. I'll never forget her. But she is a part of the past I can reconcile. With this. With you. And I'd love to give her name to our child. To allow her the childhood she never had…"

"I'm glad you feel that way," she gifted him a beatific smile, and his heart glowed.

Then stalled.

"Wait." He sat up and looked down into her eyes with a frantically pulsating heart. "Did you just say *them…?*"

Her face shone up at him, incandescent with maternal pride.

"I must have done," she said, pulling him back to collapse against her in bewildered amazement. "Because we're having twins."

Highland Warlord
Highland Witch
Highland Warrior
To Wed a Highlander

CONTEMPORARY SUSPENSE
A Righteous Kill

ALSO BY KERRIGAN
The Highwayman
The Hunter
The Highlander
The Duke
The Scot Beds His Wife
The Duke With the Dragon Tattoo
How to Love a Duke in Ten Days
All Scot And Bothered

ABOUT THE AUTHOR

 Kerrigan Byrne is the USA Today Bestselling and award winning author of THE DUKE WITH THE DRAGON TATTOO. She has authored a dozen novels in both the romance and mystery genre. Her newest mystery release THE BUSINESS OF BLOOD is available October 24th, 2019

She lives on the Olympic Peninsula in Washington with her dream boat husband. When she's not writing and researching, you'll find her on the water sailing and kayaking, or on land eating, drinking, shopping, and taking the dogs to play on the beach.

Kerrigan loves to hear from her readers! To contact her or learn more about her books, please visit her site: www.kerriganbyrne.com

CPSIA information can be obtained
at www.ICGtesting.com
Printed in the USA
LVHW032318070620
657610LV00005B/61